Applause for L.L. Raand's

The Midnight Hunt
RWA 2012 VCRW Laurel Wreath winner *Blood Hunt*
Night Hunt
The Lone Hunt

"Raand has built a complex world inhabited by werewolves, vampires, and other paranormal beings…Raand has given her readers a complex plot filled with wonderful characters as well as insight into the hierarchy of Sylvan's pack and vampire clans. There are many plot twists and turns, as well as erotic sex scenes in this riveting novel that keep the pages flying until its satisfying conclusion."—*Just About Write*

"Once again, I am amazed at the storytelling ability of L.L. Raand aka Radclyffe. In *Blood Hunt*, she mixes high levels of sheer eroticism that will leave you squirming in your seat with an impeccable multi-character storyline all streaming together to form one great read." —*Queer Magazine Online*

"*The Midnight Hunt* has a gripping story to tell, and while there are also some truly erotic sex scenes, the story always takes precedence. This is a great read which is not easily put down nor easily forgotten."—*Just About Write*

"Are you sick of the same old hetero vampire / werewolf story plastered in every bookstore and at every movie theater? Well, I've got the cure to your werewolf fever. *The Midnight Hunt* is first in, what I hope is, a long-running series of fantasy erotica for L.L. Raand (aka Radclyffe)."—*Queer Magazine Online*

"Any reader familiar with Radclyffe's writing will recognize the author's style within *The Midnight Hunt*, yet at the same time it is most definitely a new direction. The author delivers an excellent story here, one that is engrossing from the very beginning. Raand has pieced together an intricate world, and provided just enough details for the reader to become enmeshed in the new world. The action moves quickly throughout the book and it's hard to put down."—*Three Dollar Bill Reviews*

Acclaim for Radcly*ff*e's Fiction

In *Prescription for Love* "Radclyffe populates her small town with colorful characters, among the most memorable being Flann's little sister, Margie, and Abby's 15-year-old trans son, Blake…This romantic drama has plenty of heart and soul."
—*Publishers Weekly*

2013 RWA/New England Bean Pot award winner for contemporary romance *Crossroads* "will draw the reader in and make her heart ache, willing the two main characters to find love and a life together. It's a story that lingers long after coming to 'the end.'"—*Lambda Literary*

In **2012 RWA/FTHRW Lories and RWA HODRW Aspen Gold award winner** *Firestorm* "Radclyffe brings another hot lesbian romance for her readers."—*The Lesbrary*

Foreword Review Book of the Year finalist and IPPY silver medalist *Trauma Alert* "is hard to put down and it will sizzle in the reader's hands. The characters are hot, the sex scenes explicit and explosive, and the book is moved along by an interesting plot with well drawn secondary characters. The real star of this show is the attraction between the two characters, both of whom resist and then fall head over heels."
—*Lambda Literary Reviews*

Lambda Literary Award Finalist *Best Lesbian Romance 2010* features "stories [that] are diverse in tone, style, and subject, making for more variety than in many, similar anthologies…well written, each containing a satisfying, surprising twist. Best Lesbian Romance series editor Radclyffe has assembled a respectable crop of 17 authors for this year's offering."—*Curve Magazine*

2010 Prism award winner and ForeWord Review Book of the Year Award finalist *Secrets in the Stone* is "so powerfully [written] that the worlds of these three women shimmer between reality and dreams…A strong, must read novel that will linger in the minds of readers long after the last page is turned."—*Just About Write*

In **Benjamin Franklin Award finalist** *Desire by Starlight* "Radclyffe writes romance with such heart and her down-to-earth characters not only come to life but leap off the page until you feel like you know them. What Jenna and Gard feel for each other is not only a spark but an inferno and, as a reader, you will be washed away in this tumultuous romance until you can do nothing but succumb to it."—*Queer Magazine Online*

Lambda Literary Award winner *Stolen Moments* "is a collection of steamy stories about women who just couldn't wait. It's sex when desire overrides reason, and it's incredibly hot!"—*On Our Backs*

Lambda Literary Award winner *Distant Shores, Silent Thunder* "weaves an intricate tapestry about passion and commitment between lovers. The story explores the fragile nature of trust and the sanctuary provided by loving relationships."—*Sapphic Reader*

Lambda Literary Award Finalist *Justice Served* delivers a "crisply written, fast-paced story with twists and turns and keeps us guessing until the final explosive ending."—*Independent Gay Writer*

Lambda Literary Award finalist *Turn Back Time* "is filled with wonderful love scenes, which are both tender and hot."—*MegaScene*

By Radclyffe

Romances

Innocent Hearts	The Lonely Hearts Club
Promising Hearts	Night Call
Love's Melody Lost	Secrets in the Stone
Love's Tender Warriors	Desire by Starlight
Tomorrow's Promise	Crossroads
Love's Masquerade	Homestead
shadowland	Against Doctor's Orders
Passion's Bright Fury	Prescription for Love
Fated Love	The Color of Love
Turn Back Time	Love on Call
When Dreams Tremble	

Honor Series

Above All, Honor
Honor Bound
Love & Honor
Honor Guards
Honor Reclaimed
Honor Under Siege
Word of Honor
Code of Honor
Price of Honor

Justice Series

A Matter of Trust (prequel)
Shield of Justice
In Pursuit of Justice
Justice in the Shadows
Justice Served
Justice for All

The Provincetown Tales

Safe Harbor	Winds of Fortune
Beyond the Breakwater	Returning Tides
Distant Shores, Silent Thunder	Sheltering Dunes
Storms of Change	

LOVE ON CALL

by

RADCLY*f*FE

2016

Credits
Editors: Ruth Sternglantz and Stacia Seaman
Production Design: Stacia Seaman
Cover Design by Sheri (graphicartist2020@hotmail.com)

Acknowledgments

A return to the Rivers series is like coming home to friends, family, and warm fires (or sunny afternoons, as the season dictates). The challenge of the familiar, in life as in fiction, is to embrace change as we preserve what keeps us strong. In the romance documentary *Love Between the Covers*, Jayne Krantz makes the point that readers find in romances the core values they aspire to emulate or experience in life, not "just" love and passion, but valor, loyalty, bravery, and heroism. What I love about writing and reading romances, whether stand-alones or a series romance, is the story of two people overcoming obstacles in their journey toward commitment within the context of a larger duty—to family, community, and the world we live in. Our romances tell powerful stories of individuals who risk all to live honest and meaningful lives. The Rivers community is one born of history, heritage, and inclusiveness. I hope you enjoy your time there.

Many thanks go to: senior editor Sandy Lowe for a partnership that keeps BSB running smoothly while I write, editor Ruth Sternglantz for never missing a beat, editor Stacia Seaman for her irreplaceable expertise, Sheri Halal for a perfect cover, and my first readers Paula, Eva, and Connie for encouragement and aid.

And as always, thanks to Lee for her indomitable spirit of adventure. *Amo te*.

Radclyffe, 2016

To Lee, for always answering

CHAPTER ONE

Glenn opened her eyes in the dark, not awakening so much as emerging from a void. She didn't have to look at the clock to know it was two thirty. No matter what time she fell asleep, she always opened her eyes at two thirty. She didn't dream, had taught herself not to. Sleep was a blank, an enforced respite from thought and memory. An absence of awareness wasn't exactly restful, but her body required the recovery time in order for her to perform at peak efficiency, so she maintained a regular sleep schedule, even if the actual hours she slept were erratic. She turned on her side. Two thirty-seven.

Outside the open window, the night was silent. If she listened very hard she might hear some distant sound—a freight train chugging along the river, a coyote or two calling for the pack, a branch falling from the big pines that bordered the parking lot behind the empty store beneath her apartment. Not tonight, though. The night was as empty as her dreamless sleep had been.

Her cell phone emitted a series of staccato beeps, the closest approximation she'd been able to get to her field radio, the familiarity an odd comfort. She reached for it with a quick easing of the heaviness in her chest.

"Archer."

"Hey, Glenn." Cindy Ames's soft voice was instantly recognizable. Cindy was the head night nurse in the ER, and she and Glenn had spent many hours working together over the last three years. "I'm really sorry to wake you up."

"No problem. I was awake."

Cindy laughed briefly. "If you were, I hope you're doing

something fun. But I'm in a jam and I know you're not on call for surgery anymore, but—"

"That doesn't matter." Phone to her ear, Glenn slid naked from beneath the sheet and pulled scrub pants from the neat pile she'd left on the straight-backed wooden chair next to her bed. She'd planned to wear them her first day on the job as director of the physician assistant program in the morning. "What's going on?"

"Flann's in the OR with Pete doing a blocked A-V shunt, and I can't reach Dr. Williams. He's backup for surgery tonight. I've got a lady here whose foot looks really bad. I'd wait for Flann, but—"

"I'll come over and take a look. Be there in ten minutes. Did you get X-rays?"

"Yeah, I did, and something is weird."

"Okay, you know what to do until I get there."

"You're a savior," Cindy said.

"Yeah," Glenn said flatly as Cindy rang off.

A savior.

Nothing could be further from the truth. For an instant, the tally of the dead rolled through her mind along with the memory of acid smoke and the copper taste of blood and fear in her throat. Too many to count, too many without names. But the faces never faded even though she'd taught herself not to let them haunt her, just as she'd taught herself not to dream. But some things could never be erased, not when they were tattooed into your bone and chiseled onto your soul. The dead were as much a part of her as her beating heart.

But not tonight. Tonight she tended the living.

She scooped up her keys, wallet, and phone and let the screen door click shut behind her on her way out. She didn't bother to lock up—there wasn't anything inside worth stealing. Her footsteps on the wooden staircase spiraling down the back of the building to the parking lot followed her like so many ghosts. Her ragtop Wrangler was the only vehicle in the tiny lot behind the consignment shop and its neighbors on either side, the pizza place and an antique store. Ordinarily she'd walk the mile up the hill to the Rivers where it looked down over the town and the valley like a conscience reminding everyone that life was fleeting and fickle. But Cindy was an experienced nurse, and if something about this patient bothered her enough to call for help rather than wait the hour or two for Flann or the PA to be available, then she might not have the luxury of the fifteen-minute walk. Instead, she was pulling around to the staff lot in less than five.

The ER would be empty at this time of night, unless somewhere on a nearby highway a thrill-riding teenager had misjudged a curve or a farmer had another case of indigestion that wouldn't let him breathe or a baby decided to exit the comfort and safety of the womb. But the only vehicles in the lot adjacent to the emergency entrance were those of the staff and an idling sheriff's patrol car whose occupant was probably inside scoring a cup of almost-fresh coffee. When she pushed through the big double doors into the wide, tiled corridor leading past reception, the bright lights shocked every sense sharply online. Her head cleared of memories and misgivings, and her vision snapped into crystal focus. Somewhere around the corner an elevator door clanked open, a power floor polisher whirred, and someone laughed. In the empty waiting area, a weather map scrolled across the TV screen, tracking tornados in a part of the country she'd never visited and doubted she'd ever see.

Cindy looked up at the sound of footsteps, relief erasing the lines of tension above her bright blue eyes. She must have been in her early thirties, but her creamy complexion could've been that of a twenty-year-old. "I owe you."

"You sure do," Glenn said. "Half a dozen of those chocolate chip cookies—the ones with the nuts—ought to do it."

Cindy laughed and pushed blond hair away from her face. A small diamond and accompanying gold band glinted on her left hand. "Then you're in luck, because I promised the kids I'd bake tomorrow."

"What have you got?" Glenn leaned an elbow on the high counter that sectioned off the work area from the rest of the ER. The whiteboard on the wall to her right was divided into rows, each with a number indicating the patient room and the names of those who occupied it. Only one was filled in, number seven. Down the left-hand side someone had printed the names of the doctors on call in black block letters. She scanned it, suppressing a grunt when she saw *Williams* next to surgery backup. He was notoriously unreliable, often taking hours to answer his pages and, even when he did, reluctant to come in. More often than not when she'd been taking first call in the ER and had a patient who needed to go to the OR, she'd call Flann. Flannery Rivers never complained about taking an emergency, whether she was technically on call or not. Williams would bitch and gripe if he had to get out of his warm bed in the upscale Saratoga suburb and drive down to take care of someone who might die if he didn't come. On the other hand, he never complained if he happened to hear that an emergency had come through that Flann had handled instead of him, as if it was his due that other people make his life easier.

She let go of the pulse of anger. He was an ass and not worth her time. Since returning to civilian life, she'd mostly shed the reflex need to keep everyone around her on track and doing their jobs. All she could do was give every case her best. That would have to be enough. She told herself that a dozen times a day, and someday she might even believe it.

Glenn focused on the vital signs and brief history recorded on the ER intake sheet Cindy handed her.

"Naomi Purcell," Cindy recapped as Glenn read. "Thirty-five years old and healthy. Married, three kids. They have a small herd of dairy cows down on Route 4 by the river. She came in with a fever and an infection in her left lower leg. It seems she got tangled up in some old barbed wire pulling a calf out of the brush this morning. Now her leg is red and hot and tender."

"Is she diabetic?"

"No—not that she knows of. I sent off bloods and don't have them back yet. But her temp is a hundred and three and the wound looks nasty. Swollen and draining."

On the surface it sounded like a virulent cellulitis, but Cindy wouldn't have called her for a straightforward infection. She'd have called one of the medical doctors for antibiotics and possible admission.

"What else?" Glenn asked.

Cindy shook her head, her eyes troubled. "She just looks really sick, Glenn—a lot sicker than something like a fairly superficial trauma should account for. And there's a lot of swelling. I was afraid something might've gotten in there that she didn't realize, some kind of foreign body, so I sent her to X-ray."

"You know," Glenn said, impressed as always by Cindy's clinical sense, "there's an opening in the rotation for first-year PAs. You might consider—"

"No way. I'm done with school, even if I do have an in with the new program director."

The title still felt like a too-tight shoe, and Glenn shrugged aside thoughts of her new job. "Where are the X-rays?"

"I put them on a box outside her room."

"Okay, I'll check her out. Let me know as soon as you get her labs back."

"I'll call now." Just as Cindy reached for the phone, the red triage phone rang. Cindy gave a little shrug and picked that one up instead. "ACH—go ahead."

Glenn walked down to cubicle seven and announced herself as she pulled the curtain aside. "Ms. Purcell? I'm Glenn Archer, one of the surgical PAs."

Naomi Purcell sat propped up on several pillows, her eyes fever bright in a pale white face. Lank strands of medium brown hair framed her face. Sweat beaded on her forehead, and her chest beneath the shapeless cotton hospital gown fluttered with quick, shallow breaths. A tall, husky man in a faded T-shirt hanging over the top of baggy blue jeans stood to the left side of the bed, his hand on her shoulder and terror in his eyes.

"She seems to be getting sicker really fast, Doc," he said in a low, tight voice.

"I'm fine, Todd." Naomi Purcell's voice was wispy and faint but she mustered a smile. "My leg feels like a nest of fire ants are having a picnic on it, though."

"Let me take a look." Glenn snapped on gloves and drew back the sheet, expecting to see the angry laceration Cindy had noted on the chart along with the bright red sheen of a superficial infection surrounding it. All the expected signs of infection were there, but nothing about Naomi Purcell's leg was typical. An irregular inch-long gash just above her left ankle gaped open, and a thin milky fluid oozed from its edges, slowly trickling down onto the sheet. Her foot was swollen to twice its size, the skin thin and tight as if trying to prevent the flesh and fluid beneath from bursting out and close to losing the battle. She checked for the dorsal pulse and couldn't find it. "Can you feel me touch you?"

"Yes, a little. My toes are numb, though."

"Do they feel cold?"

"No. More like they're just not there."

The inflammation extended up her calf following the path of lymphatic drainage, spidery fingers spreading toxins and whatever bacteria had invaded the deeper tissues. Glenn felt for the artery behind Naomi's knee and found the rapid beat that signaled Naomi's system was working hard to combat the infection. "This might hurt a little bit."

"Don't worry about me," Naomi said, as if Glenn had anything else to worry about.

Right now, Naomi Purcell was the only thing that mattered in her life. She gently probed at a distance from the laceration, and a faint crackle, like air popping in the plastic bubble things they wrapped around packages that come in the mail, crinkled beneath her fingertips. Her belly tightened and she straightened up. "I want to check your X-rays. I'll be right back."

"She should get some antibiotics, right, Doc?" Naomi's husband Todd said.

"Yes, and we'll get on that in just a minute."

His eyes followed her out of the room. Eyes that said, *Don't leave us. Help us.* Eyes she'd seen hundreds of times before. Three X-rays hung on the light box next to the curtained cubicle. The bones of the lower leg stood out like bleached driftwood, balloon-shaped shadows marking the surrounding muscles and fat. And there in the depths of the tissue, clear streaks like icing in a layer cake extended from the edges of the laceration. Air where there shouldn't be any. She found Cindy drinking a cup of coffee and making notes in a stack of charts in the tiny staff lounge. "We need to start her on antibiotics—I'll get cultures and call Flann."

"It's bad, isn't it?"

"It's necrotizing fasciitis, and she needs to go to the OR, right now. I should call Williams, but Flann's upstairs—"

"God, don't call Williams. If you do, she'll be sitting down here until after he's had his morning coffee."

"You did good calling me."

"I knew you'd come. You always do."

Of course she did, what else would she be doing. She scribbled an order for an antibiotic cocktail and called up to the OR. Dave Pearson, an OR tech, answered. "Hey, Dave, it's Glenn. Can you patch me into Flann's room?"

"Sure, hold on. You got something?"

"Yeah—do you have another team?"

"We can put something together if it can't wait until Flann is done."

"Let's see what she says."

A second later the line buzzed and a woman answered. "OR seven."

"Fay, it's Glenn Archer. Can Flann talk?"

"Hold on a second…Flann, it's Glenn. Can you talk?"

"Glenn?" Flann said. "What are you doing? I thought you'd moved on to greener pastures."

"Not until seven a.m. I'm down in the ER. Cindy called me. There's a thirty-five-year-old woman here with necrotizing fasciitis of her left lower extremity. Right now it's in the midcalf, but the wound is less than twenty-four hours old, and she looks toxic. She needs to come up."

"Damn it," Flann muttered. "We've got another half an hour before we can test the shunt. Pete can close after that. If they can set up another room, you can get started."

"Dave says they can. I'll get her upstairs."

"You started her on bug killers?"

"As we speak."

"Let me know as soon as she's asleep, and I'll put my head in if I'm not free yet."

"Okay, no problem."

Husband and wife fixed Glenn with anxious gazes as soon as she stepped through the curtain. "You've got an infection in your leg, you know that. The X-rays show air inside your tissues where it shouldn't be. That indicates a certain kind of infection from strains of bacteria that can be harder to treat than the ordinary kind. It's probably caused by whatever was on the old wire that you got tangled up in."

"But you can treat it, right? With the antibiotics?" Todd's voice was an octave higher than it had been and his face had gone from ruddy to gray. He swayed just a little.

"Sit down right there, Mr. Purcell, and I'll finish telling you what we're going to do." Glenn pointed to the plastic chair next to the bed and Todd Purcell dropped into it with a thud.

Todd repeated, "You can treat it—"

"Todd," Naomi said with gentle firmness, "let the doctor talk."

Glenn didn't bother correcting them. Almost everyone she took care of in the ER called her Doc. Everyone in Iraq had too. "We are going to treat you with antibiotics, and Cindy, the nurse you met earlier, will be starting them any minute. But that's not going to be enough. We need to take you up to the operating room—"

Naomi's husband gave a little groan. Glenn walked closer to the bed and gripped his shoulder, her gaze still fixed on Naomi, who held hers unwaveringly.

"You're not going to have to amputate my leg, are you?" Naomi Purcell asked.

"No. We're going to make an incision and wash out the deeper tissues to help stop the spread of infection. We might have to make several four- or five-inch incisions, but they'll heal. You'll have some scars, but it's early yet, and chances are good your leg will be fine except for that."

"All right," Naomi said instantly. "When?"

"Right now. As soon as we can get the antibiotic started, we'll take you upstairs to the OR."

"Are you sure you have to do this?" her husband asked, looking like a frightened deer trapped in a thicket of briars.

"I'm sure. I talked to Dr. Rivers about it, and she—"

"Harper Rivers?"

"No, Flannery."

"Harper takes care of our kids," he said, some of the color coming back to his face. "Her sister—that's the surgeon, right?"

"That's right. She'll be in charge upstairs."

"But you'll be with her, right?" Naomi said.

"Yeah, I will be," Glenn said, thinking this would probably be her last case with Flannery Rivers.

CHAPTER TWO

Mari had never lived anywhere without bus service. She'd never lived anywhere without malls and movie theaters and takeout. When she was thirteen, she'd gone to one of the big agricultural centers in LA County on a school-sponsored trip, but the miles and miles of row after row of green things had seemed foreign and boring at the time. Looking back, it had probably only been a few hundred acres of lettuce, but she'd been happy to get back to the concrete and city smells she'd grown up with. No buses meant driving, which she could do but had rarely needed to undertake back home when everything was a stop away on the subway, light rail, or bus. Who would drive in the insanity if they didn't need to?

When she'd arrived at the Albany Airport lugging everything she planned to start a new life with in two suitcases and a taped-up carton of books, she'd rented a car and, following a printout from Google Maps, driven on increasingly narrow, twisting roads through countryside vaguely reminiscent of the fields and green valleys beyond the sprawl of Los Angeles. The farms she passed here, though, were so much smaller and the land so much hillier and the air so much cleaner. Maybe the East Coast seemed so alien because she'd never known anything other than LA. She'd rarely spent much time outside the city, because why would she? Everything that had seemed important growing up was there in the teeming streets—entertainment, shopping, school. Her parents almost never took a vacation—her father was always working in the store, her mother often joining him during the welcome busy stretches, and on the rare times when they weren't both busy, there was always something going on with one or the other of Mari's siblings. With barely a year and a half between them all, the after-school sports, clubs, and social events were a never-ending cycle that repeated year after year. Dances and finals and sports practice occupied everyone's time, and when her mother was too busy with the younger ones, the older ones—the girls at least—stood in for her. Mari's life had been the family, and she'd never imagined it any differently until everything had changed.

She'd dropped the rental off at the nearest return site as soon as she'd unloaded her belongings and the household essentials she'd picked up at a Target before leaving the city. She couldn't afford to lease or buy a car, and so she would walk. She didn't mind walking and it wasn't very far from her studio apartment to the hospital. Or to anywhere else in the little village, either. Everything she needed in terms of food and necessities she could get at the grocery store she'd discovered just at the opposite end of town, its parking lot filled with pickup trucks and Subarus. She'd wondered on her first exploration of the village four days before if people drove anything else at all. Since then she'd found a surprisingly big pharmacy at the intersection of Main Street and the county road that ran through the center of town, a diner, a bakery that also served decent coffee and beyond-describable muffins and pastries, a pizza place, and a number of other shops. She could survive without a car, and walking felt good. Using her body felt good, and even after a week, her muscles seemed stronger.

And she'd better get her butt in gear now with just over an hour before she needed to start her new job. Her stomach squirmed with nerves. This wasn't at all how she'd imagined her first day as a newly minted physician assistant. The silence of her tiny apartment reminded her every minute of all the voices that weren't there, encouraging her, teasing her, quietly supporting her. Now there was only the voice in her own head telling her she could do this. She'd done much harder things. And she wanted to do it, needed to do it. Work gave her a reason to get out of bed in the morning, that and her stubborn refusal to be defeated.

She showered in the miniscule pocket bathroom, barely able to dry off without bumping her hip on the corner of the sink. She blow-dried her hair, thankful again for the natural waves that required little more than a decent cut to look acceptably stylish, and put on the minimum of makeup to cover the smudges beneath her eyes. Sleep was sporadic still, and she hadn't quite gotten over the jet lag. She'd never been very good at traveling on the few occasions she'd visited her father's distant relatives in Mexico or interviewed for PA-training positions. She always missed her pillow. The one she'd slept with forever, it seemed, shaped to her arms and the curve of her cheek.

She smiled at her weary image in the mirror and admitted what she really missed. The smell of coffee floating up from the kitchen in the morning along with her mother's voice reminding Joseph of some errand he had to do after work or calling to Raymond to get out of bed before he missed the bus or singing snatches of some old song as she fixed breakfast and packed lunches. Even with four of the kids gone, the house had still felt full with her and the two boys and Selena still living at home. The house always felt full of life.

Her tiny apartment was neat and airy and sunny, but oddly sterile, as if the silence scoured it clean. Getting to work and occupying her mind was exactly what she needed to remember she was damn lucky to be able to complain about anything—including a nice, clean, quiet place to live and a job she'd wanted all her life. Self-pity was an unbecoming pastime, and she needed to be done with it.

Feeling better for the mental scolding, she dressed in tan pants, brown flats, and a dark green cotton polo shirt, gathered the necessities into her favorite buttery soft leather shoulder bag, the one Selena had given her for Christmas two years before, and made sure to lock the door on the way out. The hospital was at the other end of town up a hill, a twenty-minute walk from the short street a few blocks off Main where she'd found an apartment in what had once been a grand mansion but was now carved up into small odd-shaped apartments. Hers was on the second floor in the back, overlooking a plain fenced yard shaded in one corner by a big tree she thought was a maple, but wasn't sure. No one seemed to use the yard, although someone cut the grass.

Traffic was heavier than she expected at a little after six, mostly those pickup trucks again, almost all filled with men and carrying logos on the side saying floor repair, general contractor, plumbing, or some other trade. The café was open, and she treated herself to a scone and a cup of very good espresso and still approached the hospital twenty-five minutes before she needed to be there. The hospital was the only building on the wooded hillside, and as she passed through the stone pillars flanking the entrance to the winding, crushed-gravel road and climbed past tall cast-iron lampposts and taller pines, she felt as if she was walking back in time.

At the top of the approach road, Mari stopped. She'd only had glimpses of the hospital through the trees that surrounded it on her walks through the village, although she'd been aware of its presence, perched above the fray like a watchful bird. It even looked a little like a bird, with its wings stretching out to either side. She'd seen pictures of it online and even found an old historical society talk about it that someone had posted along with photos, some of them decades old. She tried to imagine, looking at the faded sepia images of young women in long dresses with white aprons and frilly caps, and stern-faced men in high-collared white shirts and tailored coats with narrow lapels and high-waisted pants, what it had been like practicing medicine before the modern era had brought such astounding progress and devastating commercialization. Before the days of vast medical consortia and insurance companies and all of the other agencies that had crowded in and relegated so many of the hospitals like this to memory.

This hospital was undergoing a major transition, adding an Emergency Medicine residency program and joining with the regional medical school's PA training program. She was about to become one of the faculty of that new program. A year ago she thought she'd never have the chance to treat a single patient, and now this. Everything had happened so quickly. A job and a new life.

No one had congratulated her and no one had tried to stop her from leaving. Of course, in so many ways, she'd already been gone.

A siren wailed, drowning out her thoughts, and she jumped onto the green grassy shoulder well to the side of the curving road as an EMS van rolled around a corner and swept past. Perhaps whoever rode inside would be her first patient. Fifteen minutes from now, she'd know.

From the turnaround in front of the hospital, she took one more second to appreciate the soaring majesty of her new home—as she somehow thought of it. A fountain centered the grassy expanse in the middle of the circular drive, clear water draped in rainbows gushing into a scalloped cast-iron basin from beneath the feet of a life-sized metal sculpture of a woman with a child by her side, their hands clasped together. The hospital itself was anchored by the central structure, a brick edifice six stories high, ornate white columns surrounding the broad entrance, and wings extending from either side like arms clasping the forested hills towering behind it. She turned and looked at the village down below, dappled in sunlight and shrouded by tree branches—seeming so peaceful, as if nothing could ever disturb its tranquility. She knew she was only wishing such a place existed, a foolish wish. The past could not be undone or relived. Harsh words could only be forgiven and someday, she hoped, forgotten.

And none of that mattered now. She turned back to the hospital and took a deep breath of the cleanest air she thought she'd ever experienced. So fresh her lungs actually tingled. Smiling at the thought, she followed the drive in the direction she'd seen the ambulance take and found the emergency room entrance without any trouble. At six forty-five in the morning, it was already busy. Several people stood in line at reception, waiting to sign in with the woman sitting at the counter. A line of gurneys waited along the wall on either side of big double doors that stood open at the entrance to the treatment area. An orderly pushed a woman in a wheelchair around a corner, and an elevator dinged. The murmur of voices drew her down a short hall to the nurses' station. She stopped by the desk and waited until a middle-aged man with thinning brown hair wearing khaki pants and a camo scrub shirt adorned with Snoopy looked up at her and smiled.

"Can I help you? Are you here with one of the patients?" he asked in a surprising lilting tenor.

She held out her hand. "No, I am Mari Mateo. A new PA. I was wondering—"

"Oh, right. That's today—welcome. Glenn's not here, but come with me."

Mari hesitated as he swept around from behind the counter. "If you could just point me to the conference room—"

"I'm Bruce Endie—one of the nurses. This way," he said over his shoulder as he hurried along. Mari followed down the hall and around the corner before he disappeared completely.

He stopped in front of an open door, rapped quickly, and said, "Dr. Remy. New troops."

Mari halted abruptly beside him and glanced into a small office where a woman sat behind the desk. She felt her face color when she recognized the head of the ER. They'd only talked via Skype, but Dr. Remy wasn't someone she would easily forget. "Oh, Dr. Remy! I'm really sorry. I think I was supposed to be in the conference room."

The blonde with the emerald green eyes, sculpted cheekbones, and warm smile motioned her in. "That's okay. Mari, isn't it? Call me Abby. Have a seat."

"Thanks." Mari sat in one of the two chairs in front of the ER chief's desk. "I'm afraid I'm early."

Abby grinned. "You'll never hear complaints about that. I'm sorry Glenn isn't here to—"

"Am I late?" a low, smooth voice inquired from the direction of the open door.

"Not at all," Abby said. "This is Mari Mateo, our new PA. Glenn Archer is our program director, Mari."

Mari turned in her seat, her gaze falling on a slightly taller than average woman with shaggy dusky blond hair, a lean face with slate-blue eyes, and a wide sensuous mouth above a square chin with a shadow of a cleft. The expression in those intense eyes was appraising and cautious. No quick smile and friendly welcome here. Not unfriendly, just remote.

"Good to meet you," Glenn said in a slow, sensuous drawl. A smile flickered and was gone.

"Glenn will take care of getting you settled," Abby said.

Mari rose, wondering just how settled she'd be when just the slow sweep of Glenn Archer's gaze over her face made her pulse quicken.

CHAPTER THREE

G lenn strode silently down the hall toward the main area of the ER with the new PA keeping pace. Why the hell had she let Abigail Remy talk her into giving up her position as Flann Rivers's surgical first assistant to head up this new training program? Abby hadn't even had to work hard to convince her. It hadn't been flattery, she wasn't susceptible to that. Sure, Abby had said she'd needed her, needed someone with experience who was used to leading a team to be sure the PA training program got off the ground and running without any hitches. The new cooperative programs between ACH and the area medical centers were vital to keeping the hospital healthy. The ER, hell, the whole hospital had been in trouble not long before, and there'd been talk of the place being bought out and closed. Everyone thought Presley Worth, the new CEO, had come here to do exactly that. Maybe she had. But not now. Presley, medical staff president Edward Rivers, and every member of the staff were united in turning the place around. So how could she have said no—when had she *ever* said no when she believed in something and duty called? She'd been happy working as Flann's second, satisfied with her solo responsibilities. Comfortable. Safe. Hell. She knew what the problem was. She didn't want to be a team leader, didn't want to be responsible for success or failure. Didn't want to be anyone's go-to. Not again. But she'd signed up for it, hadn't she? Reenlisted just as automatically as she had the last two times. So here she was, the PA director, with a new staff PA, and she still hadn't said anything more to Mari Mateo than "Come on, I'll show you where your locker is."

Glenn stopped so abruptly Mari took a step past her, then turned back and stared at her with a question in her eyes.

"You drink coffee, don't you?" Glenn said.

Surprise registered in the deepest, darkest, richest brown eyes Glenn had ever seen. Streaks of gold splintered through the chocolate, making Glenn think of sunrise over the desert, of the piercing shock of unexpected splendor in a desolate landscape. A smile rode the sunrise, cresting on Mari's wide, full rosy lips, and Mari went from pleasantly attractive to knockout beautiful in a millisecond.

"No, I don't think much of coffee."

Still caught in the storm of sudden beauty, Glenn wordlessly shot a raised eyebrow. She frantically tried to envision getting through morning report without coffee. Some people drank tea, sure. On occasion she had done that herself. But coffee was tradition, and for most medical people as precious as blood. But she could deal with a tea drinker. Somehow. "Oh. Okay. Well, uh, then…how about—"

"On the other hand," Mari smoothly went on, an amused glint in her eyes, "I particularly enjoy an espresso—especially when it's made from a good Mexican bean."

Glenn narrowed her eyes. "Espresso."

"Mm-hmm."

"That was cruel. I was imagining teabags at six a.m."

Mari laughed. "Hardly a toxic substance. Although I didn't realize how sensitive you were."

Glenn grinned. "Let's grab some coffee, and I'll give you a rundown of the day-to-day."

Mari frowned and glanced in the direction of the ER proper. "What about the patients? Shouldn't we be checking on them?"

"Yeah, we should." Glenn nodded, impressed and pleased. "And we will. But I checked the whiteboard on my way through just now, and there's nothing urgent that needs our attention. I've got my radio—" She winced and patted her pants pocket. Even after years out of uniform she couldn't get used to not having a radio and being patched into com central. "Phone. I've got my phone. They'll text us if anything critical comes in. Otherwise, we're waiting on some labs on the patients who came in before change of shift. Everyone at intake looked like walking wounded. So we're okay for a few minutes."

Mari cocked her head. "All that from a quick glance at the whiteboard?"

"And a fast sit rep from Bruce."

"Oh, I met him. Is he ex-military too?"

Glenn stilled. "Sorry?"

"You are, aren't you? Ex-military? You remind me a lot of my training instructor. He was a Navy corpsman, not this time around—Vietnam. But it's more than just the lingo, it's everything—the way he…you…process information, the quick-look rapid-fire assessment and fast decisions. That must be something that never leaves. He sounded a lot like you."

Ice trickled down Glenn's back, and she suppressed a shudder. A lot of things never left. Habits, instincts, reflexes. Memories. The overwhelming need to act. Quickly, while there's still time. Before something else, some*one* else, gets you first. She took a slow breath. "You're very observant."

"Sorry, just guessing." Mari regretted her offhand comments. Whatever she'd said had triggered a response she hadn't intended. The carefully guarded personal space and profound reserve Glenn had initially projected right after they'd left Abigail Remy's office had begun to thaw as they'd talked. Now the wall was back again, a clear bulletproof barrier that left Glenn visible but untouchable. Mari regretted having hurt her somehow, for the warmth she'd felt just minutes before had been swallowed by a darkness that could only be pain. Hoping to coax some of the heat back into Glenn's expression, Mari extended an olive branch. "I could use a cup of coffee. And I would like to hear about the program."

"Even cafeteria brew?"

Mari shuddered but nodded gamely. "Bring it on."

"Sure, if you're willing to chance it." Glenn laughed, the deep chuckle a momentary breeze that blew the storm clouds from her eyes, lifted Mari's spirits. Glenn was off again in that fluid, loping gait, and Mari hurried after her.

Trying to keep a mental map of where they were going, Mari concentrated on memorizing the series of turns and staircases before they came to a pretty typical hospital cafeteria—bustling with people moving through the coffee line, grabbing food from the racks and hot trays, and clustering at round tables filling a long rectangular room. She winced at the dark brown liquid that came from the industrial urn as she filled her cup and contemplated adding cream just to dilute the acid content but didn't see any reason to start bad habits. She'd had plenty of bad coffee in her life. Plucking a decent-looking raspberry Danish from a tray, she paid and followed Glenn to one of the smaller tables on the far side of the room. She slowed and stared, coffee and Danish in hand. Windows. Big windows taking up half the height of the wall, and oh, the view.

Glenn sat and broke a bagel in half. "Something wrong?"

"I've never seen anything like this. I guess I've gotten used to being closed up inside the hospital. I mean, there were always windows, but there was nothing much to see outside them. Parking lots and other buildings. So you just sort of stopped looking, you know? As if the world outside was gone. But here—just look! There are honest-to-God flowers out there. Everywhere. And not a car in sight."

"The architects were smart when they added the lots—they're below the crest of the hill, so you still have the effect of being above it all up here. You should see it in spring. The rhododendrons and azaleas are blinding. It's even nice when it snows. The windows in the ORs face the mountains, so it's pretty spectacular."

"Oh my God. You have windows in the OR suites? How do you work?"

"It's nice." Glenn's expression grew distant. "Nice, but strange, to look up from the table and see the world out there. It kind of reminds you that this person you're working on is still connected to people and places beyond the spotlights and the machines and the instruments. Humanizes it all somehow."

"You really like the OR, it sounds like." Mari sat down across from her.

"I like doing."

"Me too, but the surgery rotation was my least favorite part of training."

"Why is that?"

"Too removed. I like talking to people, listening to them, finding out what's wrong by putting the pieces together. I'd miss the connection, I guess."

"I suppose it might seem remote," Glenn mused, "but I don't

think you can be any more connected than touching another person. Surgery's intimate, as personal as it gets."

Glenn's gaze flickered, like a page turning, and Mari knew instantly her thoughts had fled elsewhere again. She desperately wanted to know where Glenn went when memories—or something more than memories—pulled her away. What did she see, what power held her in its grip? When Glenn's gaze refocused on her, Mari knew she'd returned. Pretending she hadn't noticed the brief lapse, Mari said quietly, "I can't argue that touching is uniquely intimate."

"Different strokes," Glenn said casually.

Subject closed, but Mari wasn't ready to give up. "You were the regular first assist for Dr. Rivers in the OR?"

"I was pretty much her first assist for everything—I didn't work with anyone else on a regular basis. I saw patients in the ER when she couldn't, made rounds, took call, did cases with her."

"Like a partner."

"I suppose." Glenn sighed. "Yeah, pretty much. Flann let me do what I could do."

"This sounds like my kind of place."

"You'll have a lot of independence in the ER—if we get approval for level two trauma, we'll double our census."

"Is that likely?"

Glenn laughed. "I wouldn't be surprised if the new CEO pushed for level one. We're ten minutes by air from a major interstate with no other major hospitals around."

"I'm looking forward to the challenge."

"Where did you train?"

"USC in LA."

"Big place," Glenn said.

"Oh yes. Four hundred beds, level one trauma, Children's Hospital next door, advanced training programs in everything. Very big place."

"Cog in a wheel?"

"Maybe a little, but great training." Mari smiled, remembering how easy it was to get lost in the system. "How about you?"

"Uncle Sam," Glenn said abruptly. "So what did you do when you finished—before here?"

Mari had known this question would come up and hadn't practiced how she was going to answer. She wasn't ashamed or embarrassed or overly private about personal matters, but still, she hadn't wanted to drag the past with her to this new life. Of course, this was one thing that would never be the past. For now, though, partial truths would suffice. "I didn't—do anything, that is. I had a job lined up, but that fell through."

"How did you find out about us?"

The question was natural enough but alarm bells rang. All Mari wanted was to fit in, to have a place where she could work and be herself and not catch sidelong glances of curiosity or concern or condemnation.

"My previous program director contacted me. He'd heard about the new program and the openings here." Truth. Mari could still hear his cautious tone, his careful question as to whether she was ready to go to work. The opportunity had seemed heaven-sent, and the interview she'd had on Skype the next day had almost been a dream. She'd been so anxious for her long-distance face-to-face with the ER chief, she'd checked and double-checked her computer to make sure she could connect and was sitting in front of a blank monitor ten minutes before the appointed hour. Abigail Remy had been friendly and straightforward. She'd also said Max Gardner had talked to her personally and told her Mari was one of the best graduates he'd had in years. After twenty minutes, Mari had a job. She left all that out when she recounted the story to Glenn. "I guess you were busy that day. We didn't get a chance to talk."

"Abby hadn't convinced me to take the job yet." Glenn studied her. "So you're new at this."

Mari tried not to bristle. "Not exactly. I've had plenty of hands-on experience. Our program was very intensive, one of the best."

"I don't doubt it. We put on a big push to fill our instructor slots with good clinicians, and Dr. Remy wouldn't have taken anyone who wasn't the best. But there's a difference between boot camp and boots on the ground."

"I assure you, my boots are ready."

Glenn laughed again, such a rare sound it was as surprising as it was pleasing. She nodded and glanced at the coffee, untouched in front of Mari. "You ought to try it. Start getting indoctrinated."

Mari sighed and sipped. She tried another swallow. "Huh. It's quite good."

"That's Flann's doing. She got them to upgrade the brand of coffee and change out the urns every couple of hours. One of the perks of a small place like this. You won't be a cog in a wheel here."

"I'm glad." Maybe this place would be the community she'd lost. "I think I'll like—"

"Hey, Archer. Seven ten and you're still lounging over coffee. No wonder you jumped ship."

Mari stared up at the woman in navy scrubs and a wrinkled, shapeless green cover gown, rather like a giant cloak, standing beside the table. A surgical mask dangled around her neck and her disheveled mop of dark hair still showed the imprint of a surgical cap. Her face was all edges and long lines, attractive, Mari supposed, if you liked the dark, edgy type. She preferred Glenn's cooler, classic contours...and stopped herself before *that* thought went any further. Glenn was very good-looking, and the swift changes that came over her face—from light to dark, cool to warm—along with the fleeting hints at whatever she kept so close were fascinating. Mari had never looked at a woman and thought *fascinating* in her life, which ought to be caution enough. Glenn had secrets, just as she had, that was all. She felt a flush rise in her neck when she realized the newcomer was studying her with unapologetic frankness. She lifted her chin, refusing to be embarrassed by the scrutiny.

"Actually," Glenn said with that faint hint of a drawl, "we're in the midst of orientation."

"Ah. Fresh boots?" Grinning, the woman held her free hand out to Mari and sipped from the cup of coffee she held in the other. "Flannery Rivers. Welcome aboard."

Mari smiled and took her hand. The long fingers that closed over hers were firm and smooth and certain. "Mari Mateo, and my boots are already well broken in."

"Good to hear. Glenn will probably need all the help she can get."

"Thanks," Glenn said good-naturedly. "How's the patient from last night?"

"Just saw her. Temp's down and the leg looks good. Nice work."

"Thanks," Glenn said quietly.

Flann pulled a chair over from an adjacent table and settled in between Mari and Glenn at their small table. "How many more recruits do you have coming?"

"One more new staff and four students."

Flann laughed. "It'll be a hell of a day down there."

"We'll handle it." Glenn smiled. "Dr. Remy has put together an amazing program in an incredibly short time."

"You helped," Flann said.

"I followed orders," Glenn said.

"Well, Abby is very efficient when she wants something done." Flann glanced at Mari. "Dr. Remy managed to seduce Glenn away from the OR in record time." She shook her head. "First she takes my job, then she takes my right hand. It's a damn good thing I love her."

"Um…" Mari was at a complete loss and sent a helpless look in Glenn's direction.

Glenn laughed. "Dr. Rivers is chief of surgery, Mari, and for a while she wore another hat—heading up the ER too. Until Dr. Remy came along."

Flann sighed. "Yeah. Then Abby decided that Glenn belonged in the ER full-time, and she took her too."

"It seems that Dr. Remy has very good judgment," Mari said.

Flann grinned. "She has to, she's going to marry me."

"Oh." Mari laughed. Flannery Rivers might like to tease, but her fondness for Glenn was obvious, and the way her eyes sparkled every time she said Abigail Remy's name told exactly how she felt about her. Flann reminded her a little bit of her oldest brother Hector, always high on life, playful and charming, when he wasn't being downright annoying. A swift shock of sadness and unexpected longing shot through her. She caught her breath and forced a smile. "Congratulations."

"Thanks. I'm hoping Glenn gets bored fast and comes back where she belongs." Flann stood. "But in the meantime, good luck." Her voice had gone from teasing to sincere, and the warmth with which she looked at Glenn gave Mari some idea of the depth of the friendship between the two. She was glad. Glenn seemed so very alone.

"Don't get into too much trouble without me," Glenn said.

Flann squeezed Glenn's shoulder. "Wouldn't think of it. Don't forget to tell Mari and the rest of your new boots about the barbecue."

"Right," Glenn said, pulling her phone from her pocket as Flann walked off. She glanced down and then at Mari. "Incoming. You ready to go to work?"

Mari stood. "You have no idea."

CHAPTER FOUR

Mari raced at Glenn's side, threading between the tables on the way to the nearest exit. Most people barely gave them a glance, used to seeing staff race off to an emergency. Glenn didn't return the way they'd come, and Mari was quickly lost and didn't bother trying to follow their route. She just focused on keeping up with Glenn as they jogged around corners, through a fire door, and down a concrete stairwell lit by bare bulbs in metal cages.

"You run?" Glenn asked, not the least bit breathless.

"I did," Mari said, trying valiantly to sound as unstressed as Glenn. Her heart pounded against her ribs, but her wind was holding. Her legs were nearing jelly status, but then, she hadn't used them much in the last half a year or so. They couldn't have that much farther to go, could they? "I'm a little bit out of training just lately."

"You move like a runner."

Mari was oddly pleased by the comment but barely had time to appreciate it before Glenn pushed through another unmarked gray metal door and delivered them into the center of a tornado. A blast of disorienting noise and a flurry of rushing people sent a surge of panic racing through her. Nothing looked familiar—what was she supposed to do? After a second, Mari's pulse calmed and she made sense of the controlled chaos in the hallway. She'd seen this before. ER staff pushed gurneys toward the ambulance bay to await the injured, pulled back the curtains on examination cubicles, and opened equipment packs. Lights came on in a big room Mari barely had a chance to glance into as she hurried by, but even a quick look was enough to tell her it was a pretty fully staffed operating room.

"What have we got?" Glenn called to Bruce, the nurse Mari recognized from earlier.

"EMS is five minutes out. Grain silo collapse."

Glenn's face set into grim lines. "How many?"

Bruce shook his head. "We're not entirely sure. First report was three, then another unit called in and they're bringing two, and we think there might be more. Could be upward of ten." He grimaced. "Apparently a couple of people went in to try to help and ended up getting trapped themselves."

"How many people do we have down here?"

"Never enough for this kind of thing," Abigail Remy said, emerging from the reception area wearing scrubs and a white coat, her expression intense and hyperfocused. "Bruce, call up to the SICU and see if they can spare us a couple of nurses. Then get the respiratory techs down here—every one we have in-house. You'll be triage."

"Yes, ma'am," Bruce said, practically saluting. He spun on his heel and strode away.

Abby turned to Glenn and Mari. "Glenn, I want you to take the criticals, anyone that looks like they need immediate surgical intervention, get them into the trauma bay stat. I'll call Flann and alert the OR to put a room on standby."

"Roger." Glenn leaned toward Mari and lowered her voice. "How are you feeling?"

"Fine," Mari said. "I'm good."

She was. Her heart galloped with the adrenaline rush, but she wasn't nervous and she wasn't afraid. She also wasn't alone, and she knew it. If she got something she couldn't handle, she'd have backup. Glenn was here, looking solid and sure, as if she'd seen and done this kind of thing a hundred times before—because she had. Dr. Remy too. But most of all, Mari trusted her training.

"Good," Glenn said. "You'll take anyone who isn't actively hemorrhaging or in full arrest. Use room one."

"Okay—you better tell me about grain silos. What can I expect?"

Glenn's gray-blue eyes darkened to nearly black. "Don't see much of that in LA?"

"Try never."

"Depends on what was in the silo, but usually corn or wheat, which generates heat, toxic gases, and a hell of a lot of dust. When the structure collapses or the contents avalanche inside, whoever's buried will suffocate in seconds or be crushed, but they can also get sucked into the augers and mixers—meaning broken or severed limbs." She spread her hands. "If it takes more than a minute to extract the ones who are completely submerged, their lungs will be full of dust and even if we intubate, it's not going to be enough."

"So blood gases on everyone," Mari said, trying to formulate a treatment plan on the fly. This was nothing like a multi-vehicle pileup on the interstate, but the principles were always the same. "What else? Injury-wise?"

"Compression syndromes, fractured ribs, open and closed extremity type injuries. The fractures can all wait unless there's vascular compromise."

"Right. Airway will be the thing."

Glenn nodded. "If you need an assist, holler. I'll be right across the hall."

Bruce appeared around the corner. "The first bus is here."

Abby strode confidently into the center of the waiting staff. "All right, everyone, you know what to do. Let's go to work."

Mari took a deep breath and hurried into her room, quickly scanning the instruments set out beside the exam table. She pulled on gloves just as a stream of first responders burst into the ER pushing stretchers toward the rooms where Bruce had directed them. Two EMTs angled a stretcher into Mari's cubicle with a small form nearly dwarfed by oxygen tanks, an EKG monitor, and IV bags. All Mari could make out beneath the tape and O2 bag was a blue-tinged face and a shock of yellow hair.

A heavyset redhead at the front of the stretcher croaked hoarsely, "Juvenile, maybe ten years old, buried in three feet of dust—" He lost his voice for a second, then continued, voice steadier although agony misted his eyes. "The family had already dug him out, and the dad was doing mouth-to-mouth. We intubated in the field."

"Pulse ox?"

"60."

Mari's stomach plummeted. 60 was barely compatible with life and not enough to sustain brain function. She quickly listened to the boy's small chest and could hear no air moving in the lower two-thirds of his lungs. Thankfully she detected a rapid heartbeat, but that wouldn't last long if they couldn't ventilate him. "On a hundred percent O2?"

"That's what's running, but it doesn't seem to be doing much good."

Mari glanced at Beverly, a middle-aged brunette nurse who'd arrived to help. Her mouth set into a tight line, and Mari didn't have to ask why. If they did nothing, this child was dead. But no matter what she did, it probably wouldn't make a difference. Still, her job was to fight, as long as reasonable, and fight she would.

"All right," Mari said, hoping she sounded confident, since she hadn't actually heard of what she planned to do being used for anything like this. Although she hadn't heard of *this* until ten minutes ago. "Let's set up a saline lavage, get another pedi tube ready." She looked up at the two EMTs. "What size do you have in there?"

"Six," replied the second EMT, a thin young blonde with a silver hoop through the corner of her left eyebrow.

"Who intubated him?"

"I did," the blonde said.

"Did you see debris in his trachea?"

"I didn't see anything. It was a blind intubation."

"All right then, let's see what we can see." She ought to clear this treatment with someone before she went much further. "Beverly, can you get Dr. Remy or Glenn for me?"

"Not for a few minutes," Beverly said. "I saw them both at a resuscitation on my way in here."

"We don't have a few minutes," Mari muttered.

"Let's not waste any time, then," Beverly said briskly, as if telling her to do what she needed to do. She stood by with suction and a small-bore catheter connected to a saline bag under pressure.

"Time me." Mari took a deep breath and slid out the breathing tube, removing the only thing keeping the boy breathing—and alive. She didn't have long, but then, neither did he. She slid in her laryngoscope and lifted his chin, giving herself a narrow tunnel down which to evaluate his airway. The thin light at the end of the instrument illuminated the back of his throat and the upper part of his trachea. Where she should have seen glistening pink mucosa she saw only thick clumps of dark debris. It looked as if someone had poured concrete into his windpipe. No wonder he couldn't breathe.

"Let me have the lavage catheter."

Beverly slid the thin tube into Mari's hand and she threaded it down into the debris and hopefully into his trachea. "Go ahead, open up the bag and get the suction ready." Fluid shot into his trachea, completely blocking what remained of his airway. If this didn't work, he'd drown. The saline mixed with the dust from the grain silo, threatening to glue shut any possible avenues for airflow, and Mari frantically suctioned before the mixture turned into paste.

"Time?"

"Thirty seconds," Beverly said.

"Another fifteen seconds," Mari said, the muscles in her shoulders starting to ache.

The curtain twitched back and Abby Remy looked in. "What's the story?"

"Foreign material in the airway. Some kind of thick, particulate matter—dust, I guess," Mari said without looking up. "He was tubed on arrival, but not oxygenating. We're lavaging to clear the trachea and mainstem."

Abby threaded her way between the EMTs, who hadn't budged, to the head of the table and looked over Mari's shoulder. "Lift the laryngoscope a little bit more so I can get a better view."

Mari took a deep breath and lifted. Now her arm was beginning to shake. Keeping the jaw open and the airway exposed was strenuous, and she hadn't intubated anyone in almost a year.

"How long on the lavage?" Abby asked.

"Forty-five seconds."

"O2 sat?" Abby called out.

"58," the male EMT reported.

Mari's stomach plummeted. She was going to lose this boy.

"Keep going. You've almost got it," Abby said quietly, her sure, certain tone injecting much-needed strength into Mari's aching arm. "You want me to take over?"

"No," Mari said just a bit breathlessly. "He's almost clear."

"There you go," Abby said with a note of victory. "The suction fluid is coming back clear."

Mari finally breathed. "Turn off the saline and let me have the new ET tube."

"Here you go. A pedi six," Beverly said and slipped the curved plastic endotracheal tube into Mari's outstretched hand.

Never moving her gaze from the small dime-sized opening that led down into the boy's trachea, Mari slid the tube between his vocal cords and toward his lungs. "Hook us up?"

The ventilator began to hiss, and Mari slid out the laryngoscope and stepped back.

Abby listened to his chest with her stethoscope, nodding as she quickly moved the diaphragm over his chest. "Breath sounds are good. Pulse ox?"

"65," Beverly said.

"Increase the rate to twenty and decrease the volume. Let's rapid pulse him."

The pulmonary tech adjusted the ventilator, and the machine cycled quickly in short, sharp bursts as if it was panting.

"Suction him down the tube, Mari," Abby murmured.

Quickly, Mari complied, barely able to take her eyes off the pulse oximeter, hardly breathing herself as the numbers began to edge up. 68, 72, 75, 80, 85, 90.

"Holy Jesus," the big burly EMT muttered. "You got him back."

"Let's get a chest X-ray," Mari said, tempering her elation. A million things could go wrong, and if he'd been without cerebral perfusion for too long, she might not have saved him after all. Now only time would tell if he would recover. She had to be sure he didn't have other injuries that could complicate his recovery, and then they would wait.

Abby said, "Draw a full panel of bloods and get him up to the intensive care unit." Abby squeezed Mari's shoulder. "Very nice, Ms. Mateo."

"Thank you."

As quickly as it had begun, it was over. Beverly drew bloods from the IV line and the two EMTs, who appeared to have no intention of leaving their charge, pushed the stretcher out into the hall. Another stretcher materialized in her cubicle, this one with a young man whose right arm was misshapen and bloodied.

"Hi, I'm Mari Mateo, a PA," she said, and got back to work.

❖

Mari had no idea how much time had passed by the time the last patient left her cubicle for an observation room upstairs. It might've been ten minutes, it might've been ten hours. All she knew was she'd never felt so exhilarated in her life. She'd splinted fractured limbs, inserted a chest tube under local anesthesia, and treated an acute case of asthma with inhalation agents and intravenous medications, avoiding a dangerous intubation. She'd evaluated more complex cases in one day than she had in a month of training, and she'd managed mostly on her own. She'd been dimly aware of the seething activity around her as she'd worked—once she'd heard the high-pitched wail of someone's heart breaking, and a moment later Glenn's low-pitched, melodious cadence calling for a cutdown tray. Dr. Remy popped in and out of her room, checking patient status, reviewing a treatment plan, offering suggestions.

As soon as the transport orderly took her patient, a forty-five-year-old fireman with an impending MI, to the medical intensive care unit and no one brought another patient to replace him, she sagged into the hard plastic visitor's chair against the wall of her treatment room and stared at the litter-strewn floor. An errant glove someone had tossed toward the trash can and missed, an IV tube dangling from a metal stand, the saline slowly dripping into a clear puddle, bandage wrappers, a plastic cap from a syringe. A war zone.

"How'd you do?" Glenn asked from the doorway.

Mari glanced over at her. "Okay, I think. I didn't lose anyone."

"That's a good first day, then." Glenn grinned and checked her watch. "Of course, you've still got another eleven hours to go."

"You're kidding."

"Nope. It's just a little bit after 0830."

"Oh my God." Mari blew a strand of hair from her eyes. "Is it over? Did we win?"

Glenn's eyes clouded. "Mostly. Two fatalities, both submersion casualties—a twenty-year-old farmhand, first day on the job, and the thirteen-year-old daughter of the farm owner."

"Damn," Mari whispered, sadness blunting the thrill of victory she'd experienced just moments before.

RADCLY*f*FE

"But I hear you saved her brother—smart thinking. A gutsy call."

Mari shrugged. "Probably more beginner's luck."

"I don't believe in luck—unless it's bad."

At the sudden dark tone in Glenn's voice, Mari took a hard look at her. Her skin was pale beneath her tan, her face drawn and tired. She'd had the critical patients and had probably been involved with the fatalities. "Are you all right?"

"Me? Sure. Fine." Glenn shrugged and her usual mantle of calm control fell back into place. "Come on, I'll show you where the locker room is. You can get clean scrubs and shower if you need to."

Following Glenn's pointed gaze, Mari looked down at herself and realized that a spray of blood from one of the IVs she'd started had left a crimson crescent across her chest. Another splotch of blood marred her thigh. She couldn't see patients the rest of the day like this.

"You're right. I need to get cleaned up."

"You probably ought to have something to eat. This kind of thing burns off a lot of energy, and you don't want to crash later."

"I'm not eating anything until…" Mari made a face and indicated her blood-soaked scrubs.

"I'll grab something for you while you shower. Cereal is always a good quick fix."

Mari grimaced. "How about a bagel."

"I can always dig up a bagel. Cream cheese?"

"Peanut butter. More protein."

Glenn grinned. "You got it."

The women's locker room occupied the opposite end of the ER from Dr. Remy's office. Glenn tapped a locker with a small metal tag stamped with the number 37. "This is yours. You'll need to bring a lock from home, but truthfully, no one is going to take anything."

"I don't really have much to take. A five-dollar bill is all the money I brought with me." Mari shook her head. "I should've thought to bring a change of scrubs."

"Don't worry about that. The hospital provides. Towels are in the shower room."

"Thanks."

"Don't mention it." Glenn hesitated for a second. "And you're right, you're not all that green."

Mari smiled to herself as Glenn disappeared, leaving her alone.

• 42 •

She chose the farthest of the three shower stalls, found the clean stack of white towels, and grabbed two. She left her clothes in a pile on a narrow bench outside the stall and stepped into the hot water. She kept her hair dry as she slowly turned in the strong jet, reveling as the heat soaked into her muscles and eased away the tension and stress. Tilting her head back, she closed her eyes and emptied her mind.

"Hey, you need anything?" Glenn's voice called from somewhere nearby.

Mari's eyes snapped open. She thought she might actually have been asleep.

"No. Thanks. I'll be right out." She quickly turned off the water and stretched an arm outside, feeling around blindly for the bench where she'd left the towel. Only then did she realize she couldn't reach it without stepping out. "Um…do you think you could hand me the towel?"

For a long moment, she thought Glenn had left.

"Sure," Glenn said at last.

Suddenly shy and having no idea why she should be, Mari curled the curtain back but kept it covering her body. Glenn stood three feet away, one arm extended, the white towel dangling from her hand, her face averted.

Mari took the towel. "Thanks."

"You're welcome," Glenn said in a slow, soft, impossibly sultry voice. Slowly, Glenn looked in her direction.

Mari could've ducked back into the shower, but why should she? She certainly wasn't ashamed of her body, and she wasn't bothered by Glenn seeing her. Besides, she was pretty much completely covered by the very not-sexy shower curtain. "I'll be right out."

"Got your bagel out here." Glenn turned away.

"Glenn?"

Glenn spun back around. "Yes?"

"I forgot to get scrubs."

"They're in the other room."

"I was afraid of that." Mari wanted to laugh, but Glenn's expression was so intense, so serious, so *focused* on her.

"Smalls?" Glenn asked, making the word sound ridiculously personal.

"Medium. I like them roomy."

Glenn gave a little bow. "At your service."

Mari finally laughed. "I don't usually require this much service."

"I don't mind."

Mari let the curtain fall closed, holding the towel between her breasts. Nothing had happened. But she felt as if it had.

CHAPTER FIVE

Abby ought to be celebrating, but she couldn't shake the bittersweet taste of flawed victory from her mind. Her ER staff had earned high marks for their handling of their first mass casualty alert. Everything had gone well, by the book. But by-the-book success didn't make her feel any better when she'd had to tell the parents of a thirteen-year-old girl that she hadn't been able to save their child. Telling a family member they'd lost a loved one was never easy, no matter the age of the patient. Everyone always thought the death of an older individual was easier to accept, but it wasn't. Everyone was important to someone—loved and cherished and depended upon. Everyone, she'd come to learn, was woven into the fabric of life in some way, even those who seemed to be most disenfranchised. She could still remember the day a homeless person, one of the favorites of just about everyone at the otherwise big impersonal city hospital, had died in his sleep on the corner by the main entrance, wrapped in his many layers of clothing and surrounded by his tattered grocery store bags filled with what remained of his earthly possessions. Everyone mourned, perhaps more than would have mourned the loss of someone known to far fewer people. Perhaps more than anyone would mourn for any of them. Benny the Bagman. She smiled sadly at the memory.

Flannery Rivers tapped on Abby's open door and strolled in.

"Hey," Abby said softly. Just the sight of her lifted Abby's spirits.

"Hey yourself, Dr. Remy." Flann turned, eased the door closed behind her, and came around behind the desk. She crouched, cupped Abby's cheek, and kissed her.

"Flann," Abby murmured. "Not appropriate behavior for the work environment."

"Hey, this used to be my office. It's seen worse."

Abby laughed and some of the pall lifted from her heart. "I actually believe you, and I'm very glad to know that your new office is about the size of a telephone booth and not very private."

"Why would I want to have sex in a telephone booth when we have that spacious eight-by-ten bedroom at home with a sixteen-year-old sleeping in the loft?"

"Oh, come on. It's at least ten by twelve." Abby sighed, aware their courtship was far from typical—they hadn't had much chance to bask in the insanity of falling in love when she had a teenager to raise. A particularly vulnerable teenager at that. She couldn't be more in love or more ecstatic, but she still wished she could be as free as her friend Presley seemed to be in *her* new love life. For all appearances, Presley Worth and Harper Rivers spent every spare second enjoying one another. Abby didn't want Flann to miss a second of that kind of pleasure. "I know, I'm sorry. It *is* crowded."

Flann ran her thumb along the curve of Abby's jaw. "It's perfect. I wouldn't change a thing—well, I'd like a bigger bedroom with a slightly more substantial door on it."

The light in Flann's eyes telegraphed exactly what she was thinking about. Abby blushed.

"Really, Abs?" Flann murmured. "After what we did just last night, you're blushing at the mere suggestion of carnal pleasure?"

"Stop," Abby whispered, struggling not to touch her. "I can't be thinking about that right now."

"Funny, I can hardly stop thinking about it." Flann traced a finger along her jaw. "Besides, we won't be there much longer."

"God, I hope this contractor turns out to be someone we can work with. I really want to get the new place renovated so we can move in before winter."

"Baby," Flann murmured, "winter comes early in these parts."

Abby's eyes took on that fierce light Flann had come to recognize as absolute determination. "The first snowfall is five months away. That's plenty of time to get us two working bathrooms and a decent kitchen."

"And a roof that doesn't leak and some modicum of heating," Flann added.

"You said one of those pellet stoves would heat the whole place."

"Probably. I said probably."

Abby tapped Flann's chest with a fingertip. "We paid cash so we could get our family moved in as soon as possible. And that does not mean next year. I want to have our own *private* bedroom."

"I'm sure Blake would like a bedroom too."

Abby laughed. "I think he only mentions it once a day."

Flann's heart gave a little jog at the words *our family*. She had her own family to look after now, and she hoped to God she was anywhere near as good at it as her mother and father were. "I take it the excitement is over down here. Sorry I missed the fun. How did it go?"

"Good," Abby said quickly. "Good. Everyone held steady and did their part. We admitted five, streeted three, and didn't have to transfer anyone."

"Good for you." Flann rose and settled her hip onto the corner of the desk, playing with a strand of Abby's golden hair. She loved the color, like sunshine on a wheat field, and the texture, soft and silky as the strands of fresh young corn. "So what did I see in your eyes when I walked in? Some kind of trouble."

"I hope you're the only one that can read me that well," Abby muttered.

"I better be."

Abby caught Flann's hand and kissed her palm. "Believe me, you're the first to do it and the only one who is ever going to see inside me."

"What happened?"

"We lost a teenage girl, just a couple years younger than Blake. It was horrible. She suffocated in the silo."

"Damn," Flann murmured. "Every couple years something like that happens around here. Who was it?"

"A farm family up the Hudson a ways. Hoffertin. The girl's name was Annie."

"I knew a Jim Hoffertin, used to be a quarterback for Granville High. About four years older than me, I think. I know his family had a farm."

"That's the father."

"Man, that's hard."

"It's worse, I think, because the girl went in after her brother when the silage funnel collapsed and they managed to get him out but not her."

"I'm sorry."

"Yeah, so am I."

"But the brother made it?"

"He did, at least we think so. He's still on a blower and probably will be for at least twenty-four hours, but his vital signs are good and preliminary EEG shows pretty normal activity. We were lucky—our PA started to lavage him right away and cleared his lungs enough to ventilate him."

"Nice. Pretty sweet trick for the ER."

Abby smiled. "Eventually you'll learn to respect what we can do down here."

Flann spread her hands. "Hey, I'm not arguing. The more you do, the more time I have to take care of the real emergencies."

Abby snorted. "God, I don't know why I love you as much as I do. You're such an arrogant ass sometimes."

Flann leaned down and kissed her. "It's because I'm so good in bed."

"That must be it, because it's certainly true."

"Replay tonight since neither one of us is on call?"

"Tonight, sometime. I think Blake and Margie need a ride to some event at the fairgrounds, and we'll probably have to pick them up."

"Not one of the music festivals, is it?" Flann frowned. "Those crowds are rough and there's alcohol and every other thing around."

Abby smiled. "Take it easy there, cowboy. You know those two aren't going to get into that kind of thing—they have good judgment, but even so, I'm not that naïve. It's a rodeo."

"Huh. Slightly better. Okay. Sex between chauffeur trips, then."

"It's a date, Dr. Rivers."

Flann rose. "I'll be thinking about you the rest of the afternoon. Text me when you're ready to leave, and I'll see if I can get away. We'll grab dinner somewhere."

"I'll do my best. We've got new students today and a couple of new staff and it's already been a hell of a morning."

"Hey, you wanted to run the ER. It takes a unique level of skill and—"

"Go before your head doesn't fit through the door." Abby made shooing motions.

Laughing, loving to tease and loving that Abby let her, she headed down the hall and nearly ran into the other member of her family. He'd grown two inches since that morning, and she was pretty sure his voice was lower. He was still skinny as a beanpole in an oversized T-shirt and baggy shorts, though. "Whoa. Hey, Blake. What are you doing here?"

Blake shoved a thick lock of dark hair off his forehead, a habitual motion when he was nervous. He had his mother's intense eyes. "I just wanted to talk to Mom for a few minutes. Is she busy?"

"You'll have to check with her, but I think she's still free. Everything all right?"

"Yeah, sure. Great."

Flann was getting used to teenage speak, since her sister Margie was just about Blake's age and about as communicative. When Margie'd been a little girl, you couldn't shut her up. Why this, how that, what are you doing? Now she was usually lost in a book or off with Blake or doing other things that were clearly unexplainable, because when asked, her usual response was *nothing special, not much, whatever,* and *really* with several exclamation points. Flann hadn't been a teenager for a decade plus some, but she did remember when she'd reached the monosyllabic stage, she'd mostly been thinking about sex. She didn't really want to think about her sister Margie and sex, or Blake for that matter, and especially not the two of them and sex together. Her head hurt all of a sudden, but now she was a parent. "You can talk about it, you know, whatever…it is…you know?"

Blake stared at her. He'd only ever talked to his mother about things that really mattered, the things that scared him, and that probably scared her too. And then Flann had come along and his mother had fallen in love with her and he'd pretty much fallen in love with her too. Not the same way, for sure, but he couldn't think about the future now without seeing Flann and his mother and him all together. Still, it was hard to trust someone who hadn't been there his whole life, especially with things that nobody seemed to understand. Not even his mom sometimes. "Yeah. I know. It's not that."

Flann grinned. "Well, if it ever is…that—one of us, me or your mom, we'll probably know something about whatever *that* is."

"Yeah. Maybe. Sure."

Flann resisted the urge to tousle his hair, but she really wanted to. He was so sweet, although she'd never say so. Teenage boys weren't sweet, not in their minds. But he was. He was good and kind and sensitive. She deeply, deeply feared he was going to get his ass kicked more than once, more than most teenagers. She didn't want that to happen. Wouldn't let it happen if she could help it. She squeezed his shoulder. "I gotta get back to work. I'll see you at home tonight."

"Right."

Flann turned away, and Blake called to her. "Hey, Flann?"

Flann looked over her shoulder, one dark eyebrow raised.

"Thanks."

"Don't mention it."

Blake peeked into his mother's office. She was sitting behind her desk, her head tilted back, her eyes closed. He wasn't sure if he should interrupt or not but she knew he was there, she always did.

"Come on in," she said, eyes still closed. "Is there blood?"

"No, no injuries."

"Good." Abby opened her eyes. "What are you doing here? I thought you and Margie were going on rounds with the vet."

"I was going to, and then I thought I'd come talk to you instead."

"Okay. Is something wrong?" She had a horrible thought. "Please, please don't tell me you want to move back to the city, because that is so impossible."

"No way," Blake said dismissively. "I don't ever want to move from here. But Margie and I were talking."

"Uh-oh."

"Come on, Mom," Blake said in his long-suffering tone.

Abby laughed. "Okay, okay, I'm sorry. I know the two of you never come up with anything together except brilliant ideas. So what is it?"

"We decided that we need to get as much clinical experience as we can, before we get our formal training and set up practice together."

"Meaning?" Abby said, wondering if either of them would ever go through with their teenage dream to become vets, return to the community, and set up a practice together. She'd wanted to be a doctor as long as she could remember, and she'd never wavered, but many teenagers their age changed their minds about the future along with their hairstyles. Add to that the fact Margie had never had much experience outside her hometown and Blake's big city exposure hadn't been exactly great—they both had a lot of the world left to see. "So did you change your game plan?"

"No, but we thought we should get some human experience as well as, you know, animal."

"I see. Humans not being animals."

"You know what I mean, Mom."

"It's a good idea. A lot of techniques in human medicine are applicable to veterinary medicine, and believe it or not, there's actually some crossover the other way around. What were the two of you thinking?"

"That we'd split the summer," he went on quickly. "I'd start here and Margie would start with Dr. Valentine, and then we'd switch."

"Doing what?"

"Well," Blake said slowly, "that's kind of where I thought you could help. Like…I don't know—whatever you need us to do, volunteering, I mean." He grimaced. "And I don't mean standing around greeting visitors."

"Honey, this isn't Home Depot. We don't have greeters."

"That's good."

"Give me a minute." Abby sorted facts. They were both sixteen, or Blake would be in a few days. Legally they could do volunteer work at the hospital. Unpaid, but that was only fair, considering they were also completely unskilled. They were both bright, mature, and sensitive kids. "We could use a volunteer in the ER, and I bet Flann could use one in the OR."

"Really?" Blake's heart skyrocketed. "That would be incredible."

"Do you have any idea what that would be like?" Abby said gently. "Those are two of the most challenging areas of the hospital. The patients we see are often very sick or seriously injured, even dying. It wouldn't be easy, and it might be scary."

"You do it every day. So does Flann."

"I know, and it never gets any easier." Abby tried not to think of the Hoffertins and the still, pale body of the beautiful young girl on the cold stainless steel table, her mother and father broken in grief. "And it's still hard on us too."

"I think we can do it, both of us. Please, Mom. We could help."

"It would be mostly scut—taking things to the lab, helping the nurses change sheets and clean rooms, that kind of thing."

"That's okay. We'd still see things, learn things."

"I'll have to talk to Presley and Harper and make sure they're all right with it. And clear it with Flann too, but I'm sure she would love another body up in the OR to help out."

"Thanks, Mom." Blake just about vibrated while managing to stay in one place. "I'm gonna call Margie and let her know."

"Tell her it's not a done deal," Abby called after him.

"Got it."

She smiled as his footsteps disappeared down the hall. In a few short months, he'd transformed, not just physically as he transitioned, but emotionally and psychologically. He was happy now. His happiness filled her with joy.

And his life wasn't the only one that had changed. She thought of Flann and the night ahead. Still smiling, she speed-dialed a number and waited. "Glenn? Let's get the newbies into the conference room and bring them all up to speed."

CHAPTER SIX

Mari slumped on the narrow bench across from her locker and tried to summon the energy to pull out her purse and drag her weary body down the hill, through town, and back to her apartment. Twenty more minutes of movement seemed like an eternity. She couldn't remember the last time she'd been so tired. She could, actually, but then she hadn't been just tired, she'd been drained of everything: energy, will, even hope. Not now, though. This was an altogether different form of exhaustion. This was the aftermath of a campaign waged and won. Beneath the nagging ache in the small of her back, the twinge of pain in her calves, and the faint harbinger of a headache throbbing at the base of her skull, she felt anything but hopeless. She hadn't worked so hard in over a year, and she'd been so busy all day, she hadn't been able to think of anything except the patients, their families, and her obligations. When she wasn't treating one of them, or discussing a case with Abby or Jason Monroe, the other ER doc, she was supervising one of the new students. And somewhere in the midst of all of that, she'd had to meet with Glenn to review the curriculum, only to discover she had a lecture to give the next morning at seven a.m. She looked at her watch. In exactly twelve hours.

Mari closed her eyes and groaned.

"How are you doing?" Glenn said from somewhere so close behind her, Mari jumped. "Sorry, didn't mean to bother you."

"No," Mari said, springing up on suddenly shaky legs. She caught herself with an outstretched arm on the lockers. "You didn't. I was just…thinking."

Glenn frowned. "You look a little whupped."

"Long day." Mari opened her locker, fished out her bag, and slung it over her shoulder. She smiled brightly—at least she hoped she looked perkier than she felt. She wasn't sick, she knew the difference, but she didn't want any questions about her doing the job. "Good day, though. I think I'm still on West Coast time."

"Uh-huh." Glenn leaned her shoulder against the bank of lockers. Mari was trying to pretend she wasn't almost out on her feet, and she wouldn't embarrass her by telling her the act wasn't working. She appreciated pride, and guts. It *had* been a good day, different than what she was used to, but surprisingly satisfying. If she wasn't used to eighteen-hour days she'd be beat herself. After the chaos of the mass casualty alert first thing in the morning, four bright-eyed and eager PA students had arrived on their doorstep, greener than green, and they had a full board backed up of routine patients to see. Some of them had already been waiting several hours. Glenn had planned a full morning of orientation talks and tours for the students, but patients came first. The newbies didn't seem to mind. Their first clinical rotation and Glenn had to sort them out on the fly, get them assigned to a senior supervisor, make sure they understood the chain of command, and keep an eye on them all day. Overseeing new troops in the field whose entire orientation included little more than an exchange of names wasn't anything new, and at least under the current circumstances, they weren't likely to get themselves blown up if they made a mistake. But the potential was there, figuratively if not literally, for them to FUBAR a trusting civilian, and that was unacceptable. So Glenn spent the whole day with eyes on the students even though each had their own assigned supervisor.

Mari had taken to the ER as if she'd been working there forever. Glenn clued in pretty quickly that she was a natural with patients, got along well with the nurses, and didn't ask for help unless she needed it—and knew when she did. Glenn hadn't spent valuable time watching Mari, and if she had, she might have noticed sooner the deepening shadows under her eyes. Her mistake—one she wouldn't repeat.

"Things went pretty well today," Glenn said. "You've got a knack with the students."

Mari smiled. "Thanks. They seem like a pretty good bunch."

Glenn unlocked her locker, stuffed her wallet into her back pocket, and locked up again. "So far."

"You have any worries?" Mari looked around to make sure they were alone. "I didn't notice any obvious problems."

Glenn shrugged. "No, not really. The usual pecking order—at the top is Antonelli, who's overconfident and cocky, and then there's Marcus on the bottom rung, uncertain and deferential. They'll need watching for different reasons. Baker and Hernandez are the middlemen, both solid, not flashy but they get the job done."

"Antonelli has something to prove," Mari said softly, thinking the big, dark-haired, movie-star-handsome man's attitude reminded her a little of Glenn. Although Glenn lacked the arrogance—she didn't need it. Her skill was all the swagger required to cement her place at the top of the hierarchy. "That might come from him being older than the rest. And his military service is a plus, even if it makes him a little hardheaded."

Glenn laughed. "He's got decent experience, it's true. Maybe a little too used to going it alone. Sometimes experience gets in the way."

"Double-edged sword."

"Many-edged sword," Glenn murmured. "At any rate, no clear and present danger among the group."

"I agree." Mari hitched her shoulder bag a little higher. "Well, I need to get home if I'm going to put together that talk for tomorrow morning."

"I've got a PowerPoint, if you want it, that would cover most of it. It hasn't been updated in a while, but it shouldn't take long to add a few pertinent slides. Place to start."

"I'll take it," Mari said instantly and pulled out her phone. "If you give me your number, I'll text you my email address right now. This is great."

Glenn hesitated. Flann and the hospital operators were the only ones who had it. Even Carrie didn't have it, and they often shared rides to and from events. Come to think of it, Carrie had never asked and she'd never thought to offer. "Right. Sure."

Mari tapped away, and a few seconds later, Glenn's phone buzzed. She checked the text and saw an email address. "Got it."

"You're a lifesaver." Mari started for the door. "I'll be home in twenty minutes, so send it over whenever you think of it."

"You walking?" Glenn asked. Sunset wasn't for another hour, and even if it had been dark, Mari would be fine walking home alone.

Still, unease gnawed at the part of Glenn's psyche that couldn't stop assessing, surveilling, hunting for hidden dangers. For the secret killers.

Mari nodded. "How did you know?"

"Because you can drive anywhere in town in ten minutes or less, and if you're not living in town, you've probably got at least a half-hour drive."

"Excellent deductive reasoning." Mari laughed. "I'm on Elm. No car, but it's a nice walk."

"Wait until it snows."

"Huh. I've never lived where it snows."

"Hoo-boy." Glenn grinned. "I didn't notice you taking a lunch break. Dinner either, now that I think of it."

"I didn't even notice I was hungry." Mari laughed. "I'm starting to now, though."

Glenn knew for a fact Mari hadn't taken a break of any kind all day. Maybe that was why she looked like a twenty-minute walk would wipe her out. Glenn hadn't been planning to leave, wasn't in any hurry to get home with nothing much to do, but she sensed Mari was working hard to cover up her fatigue. Surprising herself, Glenn said, "Me too. How about I walk down with you, and we get something to eat?"

Mari raised a brow. "Are you by any chance offering to cook, because a, I don't think I have anything except cereal; b, I don't really have a full kitchen; and c, I'm too famished to wait for very long."

"That's a thought that never passes my mind." Glenn held the locker room door open as Mari passed by. She smelled like the vanilla soap stocked in the shower room. Nice and clean. Her hair looked as soft as black velvet. "I'm afraid my main food group is pizza."

"That's an easy one, then," Mari said as they walked out into a hot, heavy July night. The air was nearly tangible, thick with the promise of rain. Odd, the air for all its weight was nothing like the blanket of toxic smog that sometimes hung over LA. "Where is the best?"

"Bottoms Up, the bar at your end of town, makes a good one, if you want a cold beer to go with it. I'm pretty partial to Clark's, but that might be because it's ten steps from my door."

Mari laughed. "I'll take the closest."

"My place for dinner, then," Glenn said.

"All right, yes." Mari drew a deep breath and some of her weariness dropped away. Glenn's shoulder touched hers every few steps as they made their way down the winding road, and that was nice too. They didn't speak and she didn't mind. Glenn seemed content just to walk, and she was happy for the company, even though it was unexpected. She hadn't shared a meal with anyone in months, outside family, and then rarely. She hadn't been to a movie or out to dinner or even had a decent conversation with another soul. She wasn't looking for that connection now either. She'd learned not to lean on anyone once she'd gotten to a place where she didn't have to. She would never owe anyone anything again, never put herself in a position to be unable to fight back, out of obligation or guilt, but still, Glenn's rock-sure presence in the gathering dark was welcome, even in the silence.

❖

"This is without question the best pizza I've ever tasted." Mari slid a third piece of loaded veggie onto her plastic-coated paper plate.

Glenn smiled, enjoying Mari's pleasure and the unself-conscious way she attacked her food. "I'm not gonna argue that."

"I have a terrible feeling this might become my favorite dinner spot."

"Why terrible?"

Mari laughed. "I might need more exercise than walking a mile up the hill to work every day if I do this every night."

"I wouldn't worry," Glenn said. "You'll do plenty of running in the ER, and besides…I can't see as you have anything to worry about, a few pounds more or not."

Mari felt herself blushing. The compliment was probably not even intentional, just the kind of thing everyone said under those circumstances, but she liked the idea that Glenn had noticed. And wasn't that odd. She hadn't even thought about anything remotely intimate in so long she'd forgotten that was even a possibility. "Thanks."

Glenn tilted her head, a small line forming between her brows. "You're welcome, for whatever."

As she'd thought, Glenn hadn't meant anything personal by the comment. Mari hid her momentary consternation by glancing around the small storefront pizza parlor. The ovens were in the rear, with half a dozen tables and two standing counters dividing the room, and big plate-glass windows on either side of the door. She was surprised to see the place was packed on a Wednesday night. She and Glenn had snagged one of the few remaining tables when they'd arrived, and now they were all full, mostly with teenagers, but here and there a family or lone adult occupied a spot. The front door opened and another gaggle of teens came in, rushing to the counter and talking all at once. A boy and girl came in a second later and drew up to the rear of the crowd.

Glenn glanced over and instantly her whole demeanor changed, so subtly Mari might not have noticed if she hadn't been watching her for the last half hour. Glenn's expression blanked into remote, tight lines. Her eyes narrowed and scanned the entire room before settling on the teens in front of the counter, her shoulders coiled with tension. Mari followed her gaze, trying to see what had caught her focus so intensely, but didn't see anything out of the ordinary. A couple of kids jostled a couple of the other ones, comments flew back and forth too quickly to sort out, but Glenn must've heard something Mari didn't. Suddenly Glenn pushed her paper plate away and slid her chair back several inches. Her body flexed as if she was about to launch from the chair.

"What is it?" Mari asked.

"Probably nothing. Don't worry about it," Glenn said, her flat tone clearly at odds with her words.

When a dark-haired boy and a pretty girl with long, gold-streaked curls edged away from the crowd and claimed a suddenly vacant table, Glenn walked over, leaned down, and murmured something to them Mari couldn't hear. The kids were a cute couple, fresh-faced and wholesome, terms Mari didn't usually think about when looking at teenagers. The girl wore no makeup and had the slightly gangly, long-limbed build that heralded an elegant beauty in a few years. She was dressed simply in a red tank top and skinny jeans. The boy's refined good looks could have put him in contention for a modeling job in a fashion magazine, but he seemed unaware of his appeal in his loose T-shirt, baggy shorts, and typical slumped, teenage-boy posture she'd seen on her brothers.

The boy shook his head. The girl just shrugged and gave Glenn a wry smile.

Whatever they'd said didn't seem to defuse Glenn's hypervigilant mood. When she turned and took a step toward the group at the counter, the blonde grasped Glenn's wrist and tugged her back with a head shake. After a second, Glenn nodded curtly and returned to their table.

"Is everything all right?" Mari could tell from Glenn's brusque movements she still was unhappy about something, and Mari's instinct was to soothe her.

"More or less," Glenn said.

"Who are the kids?"

"Blake Remy, Abby's son, and Margie Rivers, Flann's sister."

"Wow, are they dating?"

"I don't know," Glenn said. "They're tight friends, though."

"They're cute."

"Uh-huh," Glenn said, still looking as if she was ready to go into battle.

That was it. Glenn's entire attitude emanated an air of readiness, not exactly aggressive, but prepared. Glenn's gaze suddenly shifted to Mari, and she shivered. She wasn't afraid, didn't feel in danger, but ice swept down her spine. "What?"

"What's a mean girl?"

Mari stared, then laughed softly. "You don't know?"

Frowning, Glenn shook her head. "I guess I missed that in high school."

"Who told you, then?"

Glenn tilted her head. "Margie. She said not to worry about the mean girls. But somebody's hassling them, and I want to know why."

"Oh, wow, okay. In a nutshell," Mari said, "means girls are all about being the popular ones, and anyone who isn't one of them is fair game for taunting and teasing."

"Bullying, you mean?" Glenn got that look again—a spring coiling. Mari's karate instructor when she'd been a preteen had called it a state of readiness. Watchful waiting.

"Not necessarily anything that extreme, but I suppose it depends on the person at the receiving end and how badly they want to fit in."

"Why? What's the goal?" Glenn asked, still looking flummoxed.

"Usually it's about boys. The popular girls are most attractive to boys, especially older boys."

"Can't imagine why," Glenn muttered.

"Don't you remember high school? Everything's about status, and who you date is a big part of that."

"I wasn't part of any of that."

"Loner?" Mari guessed.

"I just kept my head down and put in my time."

The statement was cryptic, but Mari sensed the memory was a hard one. "So the girls are giving Margie trouble?"

"Something like that, I think. Of course, neither of them would tell me."

"It's probably better they sort it out themselves. It's a teenager thing."

"Yeah, probably, but this is a little different."

"Why is that?"

Glenn seemed to be giving her answer some thought until she finally said, "It's not a secret, so I don't think he'd mind me saying. Blake is trans, and he's already drawn some unwanted attention from an older bunch of ass—morons."

"He's out to everyone?" Mari asked. "And Dr. Remy is supportive, I imagine?"

"Sure," Glenn said, as if there couldn't be any other answer.

Mari sagged back in her chair, so many emotions charging through her at once she had trouble sorting them out. "I think I'm jealous."

"Of what?"

"Of Blake."

"Are you saying you're…?"

"Me? No," Mari said, enjoying the look of worry that flashed across Glenn's face. "No, I am firmly a women-only lesbian, but I didn't really get that about myself until just recently. Makes me feel a little silly when I see someone like Blake."

"Some don't make all the connections right away. No harm, no foul."

"I bet you did," Mari said.

"What makes you think so?"

"Because you seem so certain, so sure of everything. Who you are and what you're about."

"Maybe that's just a front."

"I don't think so," Mari said softly.

"You still didn't tell me why you're jealous of Blake," Glenn said, once again neatly deflecting the topic from herself.

Mari regretted her impulsive statement. She wasn't ready to expose her private hurts, especially not so soon. "It's a familiar story, I guess. It's not important."

"If it's your story, it's not familiar, and it's not unimportant." Glenn held her gaze, steady and strong. "But it's yours to tell."

Mine to tell. Maybe Glenn *was* practically a stranger, but somehow, she didn't feel that way. Glenn was so intensely present, so focused on her, Mari trusted her in a way she hadn't trusted anyone in forever.

"It is, isn't it. My story." Mari took a breath. Maybe telling it would take away some of the pain.

CHAPTER SEVEN

"What do you think they're talking about?" Blake said quietly.

Margie swallowed her bite of pizza. "Who? Queen bitch?"

Blake cut a sidelong glance at the group of girls clustered around the counter, laughing with bright eyes that took in everyone in the room and quickly dismissed them, as if no one else mattered enough to be noticed. Usually Blake preferred to go unnoticed—but in a way, being erased with the flick of an eyelash was worse. Funny, he could barely remember when he wanted to be part of a group like that, though he never was. Too shy, too weird, too wrong. "Which one is the QB? Madison or Kaylee?"

"You can't tell?"

"I don't know, I don't pay all that much attention to them."

"That's probably part of the problem." Margie snorted. "Kaylee, of course. The one everyone follows around like a bunch of baby ducks."

"Hey," Blake protested, "I like ducks."

"Yeah, me too, usually." Margie leaned back and sipped her Coke, pretending not to notice when Kaylee, who she secretly envied for her straight blond hair that probably never got frizzy every time it even threatened to rain, looked in her direction. Margie practiced what Harper called a thousand-yard stare, looking somewhere over Kaylee's left shoulder and imagining herself standing in the middle of a huge cornfield with nothing around her but miles and miles of rows of green. She'd drown herself in the horse trough before she let Kaylee know that a single snarky comment even registered in her hearing, let alone made her mad.

"I don't get it," Blake said. "Them, I mean. Why be that way?"

Margie sighed. Sometimes, Blake was clueless, but then, weren't all guys when it came to girls? She leaned forward and lowered her voice, aware that Kaylee and company were still watching them. "You're the new guy, the *cute* new guy, and you're supposed to be paying attention to them, not somebody like me."

"What are you talking about? Somebody like you? You mean smart and funny and cute, instead of stuck-up and just downright… well, *mean*?"

"Whoa," Margie said, feeling her face flame. Jeez, she didn't want to be blushing in front of those girls. They'd think Blake had just said something way personal. Of course, he had, and that was kind of weird. Nice, but, jeez. "Is that what you think?"

Blake stared at the tabletop. "Well, yeah. I just figured you knew that."

Margie laughed. "Well, how am I supposed to know that if you never said anything?"

Blake lifted a shoulder. "I don't know, don't you ever look in the mirror?"

"Not where I spend a lot of time. Do you?"

"Uh…" Blake wondered if he should answer for real or just shrug it off. But it was Margie asking, right? And she got him. She never got turned off or made him feel like some kind of freak by anything he confessed. Being able to tell someone besides his mom, *instead* of his mom, about all the things he kept hidden made him feel normal. "I didn't use to like looking in a mirror because every time I did, I got this creepy feeling that everything was all wrong. That the person looking back wasn't me." He laughed and picked the edge of his paper plate. "Now I probably look too much."

"Is the right person looking back?"

Blake grinned, still not meeting her eyes. Still a little embarrassed, or maybe not embarrassed exactly, but self-conscious. "Yeah, pretty much, anyhow. More all the time."

"Well, I've probably never said this," Margie said, "in so many words, I mean, but like I said—you're a cute guy."

Blake raised his eyes. "You think by the time school starts, everybody will know about me, and maybe it'll already be over?"

"I don't know. I don't know anybody else like you, at least not here." Margie sighed. "Some kids are just jerks, but you'll be okay, sooner or later."

"Yeah, it's the later I'm worried about." Blake straightened his shoulders. "Anyhow, I wasn't talking about QB and Co. I don't care what they have to say. I was wondering about Glenn and Mari. Do you think they're talking about us?"

Margie glanced over to where Glenn sat with a petite, pretty woman with gorgeous black hair that shimmered even in the crappy light from the dingy fluorescents. Did everyone but her have to have great hair? "How do you know her name? I've never seen her before."

"Oh, I saw her today in the ER. She's a new physician assistant. We'll be working with her."

"That's cool." Margie snorted. "They look like they're on a date. I don't think they're thinking about us."

"You don't think Glenn is gonna say anything to my mom, do you?"

"About those bitches being bitchy?" Margie shook her head. "That's not Glenn. If she's worried about them hassling us, she'll do something about it herself."

"She won't, though, will she?"

"I don't think so. Not when we asked her not to."

"That's good, because I think the best thing to do is just ignore them," Blake said. "If we ignore them, maybe they'll quit."

"Yeah, maybe." Margie caught Kaylee sneering in their direction. She could handle the nastiness—she'd never wanted to be one of Kaylee's crowd—but she wasn't so sure she could ignore them if they made Blake a target for their meanness.

Mari searched for a place to start a story she'd never told before. "My family is a big one. Seven kids."

Glenn whistled. "That's kind of unusual today."

"Catholic. Anti-contraception."

"Brothers or sisters?"

"All brothers except my sister and me." Mari's voice caught and she cleared her throat. "Selena. She's my twin. We're the oldest." When Glenn politely didn't ask, she added, "Twenty-five."

"A twin. That's got to be special."

"Oh, it was. Is—I mean." Mari began folding the straw wrapper into tiny accordion shapes, staring at her hands until she saw they were trembling. She put them in her lap. When she looked up, Glenn was studying her with that same singular intensity.

"You don't have to talk about it," Glenn said softly. "Your story, remember?"

"I want to. I haven't, with anyone. But you're a good listener."

Glenn smiled. "No one is going to be fighting for our table. Take your time."

"About a year ago, I was kind of forced to take a good look at my life, and I finally admitted to myself what I'd pretty much always known, that I was a lesbian." Mari shook her head. "Boy, does that sound dumb now. I dated on and off in high school, lots of times double-dating with my sister, but that kind of trickled off when I hit my twenties. Selena dated enough for both of us, but my mother was pushing us both to get serious."

"Let me guess," Glenn said. "Grandchildren."

"Oh, yeah. As soon as possible, now that all of her own kids are at least teenagers."

"And?"

"And I never really could see myself with any of the guys I dated. A couple of them were nice and wanted to get serious, but I felt like I was only partly there. Something was missing—not with them, or at least not anything that was their fault. But something I wanted to feel, I just didn't."

Glenn nodded faintly and said nothing, waiting. From anyone else the silence would have been unnerving, but Mari sensed her attention like a touch. "When I got to a point where lying to myself about anything seemed pointless, I needed to tell my family. I needed them to know me."

"And they didn't take it well?"

Mari laughed, feeling the tears pool on her lashes. She blinked angrily. "My father is still not speaking to me except through my mother. My mother is waiting for me to outgrow this crazy phase. The worst, though, is Selena. She hasn't talked to me since I told her."

"I'm so sorry."

"Well," Mari said with a long sigh, "like I said, familiar story."

She glanced over at Blake and Margie, who were sharing pizza and talking with their heads bent close. "I know it has to be a lot harder for him in a lot of ways, adding all the physical changes to the emotional ones, but I envy him his mother's support." She glanced at Glenn. "And that of his friends."

"He's got plenty of people on his side, and he's a really strong kid." Glenn reached across the table and squeezed Mari's hand. "Like you."

"I don't feel so strong sometimes."

"Hey, you must have suspected how your family'd react," Glenn said. "But you did it just the same, and that took guts."

"I'd do it again," Mari said finally, and knowing that helped. "I just wish they could love the person I've always been."

"Maybe they will one day," Glenn said.

"Maybe. Anyhow, thanks for listening."

"Anytime," Glenn said. There was more to the story, but she knew all too well some things couldn't be uncovered all at once.

Mari pushed away the melancholy. Whatever her family did or didn't do, she had a life to build. "What about you? Is your family around here?"

Glenn grimaced. "I don't have much family to speak of. My mom died when I was about thirteen, and my old man is a drunk. I got out of Texas as soon as I could, and we don't keep in touch."

"I'm sorry," Mari said. "I must sound like a whiner. At least my family was always there for me through everything, even when they couldn't accept who I really was." She shook her head. "Love the sinner and not the sin, and all that."

"You'll be in good company around here, with the sinners and all," Glenn said with a grin. When Mari laughed, the sadness leaving her eyes, she was so beautiful, Glenn vowed to find a way to make her laugh again.

❖

"Shh," Abby said, half laughing, half groaning. "The windows are open."

"I'm not the one calling on the deities," Flann murmured, her mouth against the pounding pulse in Abby's throat. A trickle of a breeze drifted through the open windows, stirring the sultry air that settled on her naked back like an unwanted quilt. Sweat pooled at the base of her spine, and Abby's skin was an inferno against hers. Still, she wouldn't move away, wouldn't relinquish the heady feel of Abby's body under hers.

Flann skimmed a hand down Abby's flank, over her hip and around to the back of her thigh, hitching Abby's leg a little higher.

Abby gasped when Flann's taut thigh pressed harder between her legs. "I'd really, really like it if you put your hand where your leg is."

"Is that right." Flann nipped at the underside of Abby's jaw, loving the way Abby tensed beneath her. Whenever they were in bed together, she had this all-consuming urge to make Abby come, to feel her body tighten, winding higher and higher, until she exploded. No matter how many times she vowed to draw things out, to keep Abby on the brink, she had to force herself to go slow, to tease and torture, especially when Abby demanded instant satisfaction. Flann groaned just thinking about how sexy Abby was when she wanted to come. "God, you make me crazy, you're so hot."

"Then go crazy," Abby whispered in Flann's ear, catching her earlobe between her teeth. "Get as crazy as you want, just make me come. Now, damn it."

Laughing softly, Flann shifted her hips and slid her hand between them, cupping Abby in her palm. She slid one finger lower, drawing the tip along the petal-soft channel until she circled her clit.

"God, that's exactly right. You have the best hands." Abby dug her fingers into Flann's shoulders.

"All yours, baby." Flann stroked and circled and teased until Abby's breath shuddered and broke on a cry, then slid inside her to ride the orgasm from the first crest to another, even deeper orgasm.

Finally Abby grasped Flann's wrist, stilling her motion. "Stay right there. Don't move."

"You sure you want me to stop?"

"Positive. Perfect."

Flann relaxed, working to catch her breath. Somehow she never remembered to breathe when Abby was about to come. In another minute, Abby drew Flann's hand away, nudged her over, and leaned up on her elbow.

"I'll be happy when we have our own fifty acres and I don't have to worry about who might be listening." Abby kissed Flann and sighed.

"Who's worrying?" Flann asked.

Abby laughed. "If it's all the same to you, I'd rather not advertise our carnal ecstasies."

"Ecstasies, huh?" Flann grinned. "We might need more than fifty acres, because I think there's a lot of ecstasies, carnal and otherwise, in our future."

"You're right. Starting now." Abby kissed her way down Flann's throat, between her breasts, and lower. Flann's hands came into her hair, playing ever so softly over her scalp. She loved the way Flann caressed her, as if she was everything precious in the world. When she reached the base of Flann's belly, she stroked up the inside of Flann's thigh with the tips of her fingers until Flann groaned. Flann liked to tease, but Abby liked to take.

She pressed Flann's legs apart and made room for herself, slowly kissing her way from Flann's belly downward. When she took her in, Flann arched, a strangled cry caught in her throat. Abby's heart lifted and every single thought left her mind except one—pleasing the one woman in the world who held the key to everything in her life.

"Damn it, Abby," Flann said through gritted teeth. "You'll make me come right now doing that."

Abby grasped Flann's hand as she pushed her and pushed her, until Flann broke with a long, low groan, her body bowstring tight for an endless moment. Flann sagged back, and Abby pressed her cheek to Flann's thigh, listening to the sound of Flann's ragged breathing and her own runaway heart. She'd never been so content or so satisfied in her life.

"Have I mentioned I love your mouth?" Flann muttered, her words slurred.

"Now and then."

"And your hands."

Laughing, Abby kissed her thigh. "You might've a time or two."

"And everything about you?"

Abby roused herself and curled into the curve of Flann's body. Flann barely stirred. "I love reducing you to a quivering mass of jelly."

Flann chuckled. "Consider me quivering."

Abby tucked her cheek into Flann's shoulder, drew her leg over the top of Flann's thighs, and wrapped an arm around her middle. She couldn't get any closer, and never wanted to be any farther away. "I love you."

"I love you too. Let's get married before we move into the new place."

Abby stilled. "You still mean married as in church, minister, wedding ceremony?"

"Yeah, all of that."

"When were you thinking of doing this?" Abby willed her sex-addled brain to catch up to the conversation. Her heart started pounding again.

"No reason to wait."

"Flann, honey…Harper and Presley are getting married this summer."

"Yeah, I know that. I'm Harper's best man."

"So don't you think we should let the dust settle before we spring this on everyone?"

"Okay, so how about right after them?"

Abby laughed. "Do you know how long it takes to plan a wedding?"

"Are you kidding? With all the brainpower you and Presley and Carrie and my mother and sister have at your disposal?" Flann tugged Abby's hair. "Come on, you adore me, don't you?"

"Endlessly."

"And I am yours forever." Flann cupped Abby's cheek, her expression suddenly deep and intoxicatingly intense. "At least say you'll marry me now—soon—soonest. Please."

"Of course I will. Yes, a thousand times yes."

CHAPTER EIGHT

I hate to say this, but if I'm going to get that talk ready for tomorrow, I have to head home." Mari would have been happy to sit at the rickety table with the empty paper plates and the intriguing dinner companion for another hour if she weren't so damned tired. She hadn't had such a good time in forever. Their conversation had turned from the unexpectedly personal to easier topics—work, mostly, along with books they'd read or wanted to and how they'd each ended up running to relax. While they'd talked, the pizza place had cleared out and the night outside the big plate-glass windows had drifted to full dark. Someone had propped the front door open with a chair and the street was quiet except for the occasional passing vehicle and rare echo of conversation floating from open windows.

"Listen," Glenn said. "Why don't I take that talk tomorrow. It's been a long first day, and it will be late by the time you get it together."

"No," Mari said, reflexively refusing help, although at this point if she had a million dollars she would happily give it up to not have to go home and spend time preparing a talk. But she needed to pull her weight, for her own self-esteem and especially for the respect of people who depended on her to do her part. More than anything, she needed to feel whole again. "I appreciate it, really, but it's okay. I can handle it."

Glenn shook her head, a small smile on her face. "I don't doubt you can handle pretty much anything, but I don't think switching off lecture slots really warrants much of a firefight. It just makes good sense. You'll get some rest and be fresher tomorrow, and you'll put in a better day's work."

"Ha! Appealing to my sense of duty, are you?"

"Could be."

"You're pretty good at subtle maneuvering," Mari complained with a smile.

"Lots of practice. Well, what do you say?"

Mari was tired. She hadn't worked a full day since before she'd gotten sick. "Switching off talks—when's the next one?"

"You can take mine next week." Glenn leaned forward. "It's no big deal, Mari."

Mari liked the way Glenn said her name, or maybe she just liked the way her name sounded in Glenn's lazy drawl, but she flushed with pleasure and hurried to cover her reaction. "All right, I see the logic. I'll take you up on it. And thanks."

Glenn stood. "We're a unit, remember. That means we pull together and we get the job done."

"It's been a while," Mari said as she and Glenn walked out, "since I've been part of something that mattered. This matters a lot to me."

"I can tell." Glenn paused. "Listen, I was going to head out for a run. If you don't mind waiting about three minutes, I'll change into my running clothes and walk you home."

"Oh, you don't need to—"

"Hey," Glenn said, "time to get something straight. I know I don't need to, but I want to. You don't owe me anything in return."

Mari was glad for the darkness, feeling the heat in her face. "It shows?"

"That you don't want to owe anything? Yeah, and there's nothing wrong with that at all. But sometimes it's about the other person."

"I'd like the company," Mari said cautiously. Glenn drew her effortlessly into unfamiliar territory, every step new and unexpectedly exciting. Not a single thing had happened between them that was extraordinary, nothing that people didn't do every single day—have a conversation with a colleague, share pizza after work, even keep each other company on the walk to the bus or subway. On the surface, the time she'd spent with Glenn was unremarkable, except every second with her was like delving farther and farther into uncharted depths, where every breath counted. She ought to be cautious, or at least a little on guard, but she was not. She hadn't really risked anything, hadn't revealed too much, though. And she didn't want to say good night—not just yet.

"Where's your apartment?" Mari said.

Glenn pointed a finger up and slightly to the right. "Right there."

Mari laughed, breaking through the still waters of her uncertainty and taking a deep breath of cool, clean air. Glenn's apartment was next door to the pizza place, above what looked like an antique store, closed and shuttered now. "You weren't kidding about the pizza place being close to home."

"So you coming up?"

"Yes," Mari said before she thought herself into a problem that didn't exist. She was allowed to make friends, after all.

"Watch your step on the bricks," Glenn said, leading her down an unevenly paved alley between the two buildings that opened into a small gravel parking lot lit by lights above several of the rear doors of the first-floor businesses. A wooden staircase leading to an upper floor snaked upward along the middle of the building, and Mari climbed up behind Glenn to a wood deck. A small black wrought-iron table and two chairs sat in the corner of the otherwise empty space.

Glenn opened the screen door and motioned to the little seating area. "You can come in or wait out here. I'll just be a minute. Cooler outside."

Mari pulled out one of the chairs. "I'm good right here."

"Need anything?"

Smiling, Mari shook her head. "Not a thing."

"Be right back."

Glenn disappeared and Mari leaned back with a sigh. She couldn't see much beyond the confines of the dimly lit lot below, but she didn't really need to. The air had finally cooled, and a breeze smelling of something green and alive tickled her hair. The sky was clear and starlit, an amazing phenomenon she wasn't sure she'd ever get used to. From somewhere down the road or maybe across the fields, a lilting, melodious refrain she couldn't place drifted out someone's open window, the music triggering the memory of her mother ironing or folding laundry late into the night, humming along to the radio. God, she missed her. All of them.

Glenn stepped out in shorts, T-shirt, and running shoes. "Ready?"

Mari rose quickly and swallowed the sadness burning her throat. "Yes."

"You okay?"

"Fine. Although I think I could sit out here for the rest of the night. It feels great to be outside." Mari let herself stare, hoping the almost-dark covered her interest. The half-light softened Glenn's sharply etched features, but the running clothes revealed a lot more of her body than had been apparent in her scrubs. Her limbs were lean and muscled, her trunk slender and sleek beneath the sleeveless tee she'd cut off at waist level, baring a strip of skin just above her shorts that Mari found suddenly very captivating.

"I sleep out here sometimes, when it gets really stuffy in the middle of the summer," Glenn said.

Mari pulled her gaze from the pale, smooth skin and looked around. "On what?"

"The floor?"

"I got that part," Mari said laughing, "but I mean…there's no sofa or anything."

"Oh." Glenn laughed. "I just bring out a sheet and a pillow and bed down."

"The idea is nice," Mari admitted, "but the reality might be a little rustic for my taste."

"Hey, no stones, no sand, no fleas. As far as I'm concerned, that's perfect."

And there it was, the reference point that seemed to mark everything in Glenn's experience. Mari wondered what had happened to her over there and suspected she would never really know. Even secrets shared were often only half the story.

"How long were you in?" Mari asked as she followed Glenn down the wooden stairs.

"Eight years," Glenn said.

"And…over there?"

"Fifteen months, the last time." She stopped and slipped her palm under Mari's elbow. "Watch your step right here—pothole."

"Thanks, I'm good." Glenn's hand fell away, but Mari knew exactly where she had been touched. "More than once?"

"Three tours," Glenn said, surprising herself when she answered. Like a lot of vets, she didn't talk about her service except in the vaguest of terms. Many people were interested in what it was like, and she got that. Americans had lived with war for over a decade, had watched it begin in terror and unfold in horror on television in a way no war had ever been watched before. Countless knew people who had gone away whole and come back less than that, in spirit if not in body.

Flann was the only one Glenn ever talked about it with, and then only because Flann knew what not to ask. Flann wanted to know technical details—how battlefront medics handled traumatic injuries, how they saved lives in greater numbers than in any previous war. She never asked how the pain and terror and fear of failure affected those who knelt in the dirt and blood and smoke and waged their own personal wars on death. Glenn never minded talking about the things Flann wanted to know. Medicine was medicine, and the battlefield had taught her more than a lifetime of civilian practice in a clean, bright operating room stocked with everything she might need and all the help she'd ever want ever could. She remembered the day Flann had said she envied her the experience, and Glenn got that too. No one else would really understand what it was like to be pushed to the edge of her skill and knowledge and ability only to discover it wasn't enough, that she needed to do more. Risk more.

"I'm sorry," Mari said quietly. "I imagine it's something private, something you might not want to talk about. Your story to tell."

Glenn realized she must have gone silent. "A familiar story."

"Not when it's yours."

"I'm glad I was there," Glenn said, for the first time really knowing it was true. "Someone needed to be."

"There must be hundreds, more, who are glad you were," Mari said gently.

"I didn't do anything anyone else didn't do." Glenn shrugged. "Nothing remarkable, nothing worth reliving."

Reliving. Yes, that was exactly how Mari felt every time she imagined recounting the last year of her life—she feared she'd be right back there again, amidst the fear and the pain and the desperation. She quickly brushed the top of Glenn's hand, the most comfort she could offer when Glenn so clearly didn't want sympathy. "If, when, there's something, anything, you want to talk about, I'd like to hear it. But if you never do, I understand."

"If I ever do, I have a feeling it would be you."

Glenn spoke so quietly she might have been talking to herself, but Mari heard the words, sensed them settle in the deepest part of her like a cherished gift. She took a second until the tightness in her throat abated. "Are you really going running?"

"Sure, why?"

"For one thing, it's dark, and besides that, weren't you up half the night operating with Flann?"

"Yeah," Glenn said, not quite following Mari's questions.

Mari laughed. "Well, aren't you tired?"

"Oh no, not really. I don't need much sleep."

"Apparently." Mari pointed to her house. "I'm in there. Second floor."

"I'll see you tomorrow, then."

"Thanks for dinner. Be careful running."

"I will." Glenn was pretty sure she didn't have anything to be careful about, but Mari's concern felt weirdly good. She waited on the sidewalk until Mari unlocked her door, turned, and waved.

"Night!" Mari called.

"Night," Glenn whispered, and started to run.

CHAPTER NINE

Glenn never ran the same route twice. Habit was a dangerous thing. Habit could get you killed. She usually headed for the narrow roads on the outskirts of the village and then looped around the borders between town and farmland, avoiding the populated residential streets where kids and dogs congregated in the road and on sidewalks until dark. Tonight she threaded her way through the mostly empty alleys and service roads behind the businesses on Main Street and across the abandoned, overgrown railroad tracks that once transported corn and milk and flax from the surrounding farms toward the river, where barges carried the goods south and west. The train, like an interrupted lifeline on a scarred palm, no longer linked communities in the heart of the upland farms, although a freight train cut across the countryside close enough for Glenn to hear its lonely whistle crying in the night. At dawn and dusk, her favorite times to run, the roads were mostly empty, and only her footfalls kept her company.

Within minutes, her body settled into its patterned rhythm, and her senses opened to the night. Air moist with a hint of rain and smelling of freshly turned earth, crushed blossoms, and tendrils of charcoal smoke streamed over her skin. Wisps of clouds raced overhead, daring her to keep pace on their wild dash across the face of the moon. A dog barked. A coyote answered with a distant howl. Her heart tattooed a beat that kept pace with the slap of rubber soles on asphalt. Usually this far into her run her mind had stilled, bereft of thought for the only time all day.

Not so tonight. Tonight she thought of Mari Mateo. Oddly, she didn't focus on the day they'd spent working together the way she usually considered her interactions with colleagues, although Mari had settled in seamlessly and was a welcome addition to the team. She remembered instead the easy way they'd talked about the hardest things, for both of them. She'd always been a pretty good listener, even when she'd rather shut out the shouts for *medic* or whispered pleas to make sure some loved one in another part of the world knew a soldier's last thoughts had been of them. She'd never been a talker herself— never saw the point in dwelling on what couldn't be changed—but Mari's courage in exposing her personal struggles had inspired Glenn to open up a little, hell, a lot more than she ever did with anyone else.

As she covered the miles, she replayed more than their words, although they counted for a lot. Images cascaded through her mind, of Mari engrossed in examining a patient in a brightly lit cubicle, Mari sitting across from her in the hole-in-the-wall pizza place, Mari relaxing on Glenn's pathetic excuse for a porch as if there was nowhere else in the world she'd rather be. Glimpses of gleaming hair, so black and bright, and the quick flash of warm dark eyes and an amused smile lit up her consciousness like a strobe suddenly illuminating a dark screen. She could have wiped the images from her awareness if she'd wanted, but she didn't. Memories of Mari kept her company as her limbs stretched and her lungs expanded, reminding her of something she'd forgotten or maybe never really known, that the other side of solitude was loneliness. She was used to being alone, even in a crowded camp or bustling ER, and she'd never considered she was lonely. Maybe it took not being to know you were.

Glenn let the unanswerable question flee with her straining breaths. She was doing fine, no matter how she described her life, and one shared dinner with a companionable woman wasn't about to change that, nor did she want it to. She'd faced her ghosts and was making peace with them in the best way she could. That was enough for her.

As she reached the farthest point from town and turned to circle back, traffic suddenly picked up. She slowed and stared at a light patch in the sky that shouldn't be there. Laughing, she cut down a side street and ran toward the illumination coming from the fifty-acre fairgrounds on the east side of the village that was alive with music, the roar of mingled voices, and multicolored flashing lights. Now she knew where everyone was headed on a weeknight. The rodeo.

She'd forgotten the rodeo was in town for the rest of the week. When the fairgrounds weren't home to the annual summer county fair with its vendors, barns full of animals, show rings, and carnival midway, the space hosted other events: the boat show, huge antique fairs, classic car exhibits, and the always popular rodeo. Pretty soon a steady stream of pickups and cars passed her, and on a whim, she pulled the twenty dollar bill she kept folded in the small key pocket of her shorts and purchased a ticket for the grandstand show.

She picked up a bottle of water from the guy selling soda, beer, and water from a cooler he lugged back and forth in front of the grandstand and went in search of a seat in the nearly full stands. She'd seen the barrel racing, cattle roping, bareback riding, and obstacle course races a few hundred times in her life, or so it felt, but she still watched the competitors put their mounts through their paces and clapped along with everyone else at the simple enjoyment.

"Hey, Glenn!"

Glenn scanned the bleachers and grinned when she saw Harper Rivers with her fiancée Presley and Glenn's friend Carrie, who also happened to be Presley's admin and longtime friend. Carrie had shed her stylish office attire in favor of her habitual scooped tee, shorts, and sandals. With her curly shoulder-length red hair pulled back in a careless ponytail she looked closer to eighteen than early twenties. Glenn waved and climbed between the spectators clogging the aisles. She worked her way down the already full row to where her three friends pressed together to make room for her.

"Thanks for the seat." Glenn dropped down next to Carrie. "Must be a sellout crowd. Good for the town coffers."

"Hey." Carrie gave her a shoulder bump. "If I'd known you'd be free, I would've told you we were coming tonight."

"That's okay. Hadn't planned on it." Glenn uncapped the water and drank down half. She and Carrie hadn't known each other long, but they had developed a quick, easy friendship. They often ended up together at group gatherings, especially since their mutual friends were pairing off, but things had never gone any further than that, mostly because neither one of them had ever pushed for more. "I was at the hospital pretty late anyhow. First day of the new program."

"I heard you had some excitement."

"Hasn't everyone?" Glenn smiled wryly. There were no secrets in a hospital, personal or professional. The only way to keep a secret was to keep silent. It occurred to her she'd already broken that rule with Mari, but somehow she wasn't worried. Mari would respect her secrets.

"A mass casualty alert," Carrie said. "Pretty wild first day for all the newbies. How'd they do?"

"The students missed the MCA, but the ER team handled that without a hitch." Glenn shrugged. "Considering it's the students' first clinical experience, they aren't half bad, actually."

"High praise." Chuckling, Carrie offered her half-eaten box of popcorn. "Want some?"

"Nah, I'm good."

"We're going out for pizza in a while if you want to come."

"Thanks, but I already had some."

"Really?" The look in Carrie's green eyes bordered on suspicion mixed with disbelief. "You left the hospital before sundown?"

"Oh, come on," Glenn protested. "I do…sometimes."

Carrie snorted. "It's okay to admit you don't want to come along. Just don't think you're getting out of the hospital barbecue this weekend."

"I swear! I already ate. I walked down with Mari after shift and—"

"Who's Mari?" Carrie knew everyone, considering she was the CEO's admin, and she didn't know anyone in the ER by that name.

"Mari Mateo. One of the new PAs, just started."

"Huh. Since the ER is technically freestanding, those hires went through Abby and not our HR department." Carrie gave Glenn an inquiring look. "Is she nice?"

"Nice?" Glenn felt the word roll around on her tongue like a shoe that didn't fit. Mari was a whole lot of things—smart, capable, sensitive, maybe a little vulnerable, and, well, why not admit it, beautiful. "Sure, she's nice."

"And you went out to dinner with her." Carrie's eyes narrowed. "That's almost newsworthy, considering about the only place you ever go outside of work is Harper and Flann's parents' house for Sunday dinner."

"Pizza, Carrie, pizza." Glenn sighed. "Give me a break."

"Uh-huh. Just make sure she gets to the staff cookout too."

"Flann already reminded me. I'll make sure she's aware—hell, I'm not gonna drag her there."

"Mateo, you said?" Carrie asked, looking like she was only paying half attention.

"Yes, why?"

"No reason."

Carrie fell silent, an unusual state for her. The crowd started to break up before the last competition was over. Ten thirty was late for most everybody who had to get up before four in the morning to feed the animals, milk the cows, get the work of the day started before the heat or the rain or some other unexpected event interfered.

"I'm gonna get out before the crowds," Glenn said.

"Headed home?" Carrie asked.

"Yeah." Glenn toyed with the idea of making a quick stop by the ER to check on the new attending on his first night on call. He seemed solid, but he was still fresh out of his residency, and he didn't know the place like she did.

"You know," Carrie said casually, "you don't actually have to supervise every single person in the ER."

Glenn laughed. "Are you mind-reading again?"

"Honestly, Glenn, you're not all that hard to read. I'm surprised you even left today."

Glenn didn't mention she hadn't been planning on it, at least not until she was absolutely certain everything was tight and tidy, but she'd been drawn away by Mari. "Are you trying to say I'm a control freak?"

"I wouldn't be that harsh. But seriously," Carrie said quietly, "it wouldn't hurt to ease up a little bit now and then. You deserve it."

"This coming from the woman who I know for a fact works twelve-hour days almost every day."

"Have you seen my boss? She's merciless."

From the other side of Carrie, Presley Worth chuckled. "Are you admitting defeat?"

"Me?" Carrie grinned. "Never. I love my work, and if I never had to leave the hospital, I'd be happy."

"We only have a few more major projects to accomplish," Presley said, "and then your hours will seem more human."

"Really?" Carrie snorted. "You mean after you strong-arm the construction crew into getting the new MRI wing done in six months *and* build the heliport in six weeks…Oh, and don't forget pushing through the approval for our trauma accreditation so we can actually get the helicopters to land on the heliport that we haven't built yet."

"I didn't say it would be instantaneous." Presley smiled, the kind of smile fighter pilots wear as they climb into the cockpit. "It might take a month or so."

Harper Rivers, Presley's soon-to-be spouse and current chief of medicine at the Rivers, laughed out loud. "Darling, you do realize that at most places, things like that take a couple of years?"

"Well," the new CEO said nonchalantly, "this isn't most places."

"Like I said," Carrie said with a long-suffering sigh, "I love my job and I would sleep in the office if I could find a place to put a cot."

"You can always bed down on the floor," Glenn suggested. "Plenty of room behind the desk."

Carrie gave her a raised eyebrow. "Some of us are more civilized than that."

Glenn grinned, half listening to Carrie and Presley's banter while most of her concentration was focused on several teens who'd just congregated at the bottom of the stairs, Blake and Margie in the mix. She noticed that another girl and boy joined them, and after they all spoke awhile, the four began wending their way toward the exit.

Glenn stood. "I'll see you at the staff meeting tomorrow night."

"Go home," Carrie said sternly.

"Yes, dear." Glenn didn't think it necessary to add she might take just a little detour to make sure Blake and Margie didn't run into any trouble on their way home.

Mari would have sworn on all that was holy she would fall asleep the second her head hit the pillow, but she lay awake in the half dark with all the events of her first day running through her mind like a runaway movie reel. Her first day. She'd gone to sleep in this room for a week, but it still felt like today was her first day. The first day that really counted. The first day of the life she'd fought for and made happen. She'd imagined what this day would be like, but she hadn't expected most of it. The medical part was even better than she'd hoped. It was strange, the contradiction, of loving an emergency, of thriving on the challenge of going to battle against an enemy that was as real to her as she imagined an enemy on the battlefield might be to a soldier, all as a consequence of someone else's suffering. Life was on the line, and although she might not die if she failed, someone else would, and that to her was in many ways worse than her own pain. Without the suffering of others, there'd be no need for her skills. So she'd gone to battle and loved every minute of it.

She been right that this profession was what she wanted to spend her life doing, but she hadn't expected to discover such a vibrant community inside the hospital. She had immediately sensed the currents of a unique society with its own customs and history flowing around her like so many branches of an ancient river, in the halls and nurses' stations, even the cafeteria. The village was another community, with its own rhythms and tides. Glenn, when she finally let herself think about Glenn, was the most unexpected part of all. She had hoped to connect with colleagues, make friends, but she hadn't expected to meet anyone special. Someone at once secretive and welcoming, revealing and hidden. A puzzle and an open book. All Glenn's many contrasts fascinated her, but she was most grateful to Glenn for giving her hope that she could belong somewhere again. She turned on her side and pulled a pillow close, snuggling her face into the old, familiar contours, smiling to herself as she thought about Glenn sitting across from her in the pizza parlor, still feeling the heat of Glenn's dark-eyed scrutiny and the comfort of her unpitying understanding. Yes, much, much more than she had imagined her first day would be like.

CHAPTER TEN

Glenn arrived at the small ER conference room fifteen minutes before her scheduled seven o'clock lecture and found Mari already seated at one end of the oval conference table with her iPad and a cup of coffee in front of her. Dressed for the workday in pale blue, wrinkle-free scrubs, her name tag clipped to her breast pocket and a stethoscope slung around her neck, she looked rested and relaxed. No one else had arrived yet.

"Did you take those home and iron them?" Glenn asked.

Mari frowned. "Oh! You mean the scrubs? Yes."

"When did you do that?"

"I picked them up yesterday when I was here and ironed them this morning." Mari gave a pointed glance at Glenn's equally pressed darker blue set. "Don't you?"

"I used to. Now a friend in the laundry does them for me."

"Ah—special status. Let me guess—ex-Army?"

Glenn grinned. "Navy, but us vets stick together. I'll ask him to do yours. You want the same color all the time?"

"I'm not fussy."

"They look good on you—I'll tell him the baby blues."

Mari quickly looked down at the iPad, color racing across her cheeks. "Thanks. If he can't do it, that's all right."

"Billy won't mind."

"Well then, I owe you double." Mari leaned over and lifted up a small green thermal insulated bag covered with multicolored fish. She unzipped the top and withdrew a cardboard cup with a Styrofoam lid that looked very much like the one she was drinking from.

Glenn stared at it and actually felt her taste buds start to tingle. "Is that—?"

"A little thank you for giving me a break on the lecture today." Mari slid the cup down the table toward her. "Double espresso, macchiato. I just guessed on that part."

Glenn scooped up the cup, removed the lid, and took a deep breath of some mighty fine coffee. "Perfect." She sipped and sighed. "You have my undying thanks."

Mari laughed. "I sort of owe you for rescuing me and taking this session."

"Believe me, if this is what I get in thanks, I'll do all of yours."

"Well, I stop there almost every morning, so it's no trouble." Mari smiled. "Free of charge."

Glenn settled a hip on the edge of the table. "It's absolutely not required, but whenever you happen to think of it, you will have my eternal gratitude."

"You're welcome, and let's call it done."

"Done. How did you sleep?" Glenn asked.

"Just about the best night I've had in forever." Mari paused a second. If she thought Glenn looked like she'd had less than three hours' sleep, she didn't say so. "You weren't on call, right?"

"No, I wasn't, and I decided to leave Dr. Jaspers on his own last night. I saw Baker in the cafeteria, so she survived her first night too."

Mari laughed. "Was it difficult for you, not checking up on them?"

"Actually, yeah," Glenn confessed. "A good friend of mine, you'll meet her before long, Carrie Longmire, suggested I'm too controlling."

A good friend. Girlfriend? Mari assumed Glenn's interest was in women, although she hadn't actually come out in so many words. The tone of the whole conversation the night before had left little doubt, but she hadn't considered that Glenn might have a girlfriend. But then, why *would* she think about it? It wasn't like they were out on a date. Still, she felt a moment's discomfort. "Does Carrie work here?"

Glenn nodded. "Yeah, she's the CEO's admin."

"She obviously knows you a lot better than me," Mari said lightly, "but I think you're just doing what needs to be done, especially this time of year with so many newbies aboard." She pointed to her chest. "Including staff."

"You're practically a vet after yesterday's initiation." Glenn drained her cup and fervently wished for more. She'd gone home but she'd had a hard time falling asleep. Her body had been as keyed up as it used to be waiting for a call out in the field, only last night there'd been an undercurrent of excitement in the unrest that buzzed in her veins still.

"And really," Mari continued, her tone unexpectedly urgent, "do you know anyone in medicine who would want someone taking care of them who *wasn't* a control freak? I wouldn't. I'd want someone in charge who was going to be looking at every single little detail and double-checking every single person who had anything to do with taking care of me. Believe me, when I was—" Mari broke off, embarrassed to discover she was trembling. Why was it so easy to open up to Glenn, to reveal everything she'd kept from everyone else?

Glenn glanced at the door, saw the shadow of a student pass by. They only had a few more minutes. Gently she said, "When you were what?"

"Sorry. I…" Mari shook her head. "Not exactly the right time or place."

Glenn nodded. "You're right. Your call, anytime."

"Thanks."

Glenn wanted to know more. Whatever darkness haunted Mari's past, every time Mari touched upon it, her eyes filled with sadness. Glenn ached to stanch the pain as much as she ever had a battle wound. Not the place, and not the time. The students filed in and Glenn grabbed the remote for the projector and moved to the head of the table. As she launched into her abbreviated intro at precisely 0700, she watched Mari out of the corner of her eye. When she brought up an aerial shot of the hospital to orient the students to the critical locations, Mari's attention swung back and forth from the screen to Glenn. She'd given plenty of briefings before, but she'd never enjoyed having an audience. Mari's attention wasn't really on her, but she enjoyed the fleeting imagining. Quickly, she pointed out the east administrative wing, the central building with reception, the library and cafeteria, and the six-story west wing with the ER, OR, ICUs, outpatient clinics, and the patient floors.

"And here"—Glenn tapped a spot at the west wing—"will be an open colonnade leading to the building"—she made a circle with her laser pointer a few inches away—"housing the new MRI suite."

"Nice," Antonelli said. "When do you think that will be up and running?"

"We hope to break ground before the end of the summer and have the facility opened by late spring."

"No shi—kidding." Antonelli whistled. "That's pushing things. You'll be lucky if you have your bids in by three months."

"Got some experience there," Glenn remarked.

"My old man used to be a general contractor. The company put up a lot of buildings in this area, and there's pretty stiff competition for something like this."

Glenn would have agreed if it hadn't been for Presley Worth. Their new CEO had a way of making things happen a lot faster than anyone else could ever anticipate. She had all the resources of the SunView Health Consortium, a huge international medical consortium headed by her brother, at her command and numerous contacts of her own. In addition to being the CEO of the newly minted Argyle Community Hospital System, she was the head of the eastern division of SunView. Presley had the power to get things done on her timetable and did. As much as Glenn revered Edward Rivers and the entire Rivers family, she was convinced along with most everyone at ACH that Presley Worth was the CEO they needed to keep the Rivers alive and flourishing.

"Until the MRI suite is up and functional," Glenn said, getting the discussion back on track, "we'll evaluate traumatic injuries, neurological events, acute abdomens, and the like with CAT scans and X-rays. Most things that require an MRI would be done after the initial evaluation and treatment anyhow."

"What about the helipad?" asked Baker, a short, serious, steady African American student. "I heard that could be happening a lot sooner."

Glenn nodded. "You're all here for three months. There's a good chance we'll be taking medevac patients before you're finished."

"Oorah," Antonelli muttered.

Marine, Glenn noted, dimming the lights. "So let's start with the evaluation of the multiple trauma patient."

When the hour was over and Glenn finished answering the students' questions, she waited while they all trooped out to join Mari.

"I imagine that was all pretty boring for you," Glenn said.

Mari closed her iPad. "Not at all. I think it's good to know what they know, and what I can expect them to know because I'm absolutely certain they heard it before."

Glenn laughed. "And so you can remind them when they forget?"

Mari grinned. "Absolutely."

"Speaking of remembering, or remembering to remind you," Glenn said, grinning when Mari gave her a confused look, "Carrie informed me I needed to tell you about the hospital staff barbecue this Saturday afternoon. It's an annual thing. Kind of a celebration of summer and the chance for everyone at the Rivers to get together and celebrate…well, just that we're all still here, and the hospital is still standing strong."

Carrie again, Mari thought. "Why the Rivers? Almost everyone calls the place by that name."

"Flann and Harper's great-great-great-grandfather founded the place along with a few of the town notables a little over a hundred years ago. There's been a Rivers as chief of staff here ever since. Their father Edward heads the medical staff now, but since the hospital was sold, Presley actually runs the place."

"That's some legacy," Mari said. "And of course I'll be there. It sounds like fun and it will give me a chance to meet some of the other people from the hospital."

"I don't suppose you play softball, do you?" Glenn surveyed her with unabashed eagerness.

"Ah, no," Mari said. "Is it a requirement?"

"No, not really." Glenn sighed. "We're always looking for new talent. The ER has a team and we play a bunch of other teams from the hospital, and town teams like police and firefighters. Not everybody on our team is actually from the ER—Flann and Harper play for us, and Carrie, she pitches—wicked, wicked pitcher."

"Aha." For the first time in her life Mari wished she'd been more into sports instead of clothes when she'd been a teenager. "Sorry. I'm out."

Glenn laughed. "No problem—we'll still feed you, but it is a requirement that you come and cheer us on."

"And when and where would this cheering take place?"

"Usually Wednesdays, Fridays, and Sundays. I'll take you over to the field the first time."

"You're kidding. You play that many games?"

"Only during the spring and summer," Glenn said seriously.

"That has to be, like, dozens of games."

"Well, sure. And then there are the playoffs and the finals and the championship game. That winds up by late August."

"Okay, I can see this is a really big deal around here."

"Don't you have sports where you come from?"

"I suppose we do," Mari said, "but I've never paid much attention to it. The professional sports you see on television are so commercialized."

"What about those five brothers of yours, didn't they play sports?"

"In high school, sure, and I did go to most of their games. Basketball and soccer. No baseball, though."

Glenn shook her head. "Philistines."

Mari smiled. "I hereby promise to be a devoted champion of your team."

"Your support will be greatly appreciated." Glenn glanced at her watch. "And I guess it's time for us to get to it."

"Thanks again for taking the lecture this morning," Mari said as she gathered up her things. "I really would've been beat if I'd had to stay up much longer."

"Not a problem." Glenn searched her face. "You're okay for a full shift? Over the jet lag?"

"I'm absolutely fine," Mari said, certain from the glimpse of worry in Glenn's gaze she'd been right to keep some things to herself. "Let's go clear the board."

❖

Abby tapped on Presley's door at a little before eight. She knew Presley would be in, since she kept longer hours than most of the staff. She was behind her desk with her laptop open, her cell phone by her right hand, an iPad propped up against a stack of folders, and a supersize coffee in her left hand. She looked, as always, impeccable in a navy silk blazer and open-collared white silk shirt. A multistrand gold necklace rested just below her collarbone and a square-cut diamond glittered on the ring finger of her left hand. Her blond hair was swept back from her face and fell to just above her shoulders in thick easy waves. She smiled when she saw Abby peer in the doorway. "Hey, come on in."

"Busy? Of course you are busy." Abby made for the chair across from Presley. "How many worlds have you conquered this morning already?"

"Only a few," Presley said, laughing. "What's going on? Problem in the unit?"

"No, the ER's fine. Well, we could always use more money, more personnel, more space—" Abby grimaced. "Really, we're full most of the time and believe me, I'm glad for it, but if we increase our trauma call, we are badly going to need more rooms. Plus the MRI…"

"I'm working on it."

"Believe me, I know that and I'm appreciative," Abby said. "This is something personal. It won't take long."

Presley immediately sat forward, pushing aside her computer as if whatever major undertaking she'd just been involved in was completely unimportant to her. Her gaze fixed on Abby. "Is something wrong between you and Flann?"

"No, God no. Everything's fine." She blushed. "Ridiculous, I know, but perfect is the word I use in my head."

"Blake is okay?"

"Blake is thriving. Somehow"—she shook her head—"he's talked me into letting him and Margie volunteer in the ER this summer. If you and Harper agree."

"I'll discuss it with Harper and legal, but I don't see a problem there." Presley grinned. "The two of them are scary when they get their heads together."

"Thank God it's good scary."

"Amen. So—what do you need?"

Abby didn't have much time and she knew Presley didn't either. "Flann wants to get married."

"Of course she does, she's more of a nester than Harper and doesn't have a clue," Presley said. "She took one look at you and Blake and knew where she belonged."

Abby's heart lurched. She hadn't ever expected to need anyone the way she needed Flann, the way she loved her—body and soul. "She has been using the M-word from day one."

"And is there a problem?" Presley's question was gentle. "I know we lost touch for a while, but I think I can read happy all over you."

"Oh no—I mean, yes, I couldn't be happier. It's just that you know

Flann—her idea of a proposal is let's get married and today would be time enough."

Presley laughed. "Yeah, that's Flann."

"I've managed to hold her off for a month or so, but I don't want this to interfere with what you and Harper have planned. After all, you got there first, so to speak."

"Abby," Presley said with a shake of her head, "I think it's great. Harper will be beside herself. And so will Edward and Ida. Besides, I can't wait to help plan your wedding."

"Oh, please, anything you can do. Everything." Abby pushed a hand through her hair, relief pouring through her. "I don't know anything about weddings."

"We'll be old hands at it by the time Harper and I get around to it in—God, is it really only two weeks? We've got so much to do, we need another meeting."

"Brunch this weekend?"

"At the latest."

"I'll gather the troops and let everyone know where and when." Abby stood. "Thank you, thank you."

Presley came around her desk and gave Abby a quick hug. "I am so happy for you. Flann is fabulous."

"I really love her," Abby said quietly. "And so does Blake."

"Well, Flann is lucky to have you both. Is it a secret?"

"I don't think Flann has told her parents yet, and we haven't told Blake, so I'd keep it quiet for a while."

Carrie said from the doorway, "Keep what quiet?"

Abby looked over her shoulder. "Flann and I are getting married."

Carrie gave a little victory wiggle. "Good for you. Congratulations. Oh boy, another wedding!"

Abby thought about all she had to do in the ER, and her son who still had to find his way emotionally, physically, and in the community, and stemmed the rising panic. "Oh boy, indeed."

Chapter Eleven

The board was full all morning and Mari ran from cubicle to cubicle seeing patients, checking on the students, and tracking down Abby or another ER doc for final sign-off on her own and the students' cases. They were good students, responsible and caring, but they were still students. They had no idea what they didn't know and were flush with coming out of the classroom where they thought they had learned everything there *was* to know. She'd felt the same way her first few days on her clinical rotations. Around eleven thirty, a quick wave of dizziness when she stood up after spending a precious fifteen minutes at a table in the little break room with a cup of tea while charting her last discharge notes reminded her she hadn't had anything to eat since the croissant and coffee at six in the morning. She really did need to pay more attention to eating. She couldn't do much about fretful sleeping or her frenetic pace in the ER—that was the job, after all—but she could at least try to eat. Her appetite still was nothing like it used to be, and some flavors and smells had gone off for her completely. Thank God, she still loved pizza.

Thinking about pizza made her think of Glenn, and she got that odd little twinge of heat in the center of her chest that seemed to be happening every time she thought of her or heard her voice in the hall outside a curtained room or caught a glance of her, leaning a shoulder casually against the wall while conferring with Abby or one of the students. She always looked so confident, so focused, so…sexy. Oh, hell. She had no time for out-of-the-blue thoughts like that, and no place for what they might lead to. Not for a long, long time.

Lunch. Then back to work. Just as she dropped the chart into the outbox at the nurses' station, Antonelli stormed around the corner as if leading an assault on some enemy encampment, his usual pace, and flagged her down. She wasn't actually assigned to him as a supervisor, but for whatever reason, he'd decided she was his go-to person. She didn't mind, she liked teaching.

He loomed over her, two hundred twenty pounds of barely constrained muscle and testosterone to her one twenty. "Hey, Mari, I've got a hot appy that needs to go up to the OR. I'm going to call the surgeon, okay?"

"Whoa, take five there, soldier."

"Marine." His tone suggested high insult.

"Okay, marine." Mari gestured to an out-of-the-way corner where they could talk without patients overhearing them. "Run it down for me."

He looked annoyed, his dark brows lowering for an instant, but he followed her out of the way of hall traffic. Although he was impatient and cocky, he respected the chain of command, and she respected him for that. He was smart, maybe the smartest of the bunch, but he was quick on the draw, a result undoubtedly of his military experience. She refrained from reminding him this wasn't the battlefield, and every decision didn't have to be made between one heartbeat and the next. She didn't discount his field experience and what he had learned from it, but a civilian ER was a different kind of battlefield, and sometimes, careful surveillance and planning was just as important as the ability to rapidly assess and respond.

"It's textbook," Antonelli said in his usual confident and moderately dismissive voice as soon as they were alone. "Twenty-five-year-old female, twelve hours of progressively increasing right lower-quadrant pain, nausea, low-grade temp."

"White count?" Mari asked.

"Ten point five."

"Just mildly elevated," Mari pointed out.

He lifted a shoulder. "It'll be a lot higher in a few hours if she doesn't get that out."

"Pregnancy test?"

"Pending."

"Heterosexual, sexually active?"

"Yeah. Straight, no chance she can be pregnant."

"Not sexually active, then?"

"No...I mean, yeah, she is," Antonelli said, his tone suggesting this line of questioning was annoying at best, "but she had a period a month ago, and they always use a happy hat...condom."

"Normal?"

"Huh?"

Mari almost smiled. One thing the military didn't teach medics particularly well was female healthcare. Female troops on the front lines lived with men, fought with men, and were considered one of guys in almost all ways—but they were still biologically unique. "Was her period typical for her—timing, duration, amount? Did you ask?"

"No, she said—"

"Come on, let's go ask her."

"Listen, can't we call surgery and at least get them down—"

"Why don't we make sure we have the full story so we get the right person down here."

As Mari walked back to the cubicle with Antonelli dogging her heels, she scanned the chart and didn't find anything else that teased her antennae. Antonelli was probably right. The most obvious diagnosis was usually the correct one. She smiled when she thought of the old adage, *When you hear hoofbeats in the hall, don't think of zebras.* All the same, the difference between a good diagnostician and an excellent one was both curiosity and suspicion. Probably a little OCD as well. The time to be certain was before you acted, because once you began a course of treatment, uncertainty was the enemy, especially if the treatment happened to be surgical.

She pulled back the curtain and introduced herself to the pale young Asian woman who waited alone in the cubicle. She briefly ran down the history Antonelli had already taken and noted one thing he hadn't.

"So your last period was a little late and shorter than usual?"

"Only a day and not much of that," the patient said. "But I was right in the middle of some pretty intense rehearsals, and a lot of times when I'm really stressed that happens."

"What do you do?" Mari asked.

"I'm a dancer. Modern, mostly."

"Where do you perform?" Mari couldn't imagine a local art house in this rural area, and even if there was one, she doubted it could support a dance troupe, but maybe the company was located in Albany.

Kuni Yamaguchi smiled. "We're performing at the Saratoga Performing Arts Center this summer. I'm with the New York Dance Company, but my grandmother lives here. I stay with her whenever I can."

"Wow, that's incredible. I'll have to check out the events calendar." Mari drew the sheet down and gently palpated Kuni's abdomen. When she reached the lower right quadrant, the young woman tensed and caught her breath. "So tell me about this pain."

"I didn't really pay any attention to it until last night, and then it just wouldn't go away."

Mari recalled Antonelli's history and physical. Twelve-hour history of pain. "It didn't actually start last night?"

"Well, it didn't really start bothering me until last night. I noticed it just a time or two over the last few days. Not enough to slow me down. I didn't miss rehearsal."

"Aha. I know how that is." From what Mari knew of dancers, most women in competitive fields, really, they'd have to be dead to miss a rehearsal or class or meeting. She glanced over at Antonelli, whose impatient expression had turned to a frown.

"What do you say we get an ultrasound in here," Mari suggested casually.

"Yeah, I copy that."

Turning back to Kuni, she said, "I want to do a quick ultrasound scan, that's a test—"

"I know what it is, but why? The other doctor thought it was my appendix."

"And he might very well be right. But sometimes two different things can look a lot alike at first. I just want to be sure that we're not talking about something to do with your ovaries. We can do it while we're waiting for the results of your pregnancy test."

"Oh." For an instant, Kuni looked panicked. "I can't possibly be pregnant. I don't have any time to be pregnant, and besides that, we're always really careful."

"You take the Pill?"

"I did, but it makes me bloat so I stopped. But I use a diaphragm *and* we use a condom." She laughed. "Really, nothing could get through all that."

"Uh-huh," Mari said, seeing no point in citing the statistics.

A second later Antonelli pushed the curtain aside and trundled in with the portable ultrasound machine. He set it up beside the bed and glanced at Mari.

"Have you done one before?" Mari asked.

"A couple of times."

"Good. Let's see what we see."

He squeezed the cold blue gel onto Kuni's stomach and she stiffened at the first contact, then relaxed as Antonelli, with surprisingly sensitive hands, gently guided the probe in ever increasing circles from a spot in the right lower quadrant outward. At one point he paused, backed up, and circled again. He stopped and looked over at Mari. She had been following the images on the screen, and the mass in the right lower quadrant was pretty hard to miss.

"Let's get GYN down here," Mari said, looking directly into Antonelli's eyes to make sure they were on the same wavelength. The bright snap in his dark gaze told her they were and he would make sure to request a consult stat.

Mari covered Kuni with the sheet as Antonelli stepped out to call GYN. "Did someone come with you today?"

"No, I didn't want to worry my grandmother until I knew what was going on."

"What about your boyfriend?"

For the first time, the young woman, who had to be in considerable pain, looked distressed. "He, uh, no. I'd rather not…"

"You might want to call him or a family member," Mari said. "We're going to get one of the GYN surgeons down here, but I'm pretty sure you have what we call an ectopic pregnancy. That's a situation where a fertilized egg doesn't make it into the uterus but lodges somewhere else—often on a fallopian tube."

"Pregnant? That's not possible." Kuni's strident tone suggested she didn't want to believe it, but a note of uncertainty flashed across her face.

"There isn't a contraceptive in the world that's a hundred percent, although some are obviously better than others. And if there was a time that maybe the condom slipped off or he didn't get it on until later than usual…?"

"I don't know, maybe that could have happened." Kuni passed a trembling hand over her face. "God, what a mess. If it's what you think, will I need surgery?"

"Yes, and the gynecologist will discuss all those details with you. Is there someone I can call for you?"

"My grandmother, I guess, but can you try not to worry her? She's tough as nails, but she's still eighty."

"Of course. And you're sure no one else?"

"He's…our relationship isn't public."

Mari nodded. As long as she could find someone to be there to support the patient, the nature of her personal relationship was not her business. "All right. If you change your mind and want me to call him, I can. Do we have your grandmother's number?"

"Yes, I gave that to the receptionist as next of kin."

"I'll be right back." Mari squeezed the young woman's hand and left to make the call.

By the time she was finished and assured Kuni's grandmother she had enough time to arrange for someone to get over to the house to look after her animals, the GYN attending, of all people, was in the cubicle. She'd expected a resident, as had been the norm at the LA medical center where she'd trained, but then she remembered that most of the departments here didn't have a residency program. Yet. Many of the doctors worked with nurse practitioners or physician assistants instead, but the staff physicians often answered their own ER calls out of necessity and expediency.

The gynecologist, a rugged middle-aged man with thick brown hair, a lantern jaw, and an incongruously soft, melodious voice, was in the midst of repeating the ultrasound when Mari walked back in.

"What I'm seeing here," he said in his soothing baritone, "is a mass about the size of an orange sitting on your right fallopian tube that shouldn't be there. That's probably where the egg attached itself and is now bleeding."

"It's not my appendix?"

"Definitely not. We need to go in and remove what shouldn't be there and stop the bleeding."

"When?"

He set the probe aside and gently wiped the ultrasound jelly from her abdomen with a cotton four-by-four. "Right now."

She caught her breath. "Can I wait for my grandmother so we can talk it over?"

"We'll get the operating room ready, but this isn't something that can wait too long, and surgery isn't optional. If this bursts, the bleeding will pick up quite a bit." He didn't mention that catastrophic hemorrhage was a possibility or that ruptured ectopic pregnancies could be lethal. He smiled, but his expression was uncompromising. "So we'll wait as long as we can."

Mari said, "Your grandmother should be here any minute, Kuni. She was leaving as soon as she made a phone call."

Kuni nodded and closed her eyes in acceptance or defeat, or probably a little of both.

Mari, Antonelli, and the GYN attending all stepped outside, and the attending, whose name tag read Brian Brownell, MD, looked at Antonelli and said, "Good pickup."

"Mari's call, not mine." Antonelli scowled. "I would've missed it. Thought it was appendicitis."

"Yeah, they can look a lot alike." Brownell clapped him on the shoulder. "But you won't miss it next time, will you?"

"Damn right," Antonelli muttered. Brownell sauntered off to make arrangements with the OR, and Antonelli grimaced at Mari. "Fuck me. I blew that."

"How many women with noncombat injuries did you treat over there?"

"I was assigned to a forward operating base, meaning pretty much no one we got had anything *but* combat trauma."

"Then I wouldn't be too hard on myself."

"Yeah." He glanced down the hall, as if seeing someone even though the way was empty. "Bet Archer would have picked it up first time, and she was frontline, closer than me even."

"How do you know that?" Mari didn't want to imagine Glenn in the midst of a firefight or in a jumble of bombed vehicles, trying to save lives while her own could end at any second. She didn't want to see it, but she could, and her stomach protested.

"I asked her." He shrugged. "And she's got the look. Anyhow, thanks for the backup."

"Anytime."

Mari checked the board—as clear as it had been all day—and the clock. Another hour had passed since last time she checked, and if she didn't eat before the midafternoon rush when people finally decided that whatever had been keeping them up the night before or bothering them all day couldn't wait another hour rolled in, she'd never get food. Maybe Glenn would be free. "Hey, Nancy, have you seen Glenn?"

The statuesque blonde pointed in the opposite direction. "She's riding herd on a twenty-year-old in CAT scan. Baseball bat to the forehead."

Mari winced. "Okay, thanks, I'm going to—"

"Excuse me." A young, vivacious redhead who looked like she belonged in a Fortune 500 front office in her stylish royal blue suit and low heels homed in on Mari. "Are you Mari Mateo?"

"Yes," Mari said.

The redhead smiled, her celery-green eyes sparkling. "I'm Carrie Longmire. I'm pretty sure I'm your cousin."

CHAPTER TWELVE

Mari stared at the redhead who regarded her with eager anticipation. Carrie. Carrie. Wasn't that the name of Glenn's friend—possible girlfriend—the only person other than Flann Glenn had actually mentioned? *Cousin?*

"Cousin? I don't see how that's possible," Mari finally said. Nothing about this ivory-skinned, green-eyed Irish girl could be farther from her own Mexican American heritage. True, her mother was not Hispanic, but she couldn't see any resemblance at all between her dark-haired, brown-eyed mother and Carrie. No, this crazy idea couldn't be true. "I know all my cousins, and they're all on the Mateo side of the tree."

"I know, sounds wild, huh?" Carrie smiled again and grasped her arm. "Come on, I'll buy you lunch. Have you had lunch?"

Mari shook her head, trying to keep pace with the rapid-fire conversation and Carrie's supercharged energy level.

"Great. I'll tell you all about it then." Carrie gave Mari's arm a little tug.

Mari glanced at the board again. Still only a few patients, all currently being seen, and the ER was probably the quietest it would be for the rest of the day. She had her phone, she'd only be a minute away. And she did need some food. Besides, Carrie's wide-open friendliness and exuberance were hard to resist. "I don't have much time—"

"Believe me, neither do I. Have you met my boss yet?"

"Uh, no."

"Presley has two speeds—fast and hyperdrive." Carrie grinned. "If I'm gone more than half an hour, it will take me a day to catch up."

"Well, half an hour is about all I'll have." Curious and intrigued, Mari glanced at Nancy who, watching them with obvious interest, shrugged as if to say *go for it*. "Okay, sure. Lunch."

Carrie was already striding away and Mari hurried to stay with her. By the time they'd raced down a hall, up a staircase, and into the cafeteria, she was winded. Definitely time to start running again. Getting back into a regular exercise regimen would be another step toward reclaiming her life.

The cafeteria was nearly empty and the hot food lines closed, but the salad bar was still open and a cold case held packaged sandwiches that didn't look half bad.

"They make those at the café in town every day," Carrie said, seeing Mari look them over. "They're good. I get one sometimes to take home for supper."

"If they're anything like the croissants, I'm sold."

Carrie laughed. "Chocolate or raspberry?"

"Um, both?"

"See! I knew we were related."

Smiling but skeptical, Mari grabbed a sandwich and put together a quick salad. Carrie had picked a table next to the one Mari had shared with Glenn. That first conversation felt like a week ago.

Mari tried the sandwich. Carrie was right. Delicious. "I don't see how we could possibly be related. I'm not even from around here."

"Neither am I."

"But how could I never have heard of you before now?"

"Well that's the thing," Carrie said nonchalantly. "Our extended family is a little dysfunctional."

Mari laughed, not feeling the slightest bit of humor. "I don't know about yours, but I think mine probably is."

"Yeah, I actually think most are—except possibly the Riverses. I've never seen a family quite like theirs. But you can decide that for yourself when you meet them all."

"Maybe you should start at the beginning," Mari said, suspecting that with Carrie everything was a story. She liked Carrie's energy, it was practically infectious, but totally opposite her natural tendency to be cautious and guarded. And she wasn't one for believing in coincidences.

"Before I say anything," Carrie said, her tone softening and her vivacious expression settling into one of gentle seriousness, "I want to start out by saying that I don't want to create any problems between you and your family. So if anything I say is likely to do that, just tell me and I'll just stop."

Mari pushed aside the familiar twinge of pain, tired of paying the price for refusing to live a lie. "I don't actually see how you could cause any more problems than I already have. My family has sort of shut me out these past few months."

Carrie stopped eating and gave her a long look. "That sounds like it sucks."

"More or less precisely." Mari waved a hand. "Go ahead, tell me what you think is going on with us."

"When Glenn mentioned your name…" Carrie paused, fork waving in the air like a conductor's baton. "Oh, background…last night at the fairgrounds, I asked Glenn how the first day with the new job had gone and your name came up. Mateo caught my attention."

"You and Glenn were talking about me," Mari said carefully, hoping she sounded less uncomfortable than she felt. She wasn't exactly sure how she felt being the topic of conversation between Glenn and another woman, but she was more surprised to discover Glenn and Carrie had been together last night. Glenn hadn't mentioned it when they'd talked that morning. Mari gave herself a mental shake. Why should she expect Glenn to update her on what she'd done after she'd walked Mari home. Her personal, private time was just that—private.

"Don't worry," Carrie went on as if reading her mind, "there was no good gossip. Just the usual hospital stuff, you know how that is."

"Oh, I certainly do," Mari said dryly. It didn't take her very long on her first clinical rotation to discover that hospitals were giant gossip mills, mostly due to the fact that everyone spent more time together there than they did with anyone else, including their families, and a lot of that time was stressful waiting when there wasn't much else to do except talk, speculate, and pass on snippets of juicy news. Mari pushed the niggling annoyance away. "Okay—so you and Glenn were casually chatting and somehow you decided I was your cousin."

Carrie laughed. "Not right away—by the way, it *was* totally professional, except of course, for the two of you having pizza together. That was news."

"Really? Why is that?"

"Glenn leaving the hospital before nine at night for any reason other than softball is newsworthy."

Mari smiled. She liked knowing Glenn's friendly overtures had been unusual. "She was kind enough to keep me from starving."

"Uh-huh. Anyhow, when Glenn mentioned your name, I didn't see how it could be a coincidence. You're from the West Coast, right? LA?"

"That's right. I've lived there all my life. What about you?"

"I grew up in San Francisco. Where our moms did."

"My mother did grow up in Northern California, but she never talked about her family except to say they were all gone. I'm sorry, is your mother deceased?"

"My mom?" Carrie's eyes glowed. "Not by a long shot. She's a political organizer, and when she's not doing that, she's the head of a large community food service, a nonprofit that provides meals to homeless and underprivileged people. My dad is a philosophy professor at Berkeley."

"Our families couldn't be more different," Mari said. "My mother and father own a small grocery store and, other than going to church, don't do much else."

"Mine are sort of next-generation hippies, like my grandmom, but I don't think they're called hippies anymore," Carrie said.

Mari's head was starting to spin. "Well, that can't be right, then, about us being related. I don't have any relatives on my mother's side. She told me that, told all of us kids that, whenever we asked about our other grandparents."

"Your mom's name is Diane, right? And your father is Hermano Mateo?"

"Yes, that's right. That's all in my hospital paperwork—"

"Oh, I didn't get it from there," Carrie said quickly. "That's private information. I know because my mother told me about her sister's family, the ones she's not supposed to have any contact with."

"But why?" Mari asked, her confusion turning to hurt. Could this really be true? Could her mother have actually lied to her about something so important? Could she really know so little about her parents? She'd thought the foundation of her life couldn't get any shakier, but now she wasn't so sure. "Why would my mother pretend to have no one?"

"Well, this is the part that I hope doesn't cause problems, but apparently your dad didn't get along with my mother and father. They're atheists and socialists, and like I said, modern-day hippies, I guess. And your dad is pretty…um, traditional."

Mari snorted. "That would be putting it rather mildly. My dad is *extremely* conservative and both my parents are very religious. But I can't believe my mother would just break off ties with her sister because my father didn't get along with her."

"Well, she didn't, not really. They talk on the phone at least a couple times a year, and I think this past year they might have even FaceTimed. However they manage it, my mom knows the names of her sister's children. That would be you and your brothers and sister. So when I heard your name, I just had to believe that it was you."

"Oh my God," Mari whispered. "I can't believe there's—are there more of you, more of my mother's family?"

"There's my baby sister, Kelly, and I have an uncle James, so he would be your mom's older brother. Your uncle. He lives in the UK and I don't see him very often. He's gay, and he and his husband moved there, gosh, probably twenty years ago. I guess I don't have to point out where the problem would be there."

"No," Mari said softly. "You don't."

"My mom thought it was important for me to know that there was more family, even though she said we'd probably never meet face-to-face. That's how I knew about all of you. I called her last night."

"I don't really believe in coincidences like this," Mari muttered, but she couldn't disbelieve the story, either. "We certainly don't look anything alike."

"I've seen pictures of our moms when they were younger, and they look a lot alike, but my dad is as Irish as they come and I got most of my coloring from him."

"And I got mine from my father."

Carrie nodded. "I love your hair, by the way. It looks like thick black velvet."

"Thanks. I love yours. I always wanted curls like that."

"It's funny how we always think we want someone else's hair."

Mari grinned. "I can't believe we're cousins. I have others, most of them are in Mexico, though."

"I'm not totally sure it's coincidence, you ending up here, I mean." Carrie fiddled with the cellophane wrapper of her sandwich. "My mom told your mom that I moved here because Presley's company had purchased the hospital. Mom thought your mom might have said something to one of your old instructors about the new program here."

"My mom? God, I can't see her doing that," Mari said, but she wasn't really sure about anything any longer. She clearly didn't really know her mother at all. Her program director had visited a lot, especially when she'd first gotten sick, and had helped her parents understand the medical system and the barrage of treatments that came on in rapid succession. Her parents liked him, and they'd become friendly enough she could almost imagine her mother mentioning something to him. She didn't really know her parents at all, as she'd learned the hard way the last year. If her mother had been keeping a secret relationship with her sister all these years, one that Mari's father disapproved of, she wasn't nearly as passive and nonconfrontational as she'd always appeared.

"I don't know whether to be angry at my mother, proud of her, or just plain sad."

"It seems pretty terrible from the outside," Carrie said, "but I guess we can't ever know that whole story."

"Well however it came about, I'm really happy to be here," Mari said, "and I'm really happy to meet you too."

"I know, it's great, isn't it?" Carrie touched her hand tentatively. "I hope I haven't upset you by telling you all of this."

Mari shook her head. "You haven't. And crazy as it all sounds, somehow I can totally believe it. Nothing you told me seems too impossible given the way a lot of things happen in my family."

"Now that you're here, we've got to spend more time together. Glenn probably told you about softball. Do you play, by any chance?"

"Oh my God, you too?" Mari groaned jokingly. "Glenn mentioned you pitched. I don't play. I hope you'll overlook that."

Carrie squeezed her hand. "That's okay, you're forgiven. After all, you're family."

CHAPTER THIRTEEN

Glenn's shift had been over for an hour, but they'd gotten hit with the late-afternoon rush that happened sometimes in the summer when everyone was reluctant to interrupt their vacation or poolside relaxation to deal with the irritating cough or persistent pain or low-grade fever that had been plaguing them all day. She didn't mind working late, and today she had a good excuse. She would have hung around anyhow to interact with the new staff and to see how her students did on a night rotation. Sometimes, the different kinds of cases that showed up when the sun started to go down could be a challenge. Fewer consultants were readily available, and often, the first one to evaluate the patient made more critical decisions out of necessity. Great training, but overwhelming at times for a newbie. She'd just finished signing off on her last patient when she got the text from Flann to meet her in the cafeteria. She passed Abby and Mari, who also had stayed late without being asked, on her way out.

"Staff meeting tonight," Abby called.

Glenn slowed and turned. "Yeah. Planning to be there. Flann just gave me a page, so I'm going to meet her first."

Abby laughed. "If she's trying to get you back in the OR already, tell her no."

Glenn grinned, her gaze flicking to Mari, who smiled as if enjoying the banter. "I'll do my best to resist."

"You do that," Abby ordered.

Glenn sent Mari a questioning look. "Going to the meeting?"

"Yes, I'll be there."

"See you." Glenn strode through the busy halls, puzzling over

Mari. She'd been aware of her all day, even when they weren't actually engaged. She knew where she was, like a little homing beacon in her head blinking in the background, which hadn't happened since she'd been deployed. Then she knew where everyone in her unit was every minute, acutely aware she might be called upon at any second to take care of an unexpected injury. She didn't have any reason to be that tuned in to Mari's presence—she wasn't worried about Mari settling in to the ER routine, she'd done that the first day, and she wasn't concerned about Mari's clinical abilities. Mari had been right—she was well trained and lacked the usual fresh-out-of-training dangerous tendency to make snap judgments. She was confident but careful, the perfect combination as far as Glenn was concerned. Given all that, she had no reason to be any more conscious of Mari than any of the other new staff throughout the day, but she was. That alone should have felt strange and unfamiliar, but even more unsettling was she found herself thinking throughout the day about when she'd have a chance to talk to her or maybe grab another meal again. Something else that had never happened to her before. Irritated, Glenn shrugged the tangle of thoughts aside. Since when had she wasted time studying her own navel—she had work to do after all, and Flann was waiting.

The coffee urn was warm and the coffee smelled new when she poured herself a cup. Flann and Harper, who she hadn't expected, were already ensconced at their usual table in the back corner, Flann in scrubs and Harper in her typical button-down-collar shirt and khaki pants. Glenn dropped into the free chair at the table and nodded to her friends. "What's up?"

Harper nodded a greeting and shot Flann a questioning look. "You called us here, so it's your show. Is there some kind of problem?"

Flann looked uncharacteristically uneasy for an instant, and Glenn finally pegged her expression—not uneasy, shy. Huh. That couldn't be right. Even in the midst of a FUBAR, Flann Rivers was never anything except exuberantly confident. So what could be worse than an effed-up beyond all repair situation? Harper studied her sister with the same slightly curious expression as Glenn.

"Well, the thing is," Flann said, "I wanted to tell the two of you together that Abby and I are going to get married." She glanced at Harper. "A few weeks after you and Presley, so, you know, it doesn't steal your thunder."

Harper laughed. "Jeez, you think that's going to matter to us? Congratulations, but what took you so long?"

Flann grinned a little sheepishly. "I wanted to go for it this weekend, but Abby says no."

"She's right—but not because of us," Harper said. "Your wedding should be an event all on its own, not a hurry-up thing, with all the bells and whistles. And don't let her convince you small is fine. Once in a lifetime, Flann—give her a day to remember."

"Right. Got it. Big and splashy."

Harper laughed. "There you go. Perfect."

"That's great, Flann," Glenn said, not at all surprised that her good friend wanted to formalize her relationship with Abby. Flann had always been a player, but she'd never fallen before. And when she did, like everything else in her life, she went all the way. "Anything you need, let me know."

Flann cleared her throat. "Well, actually, that's why I wanted to tell the two of you together."

Harper's brows drew down and she studied Flann intently. "What's bugging you?"

Flann took a breath. "I want Glenn to stand up with me, and I thought—"

"Hey," Glenn said quickly, "I'm totally honored, but you know, Harp's your sister and—"

"No, Glenn," Harper cut in, "I think you're exactly the right person. I love you, Flann, and you know damn well I'll always be there, but Glenn…she's really the only one who can actually put up with you on a daily basis."

Flann barked a laugh, and Glenn smothered a smile.

"She's earned it," Harper said.

"Here's the deal." Flann ran a hand through her hair, her gaze cutting from Harper to Glenn. "There's a lot of things I've done in the last few years I don't think I could've done without Glenn, but Harp has shown me the road for most of my life."

Glenn glanced at Harper. On the day her last tour had ended, she'd sworn she'd go lone wolf, that she'd never let anyone close enough to lose a piece of herself if anything happened to them. She didn't want to be responsible for anyone's well-being again, in any way. But in the three years she'd spent by Flann's side, working together, struggling together, sometimes losing together, she'd broken her own promise to herself. Flann was her best friend, and whatever she needed, whenever she needed it, Glenn would be there for her. "Whatever you want, I'm good with it."

"Totally," Harper said.

Flann blew out a breath. "So you two will both stand up with me?"

"For sure." Harper grinned at Glenn. "We're good, right?"

"Absolutely," Glenn said.

"Thanks," Flann said. "That was harder than waiting for Abby to say yes."

"Which took, what, all of a second?" Harper teased.

"About that, yeah," Flann said with her usual cocky flair.

"Does Blake know yet?" Harper asked.

"No, Abby and I are gonna tell him after I tell Mom and Dad."

"Once Margie knows," Harper said, "he'll know. You know the two of them share everything, so you probably need to make it simultaneous."

"Right." Flann shook her head, smiling wryly. "I sort of wonder what's going on with those two, but I don't actually know how to ask."

"Does it matter?" Harper asked.

"Only because I don't want to see either one of them get hurt."

"You can't protect them from falling in or *out* of love," Harper said. "Most everybody gets their heart broken at that age. Hell, I did regularly."

Glenn hadn't, but she'd never had a girlfriend in high school, or after that, either. She'd had hookups. She had natural urges, after all, and being in the kind of stressful day-to-day environment where life was pretty much on an hour-to-hour basis, the need to connect just to feel you had a little bit of a grip on life was even more urgent. But since she'd been back, there hadn't been anyone.

"It's never easy," Flann agreed, "but I know Blake is already taking flak about being trans and Margie along with him. I just want to make sure no matter what, they're okay."

"We'll all look out for them," Glenn said quietly.

"Yeah," Harper said, "but we have to let them tell us what they want us to know, if and when there's anything to tell."

Flann rubbed her face. "This parenting business is really tough. And I got one half-grown-up already."

"Hey," Harper said, "why don't you and Abby do the announcement thing on Sunday at family dinner. Then we'll all be there." She glanced at Glenn. "And you too, right?"

"Wouldn't miss it."

"Perfect." Harper dusted her hands. "That way everybody gets it at once, problem solved."

Flann nodded. "Sounds good to me. Abby can decide if we should tell Blake first."

"I suppose we better head to the staff meeting," Harper said, grinning. "Presley will not be happy if I'm late."

Glenn stood, wondering if she'd be in time to grab a seat with Mari.

❖

The staff meeting was the first Mari had ever attended, since she'd had no reason to think much about the actual running of a hospital during her training. This one surprised her. The meeting started exactly on time, for one thing. She'd been watching for Glenn and saw her slip in just a few seconds before half past seven with Flannery Rivers and another woman who looked very much like Flannery except for her opposite coloring. She must be the other Dr. Rivers—Harper. When Glenn and Flann took seats, Harper went on to the front of the room and joined an elegant-looking blonde in a bottle-green suit at the narrow podium. Mari didn't need anyone to tell her this was Presley Worth. She exuded authority simply by the way she scanned the room with a combination of command and camaraderie.

The CEO was as impressive as everyone had made her out to be. Presley quickly and concisely brought everyone up to date with the various plans for expansion of the physical hospital as well as the new ER residency and other training programs under way. A ripple of excitement moved through the audience, and something else that Mari recognized after a while...hope. She'd known that everyone had lived under the threat of the hospital closing for quite some time, but she hadn't appreciated how important the hospital was to so many people in the community. Not just because a significant percentage worked there, but because the institution represented a huge piece of the history of the town. Even though there had to be newcomers like Mari, she bet the majority of those crowding into the dome-ceilinged, wood-paneled auditorium had been born there, or their parents had been.

Strangely, she didn't feel like an outsider. She hadn't expected to feel so comfortable in such a small-town environment after growing up in one of the biggest cities in the world, but she did. Just by virtue of being part of the hospital, she had become part of the community. By the time the meeting was over, she felt even more a part of her new world. The homesickness and sadness drifted a little more into the background with each passing day.

As she made her way outside an hour later, she heard her name and turned to see Glenn coming after her with quick, sure strides. Mari waited, a swift surge of anticipation coursing through her.

"Hi," Glenn said. "Walking home?"

"Yes."

"Mind company?"

"Of course not," Mari said quickly, "although you don't need to feel you have to. It's perfectly safe." She laughed. "Not even a hint of rain."

"I know, but I've been cooped up all day and I'd like to stretch my legs, unless you want to be alone." Glenn shoved her hands in the back pockets of her jeans and, for the first time ever, appeared less than absolutely confident.

"No, I don't," Mari said quietly. "I'd love the company."

"What did you think of the meeting?" Glenn asked as they started down the winding hillside. Cars streamed past them, the staff heading home after the meeting.

"It certainly sounds like it's a busy time around here," Mari said. "An exciting one too."

"A lot of change all at once. Somehow, Presley has convinced everyone that she can work miracles, and I think she probably can."

"I'm convinced, and I've only heard her speak once," Mari said. "I could feel the sense of purpose everyone had, as if everyone counted. She made everyone feel essential."

"Everyone is," Glenn said. "Speaking of essential, are you sure you're not up for trying a little friendly softb—"

"Trust me. Very sure." Mari laughed. "But I will come cheer as promised."

"Good enough. We can head over after work tomorrow—maybe grab something to eat first if you want."

Mari hesitated. She'd never actually had a date with a woman, and she didn't think Glenn was actually asking her out, but her voice disappeared on a swell of excitement all the same. She swallowed quickly. "Sure. Sounds great."

By the time they neared the end of the road, darkness had fallen and only the occasional headlight slashed across their path. When they turned onto Main Street, Glenn asked, "How did things go today? Any problems?"

"No, at least not in the ER." Mari hadn't had time to really assimilate everything Carrie had told her, but throughout the afternoon their conversation kept coming back to her along with the disquieting knowledge that she didn't really know her family after all.

"Something wrong?" Glenn asked quietly.

"No, not really." Mari sighed. "Well, yes, sort of. I'm not really sure yet. The strangest thing happened today—maybe you already know about it. Carrie came by to talk to me."

"Carrie?" Glenn frowned. "No, why would I know what she had to say?"

"Oh, I thought maybe you and Carrie…" Mari suddenly felt foolish. "Sorry, never mind."

"Carrie and me? Oh." Glenn didn't laugh or seem put out, just contemplative. "No…we're friends, but not that way. If that's what you meant."

"Oh Lord, I *am* sorry," Mari said in a rush. "It's certainly none of my business one way or the other."

"Hey, it's no big deal. Anyhow, what happened?"

"It seems that Carrie and I are related. We're cousins."

Glenn stopped walking. "What? How is that possible—and you didn't know?"

"That's exactly the way I feel." Mari threw up her hands. "It seems my mother and Carrie's mother are sisters, and they've been carrying on a secret relationship all these years—keeping each other updated about their families, about us kids and who knows what else—while my mother has pretended that she doesn't have any family."

"Why?"

Mari sighed, partly embarrassed and partly angry. "Apparently because my father doesn't approve of Carrie's parents and convinced my mother to sever ties with them. Or pretend she had."

"Wow. That's hard."

"If it's true, and I don't have any reason to think it isn't, it's more than that." Mari's chest throbbed with suppressed outrage. "It's selfish and cruel to deprive my mother of her family, to deprive all of us of our family."

"Are you going to ask your mother?"

"I haven't quite figured out how I'm going to bring it up. We're not really communicating at all since I told them about myself." She tightened her shoulders as if that would make the psychic blow less painful. "They didn't even call me before I left to move here even though I left messages. I sent them all my new contact information and haven't heard anything—not even an email."

"I'm really sorry." Glenn's hand briefly swept down the center of her back and then was gone, a fleeting comforting touch.

"I keep telling myself it doesn't matter, and truthfully, every day it hurts a little bit less, but then something like this comes up and I wonder how much of my life has been a lie."

"Not on your account, and you're doing everything you can to make it truth," Glenn said quietly.

"You know, I'm beginning to really understand how hurtful and destructive secrets can be."

Glenn couldn't disagree, even though she knew they both had their secrets.

CHAPTER FOURTEEN

Glenn walked Mari home, said good night, and took her time walking back through town. Mari and Carrie, cousins. Nothing much surprised her anymore, but once in a while, it was nice for life to hand out a good surprise instead of one that seemed random and cruel. Now Mari would have someone, family, nearby, especially seeing as how the rest of her family had let her down. Carrie wouldn't let her be alone. Slowing at the entrance to the road up to the hospital, flanked with its stone arches and cast-iron lampposts, Glenn gave a fleeting thought to hiking back up to see what was going on in the ER, but decided to head home instead. She had a game the following night, and she was strangely relaxed. Not keyed up and agitated the way she often was at the end of the day. She smiled to herself. Walking Mari home seemed to be good therapy.

When she woke the next morning at five thirty, having slept for six solid hours, she was surprised again. She lingered in bed for a few minutes, listening to the town wake up through her open window. A distant rumble of an engine, birds singing somewhere in the fields out beyond the parking lot, the quiet tick of the refrigerator in her small kitchen just outside her bedroom door. She stretched, ran a hand absently down the center of her body, felt the quick pulse between her thighs. She let her fingers linger, trailing lower, and the answering tingle made her hips press down into the bed. She closed her eyes, savoring the first blush of morning and the slow rise of pleasure. She pressed lightly, eased a finger on either side of her slowly hardening clit, focused on the tension coiling low in her belly. Her mind drifted on the slowly building waves—stroke, circle, press—and fragments of images flickered beneath her closed lids. Long-fingered hands, teasing, tugging; a warm mouth on her belly, the moist tip of a tongue teasing lower, closer. She kicked aside the sheet, too warm now, a light sweat breaking out down the center of her chest. Her hips lifted, the muscles in her forearm tightened, her wrist brushed rhythmically across her taut abdomen. Her breath caught somewhere between her chest and her throat. She groaned softly, waiting for the warmth of a mouth to close over her, to pull her in, push her over. She glanced down, seeing in her mind's eye the dark eyes and playful smile, felt the midnight strands of hair slide through her fingers. Watching, mesmerized by need, she guided the full red lips down to her clit.

"Fuck," she gasped, jerking half upright as she exploded into her hand. "Fuck." She fell back against the pillows, trembling, unable to remember the last time she'd come so quickly or so hard. Absolutely certain she'd never had a fantasy quite like that one, so unquestionably focused on a woman she knew. Still throbbing, still lightly stroking, she couldn't even pretend she hadn't been thinking about Mari.

❖

An hour later Glenn pulled into the staff lot just as Carrie was getting out of her car. Carrie waited for her as Glenn locked up and jogged over.

"Hey," Carrie said. "What's new and exciting in your life?"

Glenn was very glad Carrie wasn't a mind reader at that moment, because she flashed back to what she'd been thinking about the last hour. Damn if she still wasn't a little turned on. "Not a thing. Business as usual. You?"

"I'm so busy I don't even feel like I'm busy. It still feels like July first to me and the month is half over."

Glenn laughed. "I think your boss works on a different calendar than the rest of the world."

"You got that right."

"Mari happened to mention the two of you are related," Glenn said as they followed the winding stone path from the lot to the back entrance.

"Amazing, isn't it?" Carrie grinned. "I'm pretty psyched about getting to know her better. Say, did you invite her to the game tonight?"

"Yeah, we're going to grab something to eat first."

"Well," Carrie said, slowing until Glenn had to stop. "That's news."

"What do you mean?"

"You're dating the new PA? Don't you think that's something that you should've told your very best friend who at one point contemplated seducing you?"

"What?" Glenn's mouth dropped open. "What are you talking about?"

Carrie made a huffing sound. "You are so clueless sometimes. Presley and Abby actually might've taken bets about whether or not I was going to get you—"

Glenn held up a hand. "Stop. I don't want to know about that. I definitely do not want to know you and...jeez, Carrie!"

Carrie jammed her free hand, the one not carrying her briefcase, onto her hip. "Excuse me? Would going to bed with me be such a terrible thing?"

Glenn actually backed up a couple steps. "Whoa. No, of course not. Where's this coming from?"

"Well, I'm available, you are available, although apparently you're not now, and—"

"I'm not dating Mari."

Carrie tilted her head. "Are you sure?"

"Yes, I am..." Glenn hesitated. "If I gave you the impression that I wanted us to, you know, you and me to, well..."

Carrie broke into a broad smile. "Have sex?"

Glenn's head felt like it was about to explode. "Carrie, I mean, you're gorgeous, and funny, and smart and—"

Carrie broke into peals of laughter and waved an arm in the air. "Stop, stop. I'm sorry. I'm sorry. I just couldn't resist. God, sometimes you're so clueless."

Glenn glowered. "You said that already."

Carrie threw her arm around Glenn's shoulder, stood on her tiptoes, and kissed her cheek. "I think you're amazingly adorable and you're exactly the kind of woman I would love to go to bed with if you weren't my best friend already."

"You know, you don't make any sense at all."

"We're completely incompatible, so any sex between us would have to be casual and probably just a time or two."

"Carrie, I think I'm not making myself clear. I'm not—"

"Theoretical, I'm talking theoretical." Carrie started walking again. "But that ship has already sailed. If we were going to have casual sex, we should've done it right after we first met. Now it's too late."

Glenn squeezed the bridge of her nose, trying to keep her brains inside her head. "I wish you'd told me all of this sooner."

"You mean you would've slept with me then? Don't say anything, because I think Presley has money on—"

"No. I wouldn't have," Glenn said. "I don't do that sort of thing, just for, you know…casual."

Carrie bit her lip, seeming to be holding in more laughter. "You *do* do it, though, right?"

"Jesus, how did we get onto this topic?"

"You were telling me about your date with Mari."

"It's not a date," Glenn shouted. A passing employee paused and stared at them. She lowered her voice. "Not a date."

"Are you sure, because you might want to think about that before, you know, you miss another boat."

"Are you mad at me?"

Carrie brushed a stray lock of hair off Glenn's forehead. "Absolutely not. You are one of my favorite people in the whole world. And I am perfectly happy with things between us just exactly the way they are." She held the door open and waited till Glenn drew next to her before whispering, "And if I'd wanted to get you into bed, I would have."

"I believe it," Glenn muttered.

"See you at the game."

Glenn stared after her as Carrie dashed off toward the east wing, wondering what the hell had just happened. And what any of it had to do with Mari. She hadn't asked her out on a date. Had she?

❖

Mari pulled the last chart from the stack in front of her, flipped to the discharge page, and double-checked that she'd filled out all the necessary sections before signing. The day had passed so quickly, she'd barely had time to think about anything beyond running down lab results, checking X-rays, reviewing treatment plans, and giving patients discharge instructions. She'd had a terrific day. Even Antonelli had been a pleasure, presenting patients to her in a thoughtful and thorough fashion. He seemed calmer than she'd ever seen him. She had no doubt in an emergency, he'd still be a take-charge, rapid decision maker, but that was a good thing too. There were times to take things slow and times to act. What was important was to know the difference.

Glenn stuck her head into the staff lounge. "Hey. Almost done?"

"Just finished." Mari smiled. When she'd had a minute's break, she'd thought about the evening to come. She was looking forward to getting out of her apartment, to meeting new people, to spending time with Glenn. "Should I meet you somewhere?"

"I drove today. I've got the team gear in the back of my Jeep. When you're ready, I'm parked out back."

Mari lifted the stack of charts. "Let me drop these off out front and I'm almost ready. I just need five minutes to change."

"Me too."

Glenn walked with her while she handed her charts to the clerk, signed out, and went to the locker room to switch her scrubs for street clothes. Mari was used to dressing and undressing with other people around, but this afternoon she felt unexpectedly shy and kept her body angled away from Glenn, who changed at her locker a few feet away. When she'd shimmied into her jeans and scoop-neck T-shirt, she sat down on the narrow bench to pull on her sandals. Glenn, already in a baseball T-shirt with a team logo, leaned back against the bank of lockers, her thumbs hooked into the pockets of her button-fly jeans.

"There's something I wanted to mention to you," Glenn said.

Mari looked up, surprised by the serious look in Glenn's eyes. "What?"

"I ran into Carrie on the way into the hospital this morning, and I mentioned we were gonna grab something to eat before the game tonight."

Mari tensed but kept her voice light. "Oh. Is she going to join us?"

Glenn's brows drew down and she shook her head. "No, but she asked me if this was a date."

Mari couldn't stop the hot flush from climbing up her throat. "I see. Is that a problem?"

"Sorry?"

"I mean, is Carrie upset that we're having dinner together? Do you want to cancel?"

"No, why would I do that?"

"Well, I thought—"

"I've been thinking about it all day," Glenn went on in a rush, as if she had rehearsed what she was going to say and didn't want to get sidetracked. "It wasn't a date, when I mentioned it to you before, but I think I'd like it if it was. So would you like to have dinner with me, tonight. The two of us, like a date."

Mari caught her breath. "Glenn…"

Glenn pushed away from the lockers. "Sorry, I didn't do that very well. I apologize. You can forget I said anything."

"No, that's not it. It's not what you think."

"What do I think?"

Mari rose so quickly her head went light again. She rested her fingertips quickly against the locker to orient herself. "I don't know how to say this without sounding incredibly clichéd. I don't date, and it doesn't have anything to do with you."

Glenn laughed shortly. "Boy, there really isn't any good way to say that, is there."

"Damn it," Mari said, knowing she was messing things up and not knowing how to make it right. "It isn't about you, it's about me. I can't date."

"Why not? You have a girlfriend, wife?"

"No." Mari couldn't even absorb the impossibility of either of those things. "Just the opposite. I've never—but that's not what I mean."

"Hey," Glenn said gently, cupping Mari's elbow in the palm of her hand. "You don't have to explain anything to me. It's okay. We don't even have to have dinner if you don't want to. I can arrange for someone else to give you a ride to the game."

"No! Will you please stop trying to fix it?" Mari heard her confusion and uncertainty coming out like anger. She *was* angry, at so many things, but not Glenn.

"Sorry. Bad habit." A muscle along the edge of Glenn's jaw jumped, but she didn't move her hand away.

Mari sighed. "I'm the one who should be sorry. Let me try to explain a little bit better."

"No, you don't have to. You really don't owe me an explanation or anything else."

"I do, I do. I need to. For me, not for you."

"All right," Glenn said.

"Can we not do this here?"

Glenn picked up her gear bag and Mari's in one hand. "Come on, there's a little garden out back with some benches. No one will be out there now. We can talk."

Feeling almost surreal, Mari followed Glenn through the hospital, down a long corridor, and out through a staff exit that led into a small grove of trees with a little fountain and a ring of stone benches. The canopy of maples blocked out most of the sun, and it was cool in the shadows. She sat, and Glenn sat a few feet away. Folding her hands and sliding them between her knees, Mari stared into the fountain, only then realizing the flickering flashes of light beneath the surface were not reflections of sunlight but koi, dancing through the water.

"I can't date, not for a couple of years," Mari said.

"Why the time limit?"

With a sigh, Mari shifted on the bench and looked into Glenn's eyes. "A year ago, right after I finished my PA training but before I started the job I had lined up at the medical center, I was diagnosed with acute myelogenous leukemia."

Glenn's face blanked. The blue of her eyes swirled to indigo. "Leukemia."

"Yes," Mari said. "It progressed quickly, and the remission I got from chemo only lasted a few weeks."

Glenn's breathing picked up, but she said nothing, her gaze cemented to Mari's. She didn't say she was sorry, she didn't act shocked, she didn't offer sympathy or condolences. She waited, she listened. She was so very good at that. Her solid, unwavering calm gave Mari the courage to keep going.

"My sister Selena, my twin, donated bone marrow. The transplant worked, so far. You know the statistics, or maybe you don't, but three years is pretty much the uncertain period in terms of delayed rejection of the transplant and disease recurrence. Once past that, I can probably count on being a survivor."

"So far everything looks good?" Glenn asked.

"Yes, as of my last checkup. There really isn't anything to do at this point except wait."

"Does Abby know?"

"I don't think so. My medical record wasn't part of the application process, and it's private. I'm in good health right now."

"This job will take a lot out of anyone."

This was what Mari feared, why she kept her diagnosis secret. Already, Glenn was worrying about her, wondering if she could do her job. This was why she didn't tell people. Oh, she hated the sympathy, and the fear that seemed to hide behind it, as if somehow whatever bad karma or ill luck had befallen her might be catching, but most of all she hated being viewed as less than capable. "I'm perfectly able to do my job."

"I know," Glenn said abruptly. "I've seen that for myself."

"Then you understand why I don't want to have any kind of serious personal relationship."

"I don't think I'm making that connection."

"Really? Then you're not looking at the long game, but I have to. How fair would it be for me to get close to someone, when I might not even be here in a year or two."

"Anyone can have an accident, come down with a fatal disease. There are no guarantees."

"Yes, that sounds great in the abstract, but this isn't an abstraction. This is a fact." Mari didn't want to argue, especially not with Glenn. "You can't win against me when it comes to these statistics. I've studied them for over a year. I could be living on borrowed time. You know that as well as I do."

Glenn let out a breath. "You know what you need to do, and you don't need to justify that to anyone."

"Good," Mari said, feeling deflated rather than happy. "Then we're on the same page about no dating."

CHAPTER FIFTEEN

W ill you do me a favor," Mari said into the silence as Glenn drove them toward the softball field.

Glenn glanced over at her, keeping her face a careful blank. Her feelings were not what mattered right now. Her anger at the random unfairness of life, something she was way too familiar with, didn't matter. Her confusion at discovering a road she hadn't thought she'd wanted to travel suddenly blocked to her didn't matter. The disappointment she hadn't expected to feel didn't matter. Mari mattered. Mari had trusted her with a piece of herself, and that trust deserved to be honored. If she needed something and Glenn could give it to her, she would. "Yes."

"Don't tell anyone what I told you just now."

Glenn stared back out to the road. Knowing someone, really knowing them, wasn't always measured by a calendar or a clock— knowing was sometimes the recognition of shared pain or joy, the communion of spirit from struggling together, the connection born of similar experiences. She hadn't been rejected by her family, but she knew what it was like to be without one. She had faced her own death countless times, not from disease but an enemy just as invisible and just as merciless. She had sealed away her pain and respected the walls Mari had built. "You don't know me well enough to know that I wouldn't do that."

"I think I do, really, or I wouldn't have been in a position to need to tell you. I wanted to tell you." Mari leaned closer, touched Glenn's bare forearm. "I needed to ask because I've kept the secret so long I feel exposed somehow."

"You're not. You're safe. I won't say anything." Glenn let out a slow breath and looked at Mari, who sat half turned in the front seat, facing her. "Harper and Flann would understand more than you realize."

Mari frowned. "What do you mean?"

"Their younger sister Kate died of fulminant leukemia. She was eleven or so, I think."

"Oh God, that's horrible," Mari whispered. "I hated seeing all the children when I was getting treated."

Glenn reached her hand. "Lots and lots make it."

"I know," Mari murmured, her fingers unconsciously twining with Glenn's. "I kept telling myself that every time I looked at them."

"And you made it," Glenn said, gently disengaging her fingers. Mari's hand was warm, soft. She would have been happy to keep holding it, but Mari probably wouldn't be pleased when she realized what she'd done. She'd just asked for distance, after all. "Will you do me a favor?"

"Yes," Mari said, not qualifying, instantly agreeing.

"Will you tell me if there's a problem, any kind of problem?"

"Why?" Mari asked.

"If I know that you'll tell me if you need your shifts adjusted— more time off between cycles or whatever—or if there's a medical problem, I'm not going to be constantly wondering." Glenn smiled, felt the cold brittleness of her own lips stretched thin. "I don't want you to feel like I'm always watching, waiting for something bad to happen."

"I like that you care," Mari said, "but that's exactly why I don't want anything—anything beyond friendship—with anyone. I don't want anyone to be watching and waiting. Something like that sucks all the joy out of life."

"I'll do my best not to do that," Glenn said.

"I know you will, and I appreciate it."

"You haven't actually answered my question. Will you tell me if there's a problem?"

"I promise I'll let you know if I'm having a problem at work or if there's a change in my condition that is going to affect my job."

"Thanks." Glenn didn't miss the careful wording and the neat way Mari had sidestepped saying she'd let her know if her transplant failed, but she couldn't ask for more, couldn't ask for any confidence that went beyond their professional relationship. Mari had made herself very clear on the limits of anything personal between them. Nothing would stop her from being on guard. She couldn't change the way she was made any more than she could change Mari's desire to be independent, to avoid ties. But she could honor Mari's request, could keep the distance Mari wanted. She'd already put up the walls. She was only surprised at how much she had wanted to breach them for Mari.

❖

Carrie jogged over to the Jeep when Glenn pulled into a place in the second row of a line of pickup trucks and SUVs. Usually she parked right behind the backstop to unload the gear, but she was later than usual after their quick stop for a burger. Dinner had been quick and mostly quiet—they hadn't mentioned their previous conversation, but she kept thinking there was more she should have said, wanted to say. She just wasn't sure what, or why.

"I was wondering where you were," Carrie called, opening the rear compartment as Glenn climbed out of the driver's side. "Let me give you a hand with everything."

"Sure," Glenn said abruptly and caught Carrie giving her a look.

Carrie grinned as Mari joined them. "Hi. How's it going?"

"Great," Mari said, wondering if it counted as a lie to keep one's personal business private. She hated feeling as if she'd lied to Glenn, even though she had every right to keep her medical condition to herself unless there was some reason other people needed to know. All the same, she'd shared some pretty important personal things with Glenn while deliberately hiding the biggest one of all. Glenn must be angry or at least feel a little manipulated somehow, but Mari couldn't read anything beneath her usual calm, cool exterior. They'd shared a meal and made casual conversation, but the distance across the table had seemed enormous. She hadn't known how to close that distance, and maybe she didn't deserve to. She'd put the walls there, and as hard as they were to accept, she needed them. She preferred anger to pity, reserve to suffocating kindness. And she would not be selfish enough to take more than she could give, and she might not have anything at all to offer. She jumped when fingers closed around her wrist.

"Come on," Carrie said. "I'll take you over to the bleachers. Abby and Presley are there. You can sit with them, and they can fill you in on all the players."

"Oh, I don't want to intrude. I can find a seat somewhere."

"Hey, no way. You're my cuz, remember? I want you to meet my friends. You'll love them."

"Well, I know Abby a little," Mari said a bit helplessly. She glanced over her shoulder as Carrie resolutely tugged her away from the Jeep. Glenn looked after them, her eyes shadowed. Mari called, "Good luck tonight."

"Thanks." Glenn hefted a duffel with bats sticking out one end and turned toward the field.

Looking after her, Mari hesitated.

"Something wrong?" Carrie asked.

"What? No," Mari said quickly. "No, everything is fine."

"Super. Should be a great game."

Surrendering to Carrie's enthusiastic tug on her arm, Mari followed her through the scattering of people who mingled around a double set of bleachers off to the left of the big tall fence—what did they call that, the batter's cage? Players were already on the field, tossing the ball back and forth, and someone was hitting another one into the outfield. She'd seen baseball games fleetingly on television and in the lounge at the hospital, but never paid any attention to them beyond the basics that every American grew up knowing. The sports channel wasn't on her list of favorites, and when the ER staff was glued to the TV in the break room during the World Series, she was discreetly reading a book on her phone.

"So how's everything going in the ER?" Carrie asked when they reached the stands. She leaned against the railing, not seeming in any hurry to get out onto the field.

"Great," Mari lied for the second time in less than half an hour. She gestured to the field. "Don't you have to go?"

"In a minute or so." Carrie grinned. "I'm the pitcher. I just need to warm up a little."

"Ah, special privileges."

"That's it—think of me as the surgeon on the team. Nothing important happens without me."

Mari couldn't help herself, she laughed. Carrie had a way of lifting her spirits despite her lingering melancholy. "Do the rest of them know that?"

"Oh, they like to pretend otherwise but we all know the truth." Carrie's mischievous grin made it impossible to take her seriously. "So where are you living?"

Mari told her. "It's a little apartment, but it's nice. You?"

"I'm out in the country with Presley and Harper."

"You're living with them?"

Carrie tipped her head from side to side. "Well, technically Harper is living with me and Presley. We were there first. The hospital had actually rented the place for Presley, and I was going to stay in town, but it's this big old rambling farmhouse with plenty of bedrooms, and it just made sense for us to live together. Plus, the house comes with a housekeeper whose cooking will make you cry. Wait till you taste Lila's muffins."

Carrie made swooning noises and Mari laughed again. She'd never met anyone who seemed to take such unconcealed pleasure in life. She envied her new cousin that ability.

"Anyhow," Carrie went on, "when Harper and Prez got involved, well, you know how that goes. Pretty soon Harper was spending almost every night there."

Mari *didn't* know how that went, but she wasn't going to say so. She'd never gone any further than kissing, and not very much of that. She'd shared a room with her sister and, until she'd gotten sick, they'd shared pretty much everything. Talk of sex wasn't one of them. Selena had a serious boyfriend, but she lived at home and Juan lived with his parents too. Mari doubted they were having sex. Selena was even more religious than their parents and had declared from the time she was twelve that sex before marriage was a sin. "Is it weird, living with your boss?"

"Oh no. Prez and I have pretty good boundaries. The only real problem is that she wants to work all the time, and I refuse to talk about business before we get to the office." Carrie laughed. "Well, I try not to, anyways, but it's just natural for her. She's always thinking about what she needs to do, and since she's always twenty steps ahead of everyone, there's always a lot of that."

"Sounds like she's lucky to have you."

"Oh, she is. But she knows it. And I love my job." Carrie laughed. "Anyhow, I'm going to be moving into Harper's in a few weeks. At least I hope it will be that soon. Harper's planning to have it renovated—add another bedroom and bathroom in case my family comes to visit or something."

"Is it in town?"

"Oh no. It's right smack-dab on the Rivers plantation. I call it a plantation, it isn't really, although it looks a lot like Tara."

Mari struggled to follow the quickly swinging conversation. "Tara? You mean like in *Gone with the Wind*?"

"Yeah, you know, the big white house with the columns and the gables and the sweeping porches and the acres and acres of green? That's what the Rivers family's homestead reminds me of. Harper's place is like a quarter of a mile away—it used to be a caretaker's house, a hundred years ago, I guess. It's got its own little barn and a garden. Do you garden?"

"You mean flowers? Um, no."

"Actually, I meant vegetables. You know, tomatoes and peppers and cucumbers. That kind of thing."

Mari couldn't keep from smiling, although she didn't feel the slightest bit humorous. "Oh my God, no. I grew up right in the heart of the city. The only things coming out of the ground that weren't parking meters were the occasional trees that the city planted, and they were so puny they hardly qualified as trees. My family lives in a row house, and my mother sometimes put a window box with flowers outside the front window, but she took care of keeping them alive."

"You'll have to come and see the place," Carrie said. "I've pretty much talked Harper into letting me oversee the renovations, since I'm gonna be living there and she's way busy at work."

"Of course," Mari said automatically.

"Great! We're having a get-together at our place tomorrow. You'll have to come and then I'll take you on a tour."

"Ah, I—"

"Oops—there's my page," Carrie said when a short, barrel-chested guy in a team shirt yelled and waved in their direction. "Come on."

Carrie vaulted up a narrow aisle between the rows of benches toward the top of the bleachers and Mari hurried after. The stands were surprisingly crowded with men, women, and children talking, eating, and laughing. Sundown was at least two hours away and the air shimmered with heat.

"That's Presley next to Abby," Carrie said, pointing as she climbed, "and Harper's sister Carson and her little boy next to her." Carrie paused one row below Abby, next to Abby's son and the Rivers girl, who Mari had first seen at the pizza place with Glenn. "Hey, move down, you two. This is my cousin Mari."

Dutifully, the teens inched down and slid closer together to make room on the end.

"Thanks," Mari said as she settled beside them.

"Hey—gotta go warm up," Carrie announced to the world in general. "Everybody, meet Mari, my cousin!"

"Your cousin?" Presley said, obviously surprised, as she held out a hand to Mari. "Hi, I'm Carrie's roomie, Presley."

"Nice to meet you," Mari said to the hospital CEO. Roomie was right.

"Yeah, neat, isn't it?" Carrie squeezed Mari's shoulder. "See you afterward for victory pizza. Bye, everybody. Look after my cuz."

Mari blushed at being the sudden focus of attention, but could hardly be annoyed. Carrie was just too damn sweet.

Abby's son turned and held out his hand. "Hi, I'm Blake Remy."

The pretty young girl, who had the same classic features as her sisters along with a glorious head of thick cascading golden tresses, grinned around him. "Margie Rivers. Hi."

"Hi," Mari said.

Abby leaned down, a hand on each of the kids' shoulders. "Ms. Mateo is one of our new PAs."

"Oh, you can call me Mari," Mari said.

"Cool," Blake said. "Margie and I are going to be volunteers in the ER."

"That's great," Mari said.

Blake glanced back at his mother. "Right, Mom?"

"Presley and Harper have approved." Abby turned to Mari. "Blake is going to start with us on Monday for four weeks, then Margie."

"Actually," Margie said in a bright, clear voice, "Blake and I were thinking that we should do our rotations simultaneously, because that

way we'll get more out of them. Dr. Valentine is okay with both of us
starting in the middle of August at the vet clinic and working until we
go back to school, and then maybe on weekends."

"Weekends." Abby looked back and forth between them. "We'll
have to see how your grades are before I'll agree to that."

Blake made a face but didn't argue.

"As for the two of you rotating together, I don't see why not. You
can both start on Monday morning. Seven a.m."

Blake winced. "Seven?"

Abby smiled just a little triumphantly. "We start at seven, which
means *you* should probably show up around ten of."

Blake glanced at Margie. "Can you pick me up? Just until I get my
license." He looked over his shoulder at his mother with a truly angelic
smile. "And a car."

Abby merely shook her head. "Those negotiations are ongoing.
What are you driving, Margie—something safe? Not a motorcycle."

"Oh, totally." Margie's face glowed. "Harper gave me her old
truck for as long as I keep it running and put gas in it."

"I'll help with that," Blake said instantly.

"Fine," Abby said. "Mari and I will be your supervisors in the
ER."

"Cool," both kids said at once.

Abby squeezed Blake's shoulder and sat back while Blake and
Margie made plans in excited whispers. Mari tried and failed to imagine
her own parents interacting with her the way Abby did with Blake and
his friend, firmly in charge but listening to them, as if their opinions
mattered. A year ago she might not have noticed, or at the most been
surprised or curious. Now she was the tiniest bit jealous, and even more
than a little sad.

CHAPTER SIXTEEN

Softball was a lot more interesting than Mari had ever realized. Maybe it was the players she found fascinating, though, and not the details of the game. One player in particular. She tended to forget the score and the number of outs, being mostly too busy watching Glenn. Glenn played the game the way she did everything else, with a singular focus that showed in her every movement, from the way she ran directly out onto the field with her baseball glove tucked under her arm, racing to her position, to settling into a loose-limbed stance, poised and ready for action. And watching, always watching. Her attentiveness was one of the things Mari liked most about Glenn—no matter what she was doing, evaluating a patient, instructing a student, listening while Mari talked, she was so unwaveringly there, totally engaged. Being around Glenn, when they talked in the ER hallway or relaxed across from each other in the pizza place, she knew without a doubt she was seen. It wasn't as if Glenn had tunnel vision and shut out the rest of the world— just the opposite. Glenn was aware of *everything*. She constantly took in all the activity going on around them, as if to be sure she was never taken by surprise. Every time the door opened to admit a new customer or someone appeared from around the corner at the end of a hall, her gaze would flicker for just a second in that direction, as if she was assessing the threat level, determining friend or foe. And just as quickly her attention would swing back to Mari, one hundred percent.

After years of feeling as if she was only partially visible, to family and friends and even herself, Mari exulted in the sensation of being seen at last. No more hiding—and now that Glenn knew all her secrets, or probably all that mattered, she couldn't take solace in the shadows even if she'd wanted to. In the weeks since she'd left LA, her life had turned upside down.

But she could handle it. She had to. She had nothing to go back to.

"Ooh, this guy can hit," Margie exclaimed. "He homered a couple of times in the last game against us."

"Yeah, I remember," Blake muttered as if recalling some grievous injury. "He pulls right, though, and Glenn wasn't playing the night he homered. He got a break, that's all."

Mari perked up at the sound of Glenn's name and studied the batter. Unassuming enough, she would have thought. A slim, young guy she recognized from X-ray swung the bat in an easy motion and didn't look to be all that strong. He swung and missed the first ball. The next he watched pass over the plate with barely a glance. Then he coiled just a little tighter, his front leg stretching out as Carrie released the ball, and his bat sliced the air almost too quickly for Mari to follow. The ball streaked away with a sharp crack in Glenn's direction. Over her head. Too high for her to possibly reach.

Mari caught her breath, edged forward on the bench while people yelled encouragement and many jumped to their feet. For just an instant Glenn seemed not to move at all, but merely lifted her head as the ball soared toward her, then she angled her shoulder, her gaze still fixed upward, and ran back and back, almost to the rear wall, as the ball arced down. With a fluid sweep of her arm, she lofted her glove and the bullet-like projectile seemed to fall into it as if that had been its only intention. As if she had drawn it to her like a magnet.

Mari knew the feeling. Glenn was magnetic.

She cheered with everyone else as Glenn's team streaked off the field. She didn't know the precise score, but she didn't have any doubt that Glenn's team had won when everyone on the bench around her jumped up, hooting loudly. She found herself caught on the wave of jubilation, amazed at the delight that buoyed her spirits. The winning wasn't what really mattered, but the camaraderie, the common bond of supporting the team, most of whom were actually strangers, united her with the people around her. It was hard to feel alone in that raucous, high-spirited community.

Abby climbed down and stood next to Mari in the aisle. "I'm surprised they haven't recruited you yet."

"Actually, that was just about the first thing Carrie said to me," Mari said with a laugh. "But I convinced her I'm much more valuable as a cheerleader than a player."

"Everyone has their purpose." Abby nodded solemnly and broke into a grin. "A bunch of us are headed out to the pub for beer and burgers. Or just beer, or just burgers. Or in my case, gravy fries. You're welcome to come."

Mari almost said yes before a sudden wave of uncertainty caught back the words. She wasn't sure she could be around Glenn any more tonight without obsessing over the conversation they'd just had, and what and how things had changed. She was emotionally exhausted from reliving the last year and didn't have the reserves to absorb any more pain for a few hours, and the distance that had descended between her and Glenn hurt. And, she admitted ever so fleetingly, she didn't want to discover she was no longer the focus of Glenn's attention. At war with herself, she shook her head. "Thanks, but I think I'll head home. I'm starting nights tomorrow, and I want to get a good night's sleep."

"Okay. See you at the barbecue tomorrow?"

Before Mari could answer, Carrie appeared beside them, her flushed face alight. "Hey, great game, huh?"

"Fabulous," Abby said.

From the row behind them, Presley yelled, "Super pitching, Ace."

"But of course." Carrie looked at Mari. "Have fun?"

"It was great," Mari said, meaning the words this time.

"You're coming out with us, right?"

"Not tonight."

"You sure? Do you drink beer?"

"Ah—now and then." That was sort of true, although Mari rarely drank anything at all. Spirits were not something her parents considered proper casual drinking, and since she'd barely dated, she didn't have much reason to drink. When she'd gone out on occasion with the others in her training program, she'd usually stuck to something nonalcoholic. And then, when she got sick, alcohol was off the table.

"Bottoms Up has a great assortment on tap, anyhow," Carrie said. "And decent food. You sure?"

"I'll take a rain check."

"Okay. So I'll pick you up about nine tomorrow."

"Sorry?"

"Remember, you're getting a tour of my soon-to-be new house before we head over to the farm. I think there'll be Lila's biscuits."

"Oh—well, there's the barbecue in the afternoon and—"

"Right. We're having a little get-together at our place, to review the last-minute details for Presley's wedding. Then we can all head over to the barbecue together."

Mari glanced at Presley, who had joined them. "Oh, well, I don't want to intrude."

Presley waved her hand. "Believe me, we love all the input we can get. This wedding is a group venture. You're more than welcome."

"Nine o'clock," Carrie called, as she turned and scrambled back down the crowded aisle.

"Well, okay," Mari said in defeat. She followed along with the throng of people clambering down the bleachers and finally found a clear space to catch her breath and figure out where she was. She was pretty sure she remembered the direction Glenn had driven, and it wasn't very far at all from the center of town. All of a sudden, she really looked forward to a few moments of being alone to regroup.

"Carrie says you're not going out with us," Glenn said, materializing by her side.

"No, I thought I'd call it an early night." Mari smiled. "Congratulations on winning the game."

A quicksilver smile flashed across Glenn's face, adding warmth to her cool attractiveness that was disconcertingly captivating. "It was a bit of a cakewalk, but we'll take it now and then."

"Oh, absolutely. Every now and then you need an easy one."

"Yeah." Glenn lightly touched her arm. "Come on, I'll take you home."

"You don't have to do that. You're going out, aren't you?"

"Maybe." Glenn's brows drew down. "But I'm certainly not going to let you walk home."

"It's not far, right? Maybe a mile?"

"That's about right, but in case you haven't noticed, it's dark. Or almost—it will be by the time you get there. You're not walking home."

"It's not safe?"

Glenn blew out a breath. "Probably it is, but you're still not walking home."

"Don't forget, I've got city smarts. I've been getting around at night by myself for a lot of years," Mari said. "Besides, you run at night, don't you?"

"Yes, and I've never had a problem." Glenn put her hand in the center of Mari's back, gently directing her out of the stream of foot traffic. "But unless you want me to worry, you'll take the ride."

Mari laughed. "That strikes me as blackmail."

Glenn grinned. "Possibly."

"Thank you," Mari said, aware of the press of Glenn's fingers along the edge of her scapula, the tiny points dissolving the terrible distance she'd felt earlier. "I'd appreciate a ride, then."

"Good. That's better."

In minutes Glenn pulled to the curb in front of Mari's apartment. As Mari was about to say good night, she regretted her decision not to go out with everyone after the game. Reminding herself of all the reasons why she had decided to pass, she pushed open the door and stepped out. "Thanks again."

"Don't forget the barbecue tomorrow. Do you need a ride?"

"No," Mari said, wishing for a second that she did. "Carrie is showing me around tomorrow, and I'll be going over with her."

Glenn nodded. "Have fun then."

Mari held the door open for a second, searching for something to say and discarding everything. She'd made the rules and wished she wasn't so sure of them. "'Night."

Glenn's gaze traveled over Mari's face, warming her skin and making her heart race.

"'Night, Mari."

❖

Glenn waited until Mari was inside before pulling away. She drove to the next corner but instead of turning left toward Bottoms Up, she turned right, and five minutes later pulled into the lot behind the hospital. In the locker room, she stripped out of her dusty softball clothes and crammed them into her gym bag, pulled clean scrubs from her locker, and turned on the shower full force. With steaming water sluicing over her head and shoulders, she braced both forearms on the shower wall and closed her eyes. With nothing but silence to focus on, her thoughts were all of Mari and what Mari had told her about the last year. Her hands closed into fists and the muscles in her shoulders bunched. She hated thinking about what Mari had endured with her illness and her family's rejection, and she hated even more imagining the uncertainty she lived with every day. She hated not being able to do a damn thing about it, and she could only imagine what the waiting must be like for Mari. She was so fucking tired of senseless waste, of cruelty and the fickleness of life. And she ought to know by now she couldn't change a goddamned thing.

Straightening, pushing the anger deep down inside, she rubbed her hands over her face and switched the water to cold. The shock against her heated skin jolted through her like a rifle crack. Her mind cleared and she accepted that reality was often unfair and inexplicable. Life, her life at least, was a battlefield, and she knew what she needed to do.

She pulled on scrubs, toweled her hair dry, and went down to the ER. Bruce manned the desk.

"I didn't know you were working tonight," he said, sounding not the least bit surprised to see her.

"I'm not, officially."

"It's Friday night, though. Should have known." He gestured at the board, which was half full of names already. "In another hour we'll really be able to use you."

"Thought I'd check in on the student. Where is she?"

He grinned. "In six with an earache. Three-year-old."

High-pitched screaming alternating with heartfelt sobs emanated down the hall from the direction he indicated.

"Oh, boy," Glenn said. "My favorite thing. Holding down a thrashing, inconsolable child to look in their ears."

Bruce laughed. "Uh-huh."

"If I don't come back in half an hour, send help."

"Oh no—you're on your own, Doc."

All medics in the field were Doc, and as Glenn headed off to give her student some backup, she was grateful for anything—even a screaming three-year-old with an earache—to dull the weight of helplessness sitting on her chest.

CHAPTER SEVENTEEN

A little before four in the morning, Flann pulled into the drive beside the schoolhouse her great-grandfather had attended and parked behind Abby's car. Before Abby came to town and into her life, Flann would've bunked the rest of the night in an on-call room reserved for docs waiting for babies to be born or for the OR to get ready for an emergency case. After a few hours of semi-sleep, she'd grab a quick breakfast in the cafeteria, shower in the surgeons' locker room, and start her day again without giving the world outside the hospital a thought. There were times when she didn't get home for a couple of days. She'd never really minded, before Abby. But everything was different now.

Now the chance to slip into her own bed for forty-five minutes, to slide her arm around Abby's waist and press against her back, to cradle her face in Abby's hair and breathe her scent, was worth every second of the rushed trip home from the Rivers and back. Maybe Abby would wake up and turn to her with a murmur of welcome and a soft kiss, and they'd have a minute or two or ten, enough time for her to feel Abby's heart quicken as she stroked her, hear Abby's low moan as she teased her. A precious minute to feel Abby turn into her with a muffled cry as she exploded. Oh yeah. A few minutes with Abby was everything.

Flann bounded up the front steps and slowed when she saw the inner door was open, with just the screen keeping out the bugs and the night. Abby tended to lock up at night—city habit, and like most doctors, she was a creature of habit. Flann frowned, wondering why Abby had forgotten to close up. She eased the screen open as quietly as she could, took two steps inside, and stopped. The sun was just rising, and dim dawn light illuminated the single big room with the living area in front and kitchen in the rear. Blake sprawled in the corner of the big sofa, his head angled in an unnatural position that was going to hurt when he woke up.

"Hey," Flann whispered, moving closer.

"Hey." Blake sprang upright, shot a hand through his tousled hair, and stared at her.

"Too hot in the loft to sleep?" Flann asked.

"Wasn't so bad."

"Okay." Flann thought about Abby behind the bedroom door down the hall. Her stomach still quivered with thoughts of warm flesh and hungry kisses. She looked at Blake. "Something going on?"

"Can I talk to you?"

"Sure. Want to take a walk so we don't wake your mom?"

"Yeah, okay."

Flann turned around, walked back outside, down the short walk, and out the picket fence. Every time she saw that fence she smiled. Yep, she had the picket fence and soon she'd have the wife, officially, and one kid and maybe another one day soon. Nothing she'd ever wanted, and all that mattered to her.

"Tough case?" Blake asked as they walked toward the center of the village.

"Perforated diverticulum—you know what that is?"

"Yes, it's an outpouching of the colon, a thinning of the muscle layer, which can become inflamed and sometimes rupture. Sort of like an appendix."

Flann laughed. "Very good. You've been studying."

"Some animals get them too."

"I didn't realize that. I'd think with their diet it wouldn't be as common."

"It isn't. Dogs get it pretty often. Volvulus and other malrotations of the intestine are more common in ruminants, because of the extra stomachs."

"Uh-huh." Flann waved to the daughter of a local farmer who beeped the horn as she rattled by in an old pickup truck loaded down with hay. "Feels like I could use an extra stomach this morning. I'm starving. Think we should pick up some breakfast for your mom?"

"The café will be open any minute," Blake said, a hopeful note in his voice.

"We'll head that way, then." Flann figured the ten-minute walk would clear the last of the churning arousal from her system and give him a chance to get to the point. A minute passed in silence.

"I want to have my top surgery before school starts. Will you do it this summer?"

Oh, boy. For one second, Flann wanted to punt. Let Abby make the decision. But Blake hadn't asked Abby, he'd asked her. They'd have to talk, the three of them, but for right now, she was the one he'd chosen. "Let's back up a couple steps, okay?"

His shoulder stiffened, as if he expected a rejection, but he nodded.

"First off, we're family now. Some people would say you ought to have a different surgeon because of that."

"Why?"

"'Cause maybe my judgment will be off because you're extra-special to me, and my focus will be split worrying about you instead of doing my job."

"Will it?"

"No."

"Okay. It's not illegal or anything. You can't get in trouble?"

"No, I can't. And just so you know, if I do it, I'll get Glenn to assist. You couldn't have a better team."

Blake nodded seriously. "I know that."

"Okay. So, you've read about it, right?"

"Lots of times, and I've read blogs, and I've seen what it looks like," Blake said all in a rush.

"What do you mean? You've seen what it looks like?"

"On YouTube, guys have documented their surgeries. You know, before and right after when the bandages first come off, and then when it's all healed."

"You realize there's more than one way to do the surgery, and everybody heals differently. You might not look at all like any of those guys."

"I know. And you have to look at me to decide how to make the incisions."

"That's right."

"I know all that. I know about the scars."

"I have to say this, okay," Flann said, halting on the corner across from the café. "It's part of what I have to do as your surgeon, not because I don't trust you or believe in you. Do you understand?"

Blake shoved his hands in the pockets of his baggy basketball shorts and looked her in the eye. "Okay. I get it. Go ahead."

"Surgery isn't like the drugs. If you stop them now, some of the physical changes in your body would be permanent, but a lot of them would go away eventually." Flann waited, let her words sink in.

"I know."

"This isn't like that. There's no going back, Blake. Once the breast tissue's gone, it is gone."

"I'm sure. I've always been sure."

Flann nodded. "I know. And you know what else I know?"

"What?" Blake whispered, a shimmer of tears glistening on his lashes.

"Your mom is sure too. You have to talk to her about this before we schedule anything. You're a minor, and she's your mom." Flann grinned. "And she's sorta the head of this household."

Blake laughed. "We've already talked about it before, some. I'll talk to her right away."

"Good. So what do you want to know?" Flann asked as they sprinted across the street.

"Will I have to stay in the hospital?"

"No, you can go home soon as you're awake from surgery. It'll take me, oh, an hour or so, but I can let you know for sure on that when I examine you."

"Everyone will know, won't they."

Flann blew out a breath, her hand on the door to the café. "Probably some. Everyone who works with me in the office and in the OR will know. A few people will probably mention it to someone, but I don't think it'll become town news."

"Okay."

"Come on." Flann pulled open the door and they waited in silence in the small room smelling of sugar and fresh dough, behind a handful of early risers at the glass-fronted counter filled with out-of-this-world concoctions. Several people greeted them in passing, giving Blake a smile or a guarded once-over. Curiosity. Small towners didn't have a lot to talk about except the weather, births, deaths, money, and who was cheating on who. Come to think of it, that was probably the same all over. And then there were the newcomers to speculate about. Presley, Abby, and Blake were all still newcomers.

"Has anybody ever had it done before?" Blake asked as they started home with two brown paper sacks filled with bits of heaven. "Here?"

"No, not someone who's transitioning like you, but the procedure, sure. About fifty percent of…" She paused, wanting to get this right. "Fifty percent of cis guys have what we call gynecomastia—their breasts develop at puberty. Too many hormones of all kinds floating around. Usually it's pretty temporary, although not temporary enough for most of them. But if it doesn't resolve by your age, it probably won't. Surgery is an option then."

"Man, that sucks." Blake sounded both sympathetic and a little as if he was glad to hear about kindred sufferers.

"Yeah, they pretty much think so too. So I've had plenty of practice doing the procedure, although in a lot of places the plastics guys do it. I don't know why, it's not that complicated." Flann grinned and Blake laughed.

"Can I go back to work right away?" Blake asked. "I don't want to miss any time in the ER or at Dr. Valentine's, depending on when you schedule it."

"Five days restricted movement and three weeks limited strenuous activity. That means no lifting at all."

Blake winced. "Okay."

"I mean it. If you bleed, it'll be a real pain in the ass for both of us. And your healing will be delayed. That's the biggest problem with guys your age, keeping you from thinking you're supermen."

Blake shot her a look. "Bet it's not just the guys. Remember way back when you were sixteen?"

"Smart-ass." Flann laughed.

"When?"

"Let's talk to your mom first, okay? And then I'll look at my schedule and give you some dates and you can decide. We want to work it so you're in good shape for the wedding."

"Huh? You mean Harper and Presley?" Blake looked puzzled. "I'm not going to do anything except sit there."

"Oh, ah…" Crap, she'd forgotten already she and Abby hadn't told him about their plans for a wedding. *Discussed* it with him.

"What?"

This time she did punt. "Let's wait till we get home and we'll wake up your mom. Good thing we got her two of those apple fritters."

❖

At ten minutes to nine, Mari settled on the wide wooden steps of the wraparound porch of the grand mansion that had once been a family home and was now home to many. Home to her. She sipped her double espresso and watched a couple of teens ride by on bicycles, pedaling with no hands and debating some sports score. While she listened to the sounds of a summer Saturday morning—a lawnmower rumbling somewhere nearby, the distant honk of a horn, the excited barking of a dog down the street—she mused on how different this Saturday was from the others she'd spent here. She had plans. Her entire day was filled with things to do, people she would be spending time with. A hospital barbecue. That was definitely a first. She was really looking forward to it and admitted that was partly because she'd be seeing Glenn. They could be friends—they already were. And she didn't have to feel guilty about how much she enjoyed just being with her. So she'd let herself enjoy the little secret thrill of anticipation.

Carrie pulled to the curb in a car that looked like a bug escaped from some automotive fun house. The little red convertible with white stripes was the size of a beanbag and ridiculously cute.

"What is that?" Mari asked, walking down the sidewalk.

"Isn't it just adorable?" Carrie grinned and actually patted the dashboard. "It's a Mini Cooper. My present to myself. It's so much fun to drive and really easy to park, and I get lots of looks."

Mari laughed and slipped into the passenger seat. "I bet you do."

Carrie's hair was down and slightly tangled from the open air drive. She wore a tank top and cut-off denim shorts. Her arms and legs were tanned, her eyes sparkling, and she was definitely lookable. The car probably wasn't necessary to get her a little attention.

"I thought we'd start at my place—well, my new place." Carrie pulled away from the curb, did a neat U-turn, and headed right on

Main Street. "Then we'll head to the farm for food and Presley's war meeting."

"Are you sure I'm not crashing a private thing?" Mari asked.

"Definitely not. Not to worry."

Carrie whipped around a corner, and within a minute, they'd left the village limits and were in the heart of farmland. Fields of corn and other green things stretched on either side of the road for what looked like forever in every direction. Every few minutes they'd pass a narrow dirt road leading through the fields, far bigger and longer than an ordinary driveway, to a cluster of barns and a farmhouse centered in the midst of the fields.

"Gorgeous, isn't it?" Carrie said.

"It's certainly beautiful. You don't mind living so far from everything?"

Carrie laughed. "You'd think so, wouldn't you? And me being a city kid too. When you get home at night, there's just you and the animals and...peace. It's never really quiet, but not the noise of other people. I never realized that I might like being away from it all until I actually was. I'm always glad to get to the hospital, or the ball field, or somewhere else with friends, but there's something really special about your own little piece of the world."

"You've really settled in here, haven't you?" Mari envied her cousin having found her place, even as she was happy for her.

"You know, I really have." Carrie's face grew uncharacteristically solemn. "Thank God Presley is so good at what she does, because I would hate to have to leave. As long as the hospital is healthy, this is home. And I guess, if for some reason I didn't have my job at the Rivers, I'd have to find something else to do here somewhere." She glanced over at Mari. "I don't think I'd want to leave."

"I'm glad you're here. I'm glad we met."

"Me too. I love my friends more than anything, but there's something special about family, isn't there."

"Yes," Mari said quietly. "There is."

Carrie's soon-to-be new home was just about as cute as her car. The white clapboard two-story square with its slate roof looked like a miniature of all the farmhouses they'd passed on the way: a wide back porch, a small barn, a big garden filled with flourishing plants, some of them already laden with ripening tomatoes and peppers and cucumbers, and a view across a sweeping expanse of meadow toward distant mountains.

"It's beautiful here." Mari sighed. "Who is looking after the garden?"

"Presley, Harper, and I take turns coming over to raid whatever's ripe. Lila—our housekeeper—stops by too."

Carrie pulled open the screen and opened the back door. "Come on, I'll show you what I'm planning."

"Doesn't anyone lock their doors around here?"

"Oh, probably. The newcomers."

Mari laughed and entered a bright kitchen, big enough to eat in, that opened directly off the back porch and ran most of the width of the rear of the house. A small table with four wooden chairs nestled around it sat in front of the windows beside the back door. Dark wood counters, oak cupboards with glass fronts, a big gas range, and a white enamel refrigerator with a rounded door that looked like it might be twenty years old completed the decor.

"This is really nice." Mari ran her hand over the enamel-topped table, like one she remembered from her visit to her grandmother when she was ten. She imagined sitting at that table with a cup of coffee in the morning before work or late in the evening, when she'd finished at the hospital. She could make that picture so easily, but everywhere else she looked was shadows. Would she be alone? Would there be a woman, a life, beyond that bare glimmer of a dream?

"I know, it's amazing, isn't it?"

Mari jumped, found a smile. "Yes. Amazing."

Carrie led her through into a living room slightly bigger than the kitchen, with a square black stove of some kind in one corner with a pile of logs beside it. "One bedroom and bath upstairs. We're going to add an extension with a bedroom, another bath, and maybe a little laundry room. That's downstairs in the basement right now."

"Quite a project."

"I know, fun, huh." Carrie's eyes sparkled with delight. "Presley talked to the contractor who's renovating Abby and Flann's farmhouse. I haven't heard the schedule yet, but if anyone can get them to run two crews at the same time, it'll be Presley."

"It sounds as if everyone has been here forever—Presley and Abby and you."

Carrie ran her fingers over the top of a corduroy-covered sofa, glancing around the room. "You'll feel the same way soon, like you've always been here."

"I'm sure you're right." Mari wasn't ready to explain why she'd be content with satisfying work and the occasional company of friends like Carrie. She especially didn't want to tell her newly found cousin why family was not something she wanted to count on—not for a long, long time.

CHAPTER EIGHTEEN

Mari sat at one end of a semicircle of high-backed wooden rockers with Carrie, Abby, Presley, and Carson on the back porch of the big yellow farmhouse where Carrie lived with Harper and Presley. She gently pushed her pale green rocker with one foot, lulled by the early morning sun and the rhythmic to-and-fro motion. The worn-smooth seat was so comfortable she'd have sworn it had been carved specifically for her backside. She had to resist searching to see if her name was written on the chair somewhere. When she and Carrie had arrived, the others had welcomed her as if she had always been part of the group. Still, the foreignness of the landscape, with the fenced pastures and hard-packed dirt barnyard populated by chickens and a handicapped rooster who had been introduced to her as Rooster, reminded her she was still very much an outsider. Despite her lingering self-consciousness, she was happy to be there and hoped she'd one day be a real part of the group.

Carrie put her iced tea on the faded gray plank floor, opened her notebook, and balanced it on her knees. "Okay, let's review."

Mari smothered a smile as Carrie worked her way from person to person around the semicircle, running down their list of to-dos and ticking off all the things that had been done. She was like a general reviewing battle plans, analyzing troop movements, and shifting assignments between her officers where needed. Presley, Abby, and Carson all accepted her directions good-naturedly, including her mild admonishments when they admitted to not having yet completed all of their tasks. These women were a family, with the same kind of teasing and occasional squabbling Mari was used to at home, although she hadn't had this many sisters. Brothers were different. As much as she loved every one of hers, they were still boys. To them, everything was a problem to be solved, and once a solution came to light, they considered the issue solved. With a quick dusting off of hands, they moved on, seemingly never troubled by the emotional consequences. Selena understood the emotional aftermath of life's big and small moments, that even good things came at a cost and unhappy ones could linger beneath the surface for a long time. Mari missed Selena most when faced with the intimacy of others, when she remembered how close they had been and their abrupt parting. She should have been prepared for Selena's rejection, but she'd let herself hope. Denial was such a dangerous and destructive form of self-delusion.

Selena had wanted to be a nun when she was twelve and used to play at it the way some girls played house, wearing a habit fashioned from a sheet she tied at the waist with a woven strand of hemp and a scarf wrapped around her hair to mimic a wimple. She'd outgrown the desire to be celibate and to devote herself solely to God around the time she discovered boys, but she was still devout, like their parents. Like Mari had never really been. Mari'd never thought to question the church or its dictates growing up—it was just a central focus of her life. But as she'd gotten older and begun to see herself apart in a way that other members in her family couldn't understand, she began to wonder and question. She'd finally decided she could believe on a spiritual level even when her life was at odds with the rules and tenets of the church. She was okay with that and hoped that God was too.

Carrie flicked her pen in Mari's direction as if it were a laser pointer. "I suppose you thought you were getting out of things."

Caught unawares, Mari straightened on a surge of uncharacteristic panic. What had she missed while she was daydreaming about the past? "Uh, well…"

Carrie grinned. "You can be my backup in the cake and pastry department. If for some reason there's a problem with delivery and I can't get to it, I'll call you."

"Backup." Mari sagged with relief. That couldn't be too hard. "Sure. That sounds good."

Presley reached across Carrie and patted Mari's knee. "Carrie tends to be eager. You'll get used to it after a while."

Carrie snorted.

"I'm happy to help," Mari said.

"Well, that's good to hear," Presley said, shooting a look at Abby. "Your services might be required in the future."

Carson, a red-haired, green-eyed older version of Margie whose face had taken on an elegant beauty in adulthood, shot up straight. Her gaze swung from Presley and finally settled on Abby. "What? What has my sister done now?"

Abby chewed her lip. "Well, it's sort of a secret—"

"Really," Carrie said with mock sarcasm, "there are no secrets between besties. I hereby propose no secrets in our enclave. After all, we don't want to miss out on all the good stuff."

"Oh no," Abby said, looking pointedly at Carson. "I'm not talking about sex in front of Flann's sister."

Carson clamped her hands over her ears. "I don't want to hear it, either."

Both Abby and Presley grinned.

Carrie pretended to pout. "Well, that's no fun, then. If we're not going to talk about sex, I suppose we could talk about—" She frowned. "Damn, that takes a lot off the table."

"Stop trying to change the subject." Carson poked Abby in the side. "What about Flann, and don't mention any sex words."

"You'll find out tomorrow at dinner, all the details, but Flann and I are going to be planning a wedding pretty soon ourselves."

Carson whooped. "That's so great. My mom and dad will be thrilled. I can't wait to tease Flann about it, the one who was never going to settle down. What did it take her, a hot second?"

Abby grinned. "More than a few seconds, but they were definitely hot."

"Na-na-nanananna," Carson singsonged, pretending to poke her fingers in her ears.

Abby smiled.

Enjoying the silliness, Mari tried to imagine telling her parents she was planning a wedding with another woman as if it would be a foregone conclusion everyone would celebrate. She couldn't see a happy reception, although she didn't have any difficulty picturing the woman who'd be part of her planning. Heat climbed into her face. She needed to stop thinking about Glenn like that, and she'd be able to, if she wasn't surrounded by women who were in love with other women.

That had never happened to her before. She knew lesbians and gay men, but only casually. None who were her close friends, anyhow.

Another seismic change in her life. Now her cousin was a lesbian and she was making friends with women who were completely comfortable with their sexuality and who seemed to have families who took it all for granted too. She wondered if her family would ever be able to do more than accept her, let alone welcome whatever joy she might find in her life with a woman. She pulled herself back from the brink of that abyss. She couldn't change what her family did or whether or not they embraced her. All she could do was live her life as honestly as possible. She knew she was right, but that was little comfort sometimes.

"By the time dinner comes around tomorrow," Carson said, "it won't be much of a secret. I guess just Mom and Dad."

"We haven't told Blake about it yet," Abby said. "We were going to do that this morning, but he had something he needed to talk to us about instead."

"Is he okay?" Presley asked.

"He's great," Abby said. "He wants to go ahead with his top surgery, so we had to have a family discussion about all the details."

"Wow," Carrie said softly. "That's a big deal."

Abby nodded. "It is, but it's also the next logical step, at least for him. He's been moving toward this since he was fourteen, and the surgery—or rather the effect of the surgery—is important for him and for his sense of self." Abby looked at Mari. "My son, Blake, is transitioning."

"He's lucky," Mari said softly. "He's lucky to have you, all of you. I...I wish..."

Carrie gave her hand a squeeze.

"It's not exactly the same thing," Mari said, tearing away another layer of self-insulating protection, "but my family has pretty much exiled me since I told them I was a lesbian."

"It is the same thing—or at least, it's all part of the same fabric of difference," Abby said gently. "I'm sorry to hear about your family's reaction."

"Thanks," Mari said. "I'm glad for you and Blake. He sounds a lot braver than I was at his age."

"Me too," Carrie muttered. "I was still trying to convince myself I actually liked kissing boys more than girls." She grinned. "I quit that after a year of kidding myself."

Mari smiled at her gratefully. She didn't feel quite so clueless knowing everyone hadn't known about themselves forever.

"Is Flann doing the surgery?" Carson asked.

"That's part of what we talked about this morning," Abby said. "Blake wants her to do it, and Flann is very experienced with the procedure. Glenn will assist, so I know they'll have a good team. It's pretty straightforward, and we're all comfortable with it."

"Well, I'd let those two operate on me anytime," Carrie said in a suggestive voice.

Abby raised an eyebrow. "I'm afraid at least one of them is off the table."

"Ah, well," Carrie said with an exaggerated sigh while shooting a glance in Mari's direction, "I guess I'm totally out of luck, then."

Mari pretended she wasn't blushing.

"And I've already got my Rivers sister," Presley said. "So there go all the hot, sexy ones—"

"Okay, I'm still here," Carson said loudly. "Sisters, remember? And I already know how gorgeous they are. I had to grow up in their footsteps."

Carrie patted her knee. "Believe me, if you had been headed in that direction, you'd have been fighting off the girls."

Carson laughed. "Yeah, I'm the outlier. Well, I don't know about Margie at this point, but I'm the boring straight one."

Everyone laughed and Mari let herself be drawn into the closeness, the easiness of being who they were, the acceptance of difference. And when her image of a sexy woman didn't conjure any of the Rivers sisters, she didn't resist. Just for a minute.

"Speaking of gorgeous women," Carrie said, "I believe I hear a truckload of them on their way."

A big dusty black pickup truck rumbled into the far end of the yard, the doors swung open, and few seconds later, Harper, Flann, Glenn, Blake, and Margie clambered out and trooped across the yard.

"What did Lila make for breakfast?" Margie called, hopping up onto the back porch.

"Too late," Carrie said. "The bread basket is empty."

"No," Blake and Margie shouted at the same time.

Laughing, Carrie pointed to the screen door. "Cinnamon rolls and blueberry muffins. There might be one or possibly two left."

Margie and Blake slammed into the house. Flann leaned down and kissed Abby as Harper slid over by Presley's rocker.

"Is everyone done with the planning?" Harper asked as she cupped Presley's nape, long fingers stroking her throat.

"You know, we could probably find some chores for you to do," Presley said, sliding her fingers over Harper's. "It's really not fair that you just need to show up and look handsome at the wedding."

"Hey," Harper protested, "I'm helping my mother with the guest list. Believe me, that's work."

"An excuse," Presley said, "but a good one."

Mari lost track of the playful back and forths, too busy watching Glenn brace her arms on the railing and lift herself up onto it in a quick fluid move. She perched at the edge of the gathering, watching, laughing occasionally, now and then making a comment. As much as she was a part of everything, she was also alone. An island. Her solitude called to Mari in some deep place and she desperately wanted to be beside her, to ask her…anything—how her night was, if she'd heard about Blake's surgery, if she thought the clear blue sky was as amazingly beautiful as Mari found it.

Glenn glanced over and met Mari's gaze. The pull on her consciousness was so fierce, Mari swore Glenn knew what she was thinking. She couldn't even pretend her next move was against her will, not when she rose, skirted the ring of rockers, and leaned against the railing on Glenn's far side, out of earshot of everyone. "Hi."

"Hi," Glenn said.

"I can't believe everybody was piled into that one pickup truck. Why didn't you all bring more cars?"

"I'm designated driver for anybody who needs a ride after the barbecue today. Well, the kids won't be drinking, but the others might want a beer or two."

"I could do that," Mari said. "I'm on call tonight, so I won't be drinking. If you wanted to have a drink."

"I can take it or leave it," Glenn said. "But thanks."

"If you change your mind, just let me know." Mari started to move away and Glenn caught her hand. She stilled, every muscle in her body instantly frozen midmotion, lest she move too far away and the contact disappear.

"If you want to ride over to the barbecue with me, I can get the kids to ride with Carrie. Flann and Harper will probably ride over with Presley and Abby."

"Thanks," Mari said. After all, that's what friends did, right? Enjoyed each other's company. "I'd like that."

For one endless moment, Glenn's hand tightened around hers before slipping away. "Good. Me too."

CHAPTER NINETEEN

"A re you about ready to head over?" Glenn asked when Mari returned to her side during a lull in the animated exchanges about caterers, menus, tents versus no tents, and the advisability of elopement. Currently the latter was off the table.

"Whenever you are," Mari said, "but I should check with Carrie first. Make sure she doesn't need me. I came over with her earlier."

"Sure. No rush." Glenn was content to sit with the sun on her back, listening to her friends plan the future and watching Mari slowly becoming one of their group. She had an easy way about her, joining in the conversations where it was natural, easing back from the personal exchanges, and absorbing the good-natured teasing that flowed between siblings and old friends in all directions indiscriminately. When Mari laughed, her face glowed and her pleasure rippled over Glenn's skin like warm currents of summer air. She wasn't just beautiful then, she was indescribable.

"Did you eat?" Mari asked.

"Eat?" Glenn flailed, still lost in the image of Mari with her head thrown back, red lips parted on a full-throated laugh. It wasn't hard to imagine her fingers trailing down that sleek throat, her mouth covering those full, moist lips. "Breakfast, you mean?"

Mari laughed. "Exactly. You know, the stuff you ingest when you wake up in the morning. In addition to that excellent coffee that... actually, did you have any this morning without my personal delivery?"

Glenn winced. "I'm sorry to report I had hospital coffee this morning. Not bad, but no comparison."

"Why?" Mari frowned, sorting through her memories of the on-call schedule. "Wasn't Adams on last night with...Baker, wasn't it?"

"Uh, as a matter of fact, yes," Glenn hedged. "Adams was on last night. Baker too."

When Glenn shifted a little uneasily on the railing, an unusual action for her, Mari took note. Glenn never appeared uneasy, but Mari had an idea she knew why. "And...are we getting to the part where you were there too?"

Busted. Glenn sighed. "I might have stopped over for a quick check on the student and...then one thing or another happened."

Mari nodded. "Friday night. It was busy?"

"Pretty steady," Glenn said, relieved that Mari didn't seem aggravated that she'd gone back to the hospital and wasn't going to take her to task for it. Nice to not have to defend herself. "I was helping Baker with a knee tap on a young guy with a traumatic synovitis and one thing led to another and by the time it got quiet it was after three. Didn't see much point in leaving then."

"Probably not."

Glenn didn't add there was hardly any point, really, in her leaving the hospital much after sundown, just to go back to her apartment and read until she was tired enough to sleep. She could do that in the on-call room and frequently did.

"Did you get a run in this morning?"

Surprised that Mari seemed to know her habits so well so quickly, and even more surprised that she liked it, Glenn nodded again. "Just after sunup. Getting too damn hot to run later in the day."

"Obviously, you have forgotten your Texas roots," Mari said, knocking shoulders lightly. "Isn't it hot there all the time, regardless of whether the sun is shining or not?"

Glenn grinned. For the first time in a long time, mention of her past and the home she had steadfastly put out of her mind didn't bother her. "Your eyeballs burn even at midnight."

"See there? This weather shouldn't bother you at all."

"Definitely not the desert, I'll give you that." Glenn looked away. She hadn't meant to bring that up. Uncomfortable that the past simmered so near the surface all of a sudden.

"Not nearly as bad as that, I imagine," Mari said quietly, dropping her hand onto Glenn's knee for just an instant, an innocent gesture of comfort that exploded in the pit of Glenn's stomach with the force of a grenade. Her spine burned all the way up to the base of her neck, but the shock was pleasure, not pain. "You're right. This is nothing like there."

"I know, and I'm glad." Mari tapped a finger on Glenn's knee. "So, blueberry or cinnamon?"

"Sorry?" Glenn murmured, entranced by the pulse of energy traveling up her leg every time Mari touched her.

"Blueberry muffin or cinnamon roll?"

"Lila's?" Glenn dragged her gaze away from Mari's hand, barely grazing her leg now. Why could she still feel it so strongly? She had to stop looking. If she didn't, in another second she was going to cover Mari's hand with hers and press Mari's fingers harder against her thigh. Pull Mari a little closer.

"Mm-hmm." Mari's soft voice slipped over Glenn's skin, fraying the threads of her sanity.

"Any chance of both?" Glenn whispered.

Mari laughed, fingertips trailing lightly over Glenn's denim-clad thigh for just an instant. "Not with those two in there raiding the kitchen, but I'll see what I can salvage."

"I can wait until later to eat," Glenn blurted. Just don't move. Just…stay.

"I'm sure you can, but you're not going to. Just in case, let me get you something to hold you over." Mari smiled. "Be right back."

"Be careful." Glenn's voice had a faraway ring, as if she were speaking down a long tunnel. As if she had drifted somewhere else.

Mari paused, waiting for the time slip to pass. Waiting to be sure Glenn was completely with her. "I'll just be a minute."

Glenn shuddered lightly, as if emerging from a half dream. "I'll be right here."

"Good." Mari left Glenn still perched on the railing, enjoying taking care of her more than she'd imagined. Of course, Glenn had been looking after her pretty much since they'd met, so returning the favor was only natural. And driving the haunted mists from Glenn's eyes gave her a bone-deep satisfaction she'd never encountered before. She pushed through the screen door, suddenly eager to get back to her.

Blake and Margie perched on stools at the big wooden center island with glasses of milk and guilty expressions.

Mari said, "Did you two leave anything besides crumbs?"

They froze like deer in headlights, each glancing at the other as if for rescue.

"Um…" Margie mumbled.

"I think there's a couple left." Blake glanced at the snowy white towel covering the wicker basket on the side counter anxiously. "Maybe."

"I suppose I could hunt up Lila for instructions on how to make more," Mari murmured as she checked out the remnants. She found an entire blueberry muffin hidden in a fold of linen and half a cinnamon scone surgically sliced in two. She was surprised to find that much.

Behind her, the sound of wood scraping on the rough stone floor and thudding footsteps signaled the rapid escape of the teenagers. The two of them made her heart hurt, happiness warring with loss. She missed her younger brothers, but the pleasure of being around two such young, vital, and enthusiastic teens warmed her. Smiling, she grabbed a couple of paper napkins, piled her trophies onto them, and carried them victoriously back outside. As she passed Carrie she leaned down. "I'm going to ride over to the barbecue with Glenn, if that's okay with you."

"Sure." Carrie shot a glance at Glenn and grinned. "You'd better feed her. She looks…hungry."

Mari glanced over and heat flashed up her throat. Glenn was staring at her, and her expression for once was anything but cool and remote. Her eyes burned, and not with any half-remembered hell, but something clear and present and very much now. Hungry was a mild word for her unmasked desire.

"I have Lila's muffins," Mari murmured, transfixed.

"That might not be enough."

Not enough. Mari jolted. What was she doing, playing at a game she couldn't fully join. Playing with a woman who deserved so much more than that. "I know."

Mari pulled her tattered senses together, joined Glenn, and pretended she hadn't noticed the gathering storm brewing between them for the past few minutes. She held out the napkin to Glenn. "All that remains of the spoils."

Laughing, Glenn broke the muffin in half and held out a portion to Mari. "Want some?"

You have no idea. Lord, neither do I. Mari groaned and patted her stomach. "I do, but I've already had more than my quota. You go ahead. If you were up all night and you ran this morning, you can handle the carbs."

"Do you moonlight as a personal trainer?" Glenn asked around a giant bite of blueberry muffin. She closed her eyes and gave a small moan of appreciation. "These can't possibly be legal."

"I know, that's why I can't eat another bite. And no, I'm far from a fitness nut, but I've always been interested in nutrition, and after last year..." Mari surprised herself at how easily she talked about her illness with Glenn. Just knowing that Glenn knew freed her in a way she hadn't imagined would be possible.

Glenn stopped eating. "What? What about last year?"

"Nothing really. Just that nothing much tasted worth eating for a while," Mari said lightly, determined not to cast another shadow in Glenn's eyes. "I try to pay attention to what I'm eating, but there's some things that you just can't relegate to a calorie count. Lila's cooking appears to be one of them."

"I agree. If you can't indulge in life's pleasures every once in a while, what's the point."

"Indeed," Mari said softly.

A minute later, Glenn wiped her hands on the napkin, balled it up, and shot it into a milk pail that doubled as a trash can next to the back door. She hopped down and brushed her fingers down Mari's arm. "Okay? Ready to hit the fairgrounds?"

"Is that where the barbecue is?"

"Yep. The hospital sets up a tent city on part of the grounds."

"Great. I'm looking forward to it." Mari waved good-bye to Carrie as she walked with Glenn across the yard to the pickup.

"Whose truck is this, anyhow?" Mari asked.

"The Riverses' farm truck—anybody who needs it just grabs i—"

"Hey, Glenn," Margie called from the porch. "Can we ride with you? We're ready to go."

Glenn glanced at Mari, one eyebrow quirked. "I guess I was wrong about there being plenty of room. You good with it?"

Mari laughed and nodded.

"Yeah," Glenn yelled back, "but you're gonna have to squeeze in."

"No problem," Margie and Blake said in unison as they tore across the yard.

Glenn opened the passenger side, pointed to the running board, and cupped Mari's elbow. "It's a big step. Slide over to the middle. Those two will have to fit themselves in next to you."

"All right." Mari grabbed the handle just inside above the door with one hand. Glenn pressed close beside her, her hand strong and firm on Mari's bare skin. As she climbed up, Mari pressed her other hand to Glenn's shoulder to steady herself. Muscles bunched and tightened beneath her fingers. When she looked down, Glenn was looking up at her, the fierce intensity back in her gaze. Mari settled her hip onto the seat and slowly took her hand from Glenn's shoulder. Glenn's hand fell away from her arm. Mari's throat was oddly tight. "Thank you."

"Anytime."

Glenn swung around the cab of the truck while Margie and Blake jumped in next to Mari and slammed the door. Glenn trailed a hand over the edge of the dusty hood, her gait not quite steady. Her thighs trembled as if she'd been running a half marathon and had just hit the wall. Mari had just neatly kicked the feet out from under her, and she'd never seen it coming. Mari was a constant surprise—beautiful, tender and strong, and somehow able to slip at will inside Glenn's defenses. Glenn didn't even have to ask herself what she wanted whenever she looked at Mari. She knew with every atom of her being. She'd wanted to kiss her.

Glenn yanked open the door, jumped in, started the engine. "Buckle up, everybody." She glanced over and saw Margie on Blake's lap. "That means the two of you too. Figure it out before we get to the road."

Beside her, Mari had already strapped in. Glenn kept her eyes face front. She wasn't quite ready to look at her again without broadcasting every damn thing she was feeling. "All set?"

"Yes, fine."

Mari's thigh pressed against the outside of Glenn's, but she had nowhere to move to escape the soul-singeing pressure. She needed to keep her foot on the gas if they were going to go anywhere, but even the slightest movement reminded her that Mari was next to her, very close. She could smell shampoo or perfume or something—a flowery sweet spicy scent that twisted her up and made her want to rub her face over the soft skin that smelled so good. She gripped the wheel until her fingers ached, and even then she could still feel them trembling. She hadn't been hungry before, but she was ravenous now. And she couldn't be. Couldn't do anything about satisfying the need clawing at her insides. Hell, she couldn't convince herself she *wanted* to.

CHAPTER TWENTY

M ari watched the fields blur by, an artist's palette of gold and yellow beneath patches of brilliant blue and gleaming white. The truck bounced rapidly along over ruts and dips in the cracked macadam road, throwing up clouds of dust that coated the windows and slowly hazed the view. On one side of her, Margie and Blake chattered on about their soon-to-be first day in the ER. Mari only half listened, and the two teens didn't seem to notice they were the only ones talking, oblivious to the rest of the world as only the young could be. On her other side, Glenn had turned to stone. If she became any more rigid, she'd shatter like a statue left unshielded from the elements for so long its substance had begun to crumble. Mari wanted to touch her, to ease the festering tension, but instinct warned that was exactly the wrong thing to do. Instead, she clenched her hands together in her lap and stared out through the windshield, seeing nothing.

A cluster of long barns, random shed-like buildings, and an oval track with a grandstand climbing upward beneath a half roof came into sight. Handmade cardboard signs written with black Magic Marker posted on stakes in the driveways of houses along the way offered parking for five dollars. Glenn passed them all by and turned into the fairgrounds, stopping to pay a woman wearing a Rivers Hospital T-shirt holding a big white plastic collection bucket. A line of signs with arrows proclaiming *Parking* directed them to the five-acre lot behind the fairgrounds buildings. The grassy lot was three-quarters full, and Glenn drove slowly down a narrow lane between two rows of parked vehicles, following the directions of a line of teenagers waving orange batons to a free spot between a minivan and a pickup truck.

"Thanks, Glenn," Margie said.

Before the truck had even come to a complete stop, Blake pushed open the door and jumped out. Margie hopped out on his heels.

"Take it easy out there," Glenn called.

"Thanks, see ya," they yelled in unison and jogged off in the direction of a cloud of smoke that smelled of roasting meat and hickory.

In an instant the two had disappeared, and Mari and Glenn were alone. Mari's entire being focused on the spot where her leg still pressed against Glenn's. She had no excuse to be so close and didn't want to move away enough to break the contact. Glenn looked straight ahead, her fingers loosely clasping the wheel.

"What shall we do," Mari asked after a moment that stretched forever.

"I thought we'd walk around a little bit, and I could introduce you to some of the people you'll be working with."

"That would be great, thanks." When Glenn made no move to get out, Mari said softly, "Are you all right?"

Glenn turned to her, eyes glinting feverishly. "I'm not exactly sure."

Mari's heart double-timed in her chest. A breathless, light-headed sensation made her feel as if she might be about to float away. Glenn's eyes bored into hers as if she was trying to read her soul. Glenn's gaze fixed on her mouth. Glenn looked anything but calm and controlled. Mari swallowed. "Have I done something to upset you?"

"You have no idea," Glenn muttered.

"I'm sorry," Mari whispered, and she was. She hadn't a clue what she'd done, but she would never want to—

"You don't need to be sorry. I should be"—Glenn cupped the back of Mari's neck, ran her thumb over the delicate column of her throat—"but I'm not."

Glenn couldn't be sorry for desire so pure it felt like a prayer. The air in the cab of the truck was still and hot. Glenn's pulse beat in her ears like the rattle of machine gun fire. She held completely still, her fingers pressed to supple flesh, waiting for Mari to pull away.

But she didn't.

"Yes?" Glenn whispered.

"Yes."

Glenn pulled her closer. Mari's skin was smooth and soft and warm, like her mouth promised to be. The pressure in her chest pushed up into her throat and her breath stopped. But she didn't need to breathe. She just needed to kiss her.

Mari's lips were as sweet and soft and hot as she'd imagined. A low groan churned in her chest. She wouldn't take much. Wouldn't presume she was welcome to more. Just a brush of her lips over Mari's, just a second's taste to dull the ache of hunger. The whisper of lips turned into something longer, something fuller and firmer and deeper. Mari whimpered and her fingers feathered into Glenn's hair. Glenn dragged her against her chest, and the kiss wasn't soft anymore. Her mouth wasn't nearly as gentle as she wanted it to be but Mari met her, stroke for feverish stroke.

Glenn kissed her until there was no room for breath. She didn't care if she died just like that, with Mari's hands on her and the hot taste of her in her mouth. Mari was so pliant in her arms, so wild and welcoming. She needed more. She was starving.

Mari pushed a palm against Glenn's chest and pulled a little away. Glenn froze.

"Glenn." Mari's voice trembled. She shivered, her breathe ragged. "Glenn, we're sitting in the parking lot. Anyone can see us."

"I don't care." Glenn leaned closer, respecting the space Mari had made between them, until she could kiss just the corner of her mouth. "God, you taste so good."

Mari's fingers brushed over Glenn's mouth. "You have the softest lips."

Glenn flicked her tongue over the tips of Mari's fingers. Mari's eyes widened.

"I feel so strange," Mari murmured. "Like I'm flying apart, and if I don't kiss you again, I'm going to go wing off in a thousand directions."

"Will you come with me somewhere private where I can kiss you again?"

Mari wasn't thinking, couldn't think, was so tired of thinking. Her lips tingled, her skin vibrated, and a huge aching ball of need filled her. So many sensations pulled at her—thirst, hunger, want. Want. Oh yes, she wanted that kiss. "Yes, oh yes, let's go."

Glenn reached across Mari, grabbed the handle on the open door, and yanked it closed. Only when Glenn gunned the engine, backed out into the narrow lane, and headed toward the exit did Mari manage a coherent thought. "What about the others. Aren't we supposed to meet them? So you can drive them all home?"

"They'll be fine. If any of them need me, they'll text me."

Mari didn't argue. Glenn would never slough off a responsibility, and if she wasn't worried about Flann and the others, Mari wasn't either.

"Don't worry." Glenn's voice was low and husky.

"I won't."

"Good."

Glenn drove at the speed limit, but it felt to Mari as if they were crawling. She pressed close to Glenn again, even though there was plenty of room in the cab now, and this time she gave in to her urge and put her hand on Glenn's leg. She needed the contact, needed to know Glenn was real, needed to believe the untamed energy swirling between them was real. Glenn dropped a hand over hers and pressed Mari's fingers into her thigh.

Mari squeezed and hard muscles flexed beneath her fingers. The quick hitch in Glenn's breath cut through her like a scalpel slash, sharp and swift and terrifyingly wonderful. She immediately wanted to feel the rush of erotic power again. Pressing closer into Glenn's lean form, her breast against Glenn's arm, she swept her palm up and down the length of Glenn's thigh. Glenn twitched as if she'd been shocked.

"Fuck," Glenn whispered. "Do you have any idea what you're doing to me?"

"No, tell me."

Glenn shot her a swift glance and then cut her gaze back to the road. Her mouth had been tight, the smoldering fire in her eyes leaping into flames. "You're making me so crazy I can't think."

"Neither can I." Mari wanted things she'd never imagined wanting. Her secret fantasies had been nothing like this. "I've never felt this way."

Something in her voice must have betrayed her uncertainty.

Glenn looked at her again, the fire banked, tempered by concern. "Are you afraid?"

"No, no." Mari gripped Glenn's leg tighter than she intended and Glenn's hips flexed. Heat flared between Mari's thighs. "Never afraid of you."

"Then you don't have to think."

Glenn swung the truck down a narrow alley and pulled in behind a building. Mari finally focused on their surroundings and recognized the rear of Glenn's apartment building. She caught her breath.

"All right?" Glenn murmured as she turned to her, her fingers tracing the edge of Mari's jaw.

Mari swallowed. If she went inside, what was she saying? What did she want? She still didn't know, but she wanted to find out. She nodded.

Glenn cut the engine, jumped out, and ran around the front of the truck. She jerked open Mari's door and reached for her hand. "Come on."

Mari slid over and started to climb out. Glenn's hands grasped her waist, and she was lifted to the ground. When her feet touched the earth, Mari wrapped her arms around Glenn's shoulders and, cleaving to her, pressed her mouth to Glenn's throat. She tasted salt and heat and desire. "You have a beautiful throat. *You* are beautiful."

With a faint groan, Glenn tilted her head back, offering herself. She buried her fingers in Mari's hair and pressed Mari's mouth closer. "If you keep that up, I won't get up the stairs."

Mari touched the tip of her tongue to the delicate skin over Glenn's racing pulse. Glenn trembled, a fine shudder rippling through her body. Mari's heart leapt and a fierce thrill raced through her. Mari laughed. "Then we should go upstairs now, because I want to do that again."

With a low growl, Glenn grabbed Mari's hand and tugged her up the winding staircase, across the narrow deck outside her door, and into a small, neat apartment.

Glenn stopped just inside the door and framed Mari's face with both hands. She kissed her softly. "Bedroom?"

"I…yes," Mari whispered. What should she say…what *could* she say? *I've never done this before, I don't know what I want, I want everything and so much more?* "But I'm not sure…"

"It's okay, I just really, really need to kiss you again. Whenever you want to stop, you just tell me." Glenn's jaw tightened, the hands cradling Mari's jaw flexing as if holding back a storm. "Please, I need you."

Mari nodded. She couldn't imagine wanting to stop, not when she'd never felt as alive as she did in that instant. "Yes. Show me."

Wordlessly, Glenn took her hand again and led her through the small neat kitchen, across an equally neat but sparsely furnished living room, and into a bedroom with a single bed against one wall, a dresser with a row of precisely arranged bottles and other objects, and a slatted wooden chair beside it. Sunlight slanted through a single window across the foot of the bed, and hazy air blanketed the room. Glenn kicked off her boots and sat on the side of the bed, drawing Mari between her spread thighs. She wrapped both arms around Mari's waist and pressed her cheek to Mari's stomach. "We'll go as slow as you want."

Mari stroked the back of Glenn's neck and shoulders. "I don't know what I want, except I want to feel you."

"Go ahead."

Mari edged closer between Glenn's thighs and caressed the length of Glenn's back, tracing the tight muscles along her spine and between her shoulders. She slid her hands inside Glenn's collar and dipped her fingertips into the delicate hollows above her collarbones.

Quivering, her insides in knots, Glenn stayed as still as she could, letting Mari explore her, every muscle so tight she felt as if they might shred from her bones. When Mari lowered her head and kissed the angle of her jaw, Glenn's vision wavered.

"Can we lie down?" Mari asked almost dreamily.

Glenn couldn't refuse her, as dangerous as that would be. She could never remember need so powerful her insides hurt. She swung around, guided Mari down to the bed, and stretched out beside her. Turning on her side, she rested her hand on Mari's hip. Mari inched nearer, her lips flushed and swollen from their kisses, her eyes wide and dark and moist. Glenn kissed her.

"You're beautiful, Mari."

Mari gripped Glenn's shirt, her hips rocking insistently against Glenn's. "Do that some more."

Laughing softly, Glenn followed orders.

Kissing Mari was like discovering water in the desert and greedily filling the barren places inside that had lain parched and empty after the wastelands of the world had drained her dry. Mari arched against her with a moan, and Glenn's body came alive with a jolt. She eased on top of her, her thigh between Mari's, her weight resting on her elbows. She kissed Mari's mouth, the tip of her chin, the hollow at the base of her throat. Mari's hands scattered over her back, exploring, restless and demanding, setting Glenn's flesh aflame.

Mari tugged Glenn's shirt from the waistband of her jeans and found skin. When she skimmed her fingers over the hollow at the base of Glenn's spine, Glenn stiffened.

"Easy," she murmured. "You'll make me forget my promise to just kiss."

"I don't care," Mari gasped. She loved the weight of Glenn's body over hers, the feel of their legs entwining, the ache that pounded in the pulse between her thighs. "It feels so good. I want you to touch me. Will you touch me?"

Glenn eased a hand under the bottom of Mari's top, caressed her middle, thumb brushing just below her navel. "Tell me what you like."

"I…I don't know. Whatever you're doing. It's wonderful. I never thought it would be like this."

Glenn stilled, her palm pressed to the bare skin of Mari's stomach. Something clawed at the surface of her addled brain, a warning bell, clear and sharp. "What do you mean, you don't know?"

"God, I just want you to make it stop—whatever, anything, I don't care." Mari bent one leg over Glenn's, lifted her hips, pressed full-length against her. God, she couldn't get close enough. Couldn't stand the churning fire between her thighs another second. "Anything."

"This isn't the first time?"

Mari struggled to make sense of words while drowning in sensation. "What? Oh. Yes."

"Ever?"

Clarity rushed in, doused the fire melting Mari's reason. She pulled back, read worry in the lines in Glenn's brow. "Does it matter?"

"Hell, yes." Glenn pushed herself off, leaned up on an elbow, and studied Mari's face. "You were the one who said no involvement, no intimacies."

"What difference does it make if I'm a virgin?"

"Because this is pretty damned intimate, especially if you've never done it before. Why now? What's changed?"

"I don't know."

"No, neither do I." Glenn didn't know what she'd been hoping to hear—that Mari had changed her mind, that she'd discarded her self-imposed exile until she was sure she would remain disease free? Maybe, if she was honest with herself, she'd been hoping to hear Mari wanted her enough to say *Fuck waiting*. But Mari hadn't changed her mind, she hadn't even been aware of where they were headed, and she'd be damned if she'd take advantage of the heat of the moment. Not when Mari was likely to regret it before morning. "But I know you ought to think about what you're doing."

Mari sat up, anger and hurt twisting in her middle. "Don't you mean you need to think?"

Glenn frowned. "What are you talking about?"

Mari drew her knees up and folded her arms around them. "You were willing to have sex a minute ago."

"No, I wasn't." Glenn ran a hand through her hair. "Maybe I was, but I thought…I don't know what the hell I thought." Only what she'd hoped. She stood up. "I'm sorry. I shouldn't have kissed you. Shouldn't have started this."

Mari jumped up on the other side of the bed and straightened her clothes with as much dignity as she could manage after being so soundly rejected. "Apparently I misread things. No need to apologize."

"Mari, I didn't mean—"

"Let's not embarrass each other anymore. It was just a kiss, after all."

CHAPTER TWENTY-ONE

Glenn left Flann's truck at the end of one of the back rows near the fairgrounds exit and texted Carrie and Abby with the location so they could find it when they were ready to leave. After locking up and sliding the keys between the front wheel and the wheel well, where they always stashed the keys, she cut across the dusty lot and threaded her way through the crowd. The celebration was in full swing and every few steps someone would call out her name. She waved and kept going, making a beeline for the big Future Farmers of America tent. The smell of grilling hamburgers hung over the crowd along with the almost palpable sense of good cheer. Neither penetrated the careful lock she kept on her thoughts and feelings. Her mind was a blank, her body registering neither hunger nor the heat of a mid-July afternoon. She spoke to no one as she stood in the line that slowly inched forward, and something about her air of indifference must have reached those around her. No one attempted conversation, and finally she reached the counter.

"I'll have a beer," she said to the balding, heavyset EMT she saw on average three times a week in the ER. When he wasn't on shift with the local emergency response unit, he was a volunteer with the local FFA chapter. An all-around good guy.

"Hey, Glenn. Coming right up."

A shoulder bumped hers. "Make that two, Jimmy."

His smile broadened. "Sure thing, Doc."

Glenn glanced at Flann. She didn't believe in coincidences.

Flann grinned, not even bothering to pretend she'd shown up by accident. "Abby said she got a text from you and you ditched your designated driver status. I figured I'd catch you here."

"Uh-huh." Glenn took her beer and turned to go.

Flann grabbed hers and fell into step. "You just get here?"

Maybe if she ignored her, she'd go away. Glenn grunted.

"Big crowd."

Glenn saw no reason to comment on the obvious. All the hospital gatherings drew big crowds. More than half the people in town either worked there, had friends who did, or came out to support what was essentially a fundraising event for the place.

"Where's Mari?"

"She's got a shift tonight and decided not to come." Glenn didn't have any better explanation, at least not one she intended to share. She'd offered to drive Mari home, but Mari had insisted she'd wanted to walk. She couldn't object and had stood by wordlessly while Mari gathered her things and left with a hasty and abrupt good-bye. The silence had been cutting, but what could she say? She couldn't apologize for the kiss, pretend it hadn't mattered. She also couldn't ask Mari to change what she wanted, and didn't want, in her life. Both of them had been riding a wave of insanity, fueled by passion and finally beached by reason. They worked together, they were already friends, more than friends, and jumping into bed together would be a huge mistake. Mari didn't want a relationship, didn't even want any kind of intimacy that might lead to one, and neither did she. There'd been nothing else to say.

"You know what we haven't done for a while?" Flann said conversationally after they'd walked in silence and ditched their empty plastic cups in a recycling bin.

"What?"

"Gone one-on-one. Let's go shoot some hoops."

Glenn stopped and stared at her. "Now? In the middle of the hospital barbecue?"

Flann lifted a shoulder. "I said my hellos to just about everybody, Abby's hanging with Carrie and the others, and I had my two obligatory cups of lukewarm beer."

"Thanks, but I don't think so."

"Out of practice, I guess."

Glenn cut her a glance. "When's the last time you played?"

"I kicked Margie's ass just a couple days ago."

Glenn snorted. "Yeah, right."

Everyone knew Margie had a wicked jump shot, and even though she was a couple inches shorter than all the other Rivers sisters—and Glenn, for that matter—she was whippet fast and had hands of gold. "That'll be the day."

"Come on. Two out of three."

The night stretched endlessly before her. Mari was working nights all week, which meant she couldn't drop by the ER and hang around at night. She had nothing to look forward to for the rest of the weekend. Hell, for the week, when it came to it. She caved. An hour of sweating and listening to Flann taunt her about how slow she was getting might chase some of the dark from her head. Maybe. Worth trying anyhow, since the prospect of drinking lukewarm, weak beer for the rest of the night held no appeal. "Sure. Why not."

"Lend me some clothes?" Flann added.

Glenn nodded, Flann texted Abby she was leaving, and fifteen minutes later Glenn pulled around behind the high school where the Rivers siblings had all gone to school. The basketball courts adjacent to the parking lot were empty. The whole place was empty. Everyone was at the fairgrounds. They piled out and silently strode to the court.

Flann played basketball the way she did everything else, with an arrogant flair that sometimes appeared like recklessness but rarely was. She drove hard, took unanticipated shots, and often managed to win by doing the unexpected. Glenn was a precision player, feinting, cutting right and left, picking the percentage positions from which to shoot. Over the dozens, hundreds of games they'd played, they were almost dead even.

Flann sank a basket and backpedaled as Glenn retrieved the ball and dribbled.

"You're off your mark today," Flann called, the merest taunting tone in her voice.

Glenn ignored her, dropped her shoulder as Flann made a lunge for the ball, pivoted away, turned, and lofted a long jumper. It hit the rim, teetered, and fell back to the court without going through. Any other day she would have made that shot.

Flann scooped up the rebound, sped back out to half court, and one-handed an impossible shot that hit the backboard, angled down, and swirled around the rim before dropping through. Luck, nothing else, riding on the wings of supreme confidence and innate skill.

"So what happened with Mari?" Flann called as Glenn went for the ball.

Glenn ignored her, dribbling, driving, shooting. Sweat dripped into her eyes and stung, the burning oddly welcome.

"You two having problems working together in the ER?"

"No. Mari's good. Fits right in."

"Abby said the same thing." Flann muscled Glenn from inside, shot out an elbow and caught her in the chest, stole the ball. She circled, dribbling casually, making no move toward the basket. "I didn't think that would bother you. Her being strong."

"Why would it?"

Flann shrugged, picked up speed, drove to the basket and hit a layup. "It's pretty much been your show for a long time."

"I'm not you."

"True." Flann grinned. "There can only be one captain, and we all know who that is."

Glenn reflexively caught the ball Flann shot at her before it struck her in the chest. Ass. She dribbled, took a halfhearted shot that didn't go in, and stalked toward the side of the court. "I'm done."

Flann took one more lofting overhand shot, sank it, and retrieved the ball. She caught up with Glenn halfway to the truck.

"What's Mari's story, do you know?" Flann asked casually.

"What do you mean?" A prickling sensation started between Glenn's shoulder blades, half itch, half irritation. She should have passed on the B-ball. Flann's competitive streak never annoyed her, but then she wasn't usually in such a black mood.

"Single, girlfriend, boyfriend, you know. A couple of people were asking."

Glenn stopped, studied Flann's face. Flann might have been baiting her, but her eyes said she was telling the truth too. And why not. Mari was beautiful, new in town, and everyone always welcomed the possibility that newcomers offered.

"If anybody wants to know, they should ask her themselves."

"I kind of got the idea you were thinking along those lines yourself."

"Let it go." Glenn yanked the cab door open, tossed the ball into the narrow space behind the seats, and jumped in.

Flann sprinted around to the other side and hopped in.

"She shut you down?"

"What part of leave it alone don't you get?"

Flann shifted until her back was against the door and she was facing Glenn. "Well, I've known you for what, three years now? I've spent more time with you than anybody I know, even Abby and Harp. I don't think I've ever known you to have a date."

Glenn started the truck, but left it in park. A tangle of angry frustration twisted in her chest. The last thing she wanted to do was talk about Mari, but something kept her pinned in place. Flann's voice droned on, and all Glenn heard was Mari's name. She could still feel her, as if the unique texture of Mari's flesh had been tattooed beneath her skin. She could still taste her, that light teasing scent drawing her into a some long-forgotten, pure place where hope still lingered. The beer and the workout hadn't drained the heavy pull of desire that thrummed in the pit of her stomach.

"There's nothing going on between us."

"Do you want there to be?" Flann's voice had lost all its levity, had taken on the quiet, steady tone she used when talking life and death with the patients they cared for.

"Doesn't matter what I want."

"Bullshit, it doesn't."

Glenn shot her a look. "She's not ready."

Flann snorted. "So you just quit?"

"Yeah." Glenn shoved the truck into gear and gunned the truck toward the street. "I do."

Glenn slept little, rose early, and didn't have the energy to go for a run. Not that she was tired, only that her spirit was weary. She made a cup of coffee and sat out on the back porch, watching the sun come up and thinking about Mari. She would've liked not to, at least part of her would. A bigger part of her enjoyed thinking about her, recalling glimpses of her sitting in this very spot, her dark hair gleaming in the sunshine, her smile open and warm; the sight of her bending over a patient, focused and empathetic and just as warm and welcoming professionally as she was personally; gently taking Antonelli to task for leaps in logic, even though more often than not he ended up at the right conclusion. Discipline, Mari reminded him, would make him stronger. He understood that logic.

Glenn smiled to herself. So did she. Mari intuitively grasped the warrior spirit.

She drained her coffee cup and considered canceling her open invitation to Sunday dinner at the Riverses'. She hadn't wanted to pull back into her own private bunker this much in a very long time. Walking wounded, they called people like her. No visible blood, a few scattered scars that didn't amount to much of anything, but inside, an indefinable place that didn't heal and only seemed to bleed when feelings got through. Mari had gotten through in the span of a heartbeat.

She stood abruptly, shoving her chair back. Enough self-pity. Flann and Abby were making their big announcement today. She said she'd be there, and she couldn't back out. She'd never been one for that. She didn't regret a single choice she'd ever made, except one. Except giving in to the sweetest enticement she'd ever known. The kiss stayed with her, still tingled on her lips, still simmered in her depths.

And she was glad.

❖

Flann greeted her on the wide back porch that looked down over acres of green to the twisting river beyond when she pulled in a little after noon.

"Glad you made it," Flann said.

Glenn hopped up onto the porch. "Did you think I wouldn't?"

Flann gave her a long look. "The thought crossed my mind."

"Well, you were wrong."

"One of those rare occasions," Flann said, grinning.

"Uh-huh."

Ida Rivers, Flann's mother, was at her usual place by the stove, the pretty flowered apron, one of many Glenn had seen over the years, covering an even prettier dress she wore beneath. She was a statuesque woman in her middle years, with hints of all her children in her face—and more wisdom in her gaze than Glenn had ever known.

"Hi, darling," Ida said, sliding a big cast-iron pot with an enormous roast into the center of the long wooden table set with a dozen places.

"Hi, Ida," Glenn murmured, kissing her cheek when Ida leaned toward her.

"How are you doing?"

The question was innocent enough, but Glenn hesitated just long enough for Ida's eyes to darken and search her face for a long moment.

Glenn lifted a shoulder. "Well enough, I expect."

"Well, sit down," Ida said gently. "I'm glad you're here."

And just like that, Glenn was surrounded by family. Edward at one end of the table, Ida at the other, Blake and Margie as usual joined at the hip next to each other, Presley and Harper, Abby and Flann, Carson and her husband Bill and their two-year old bouncing back and forth between them, Carrie and her across from each other. She didn't have any trouble imagining Mari at the table. She'd fit in right away—effortlessly joining conversations, laughing, probably taking a turn at minding the toddler who thought it was such fun to walk from one lap to the other.

Talk as usual flowed in a dozen directions at once. Glenn had a hard time swallowing the most delicious food she'd ever tasted. Her insides echoed hollowly but nothing could fill her up.

As Ida cut the steaming fresh apple pie at the end of the meal, Flann said, "Abby and I have an announcement to make."

Carson broke into a wide grin, and Harper chuckled.

"We're going to get married before the end of the summer," Flann said.

Ida glanced at Abby, who rolled her eyes ever so slightly.

"Have you actually discussed this with Abby?" Ida asked as she slid a wedge of apple pie onto a plate and passed it to Flann.

"Yeah. Mostly."

"Before you set the actual date?"

Flann grinned. "Well, that was a little more vague."

Abby squeezed Flann's leg under the table, an obvious move apparent to everyone.

"She tends to skip over some of those things," Abby said sweetly, taking a bite of Flann's pie. "But this time we agree." She looked at Flann and kissed her cheek. "I love you."

Edward said, "That's settled, then. Give us the details when the

three of you"—he looked pointedly from Blake to Abby to Flann—
"have worked them all out."

"Understood." Flann slid her arm around Abby's shoulders, as
happy as Glenn had ever seen her.

The pie disappeared in a flash, the kids took off for the tree house
overlooking the river, and after Glenn helped clear the table, she
wandered out to the back porch and sat down on the top step.

A moment later, Carrie joined her. "You're quiet today."

"Flann's show."

Carrie laughed. "Isn't it usually with the two of you?"

"More or less."

"I didn't see much of you yesterday at the barbecue. Or Mari."

"Uh-huh."

"Something happened?"

Glenn watched a fat gray cat, one of half a dozen who lived in the
big barn in the adjacent field, stalk a bird that teased it by repeatedly
flying just out of reach before landing again. "No."

"Oh." Carrie stretched both legs down to the lower step, leaned
back on her arms, and tilted her face up to the sun. She was beautiful,
her red hair catching the light and gleaming with hidden strands of
gold. "Because I thought there might be something going on."

"No, there isn't."

"Why isn't there?"

"What?"

Carrie snorted. "Come on, Glenn. She's been watching you and
liking what she saw. And yesterday you were definitely looking back."

"You should leave this one alone, Carrie."

"You're both family, you know."

"All the more reason not to go there."

Glenn stood and Carrie looked up at her. "Someday, Glenn, you're
going to need to let someone in."

"Not everyone believes in happy endings, Carrie." Glenn jogged
down the path toward her Jeep.

"Life is what you make it," Carrie called after her.

Glenn drove away, wishing she believed that.

CHAPTER TWENTY-TWO

Mari worked nights all week, and the only time she saw Glenn was at shift changeover on the mornings Glenn worked. Then their exchanges were all business and took place in the conference room with half a dozen other people. Hardly the place to discuss the kiss that was almost more, not that she really wanted to revisit a scene that still left her confused and unsettled. Every night she expected to see Glenn show up for her usual spot drop-ins, but she never did. Toward the end of the week, she overheard two of the nurses mention it was odd Glenn hadn't been around, and they laughingly conjectured maybe she'd finally gotten a girlfriend.

Mari tried not to think about that conversation, and especially tried not to imagine Glenn with another woman, kissing another woman with that most amazingly soft, incredibly knowing mouth. She didn't have very good luck. She kept trying to pinpoint the exact moment when everything had gotten out of hand between them—and just how much she had been responsible for the disaster. Of course, the first kiss was probably the mistake, but she couldn't quite bring herself to regret it. She'd been kissed before, but never like that. Never so thoroughly, so tenderly, so forcefully, so…right. Glenn's kiss had been so much more than a kiss, and Mari had been touched by so much more than just the sensual glide of her teasing caresses. Somehow Glenn had managed to make her feel exciting and excited, desirable and so eager for more of…everything. Glenn's presence, as much as her touch, had ignited some slumbering part of her and awakened a fervor in her body and her heart to experience life at the peak of passion. Beyond the safety net of caution. And of course, she couldn't, could she. Not now, not yet. Not when she'd barely begun to let herself hope the nightmare was over.

Mari sighed, shelved the last chart from a surprisingly quiet Friday night shift, and watched the clock tick ever closer to seven a.m. Antonelli came into the break room and dropped into a chair beside her.

"Did you finish your backlog of discharge dictations?" Mari asked.

He shook his head. "I got tied up playing Pokémon."

She laughed. "Do you rule?"

He grinned, looking boyishly handsome and not the least bit apologetic about ditching his paperwork. "But of course."

"Just remember, if you don't do your charts, I'll have to—and if it comes to that, you could find yourself working a lot of nights and weekends. I make the schedule, remember." Mari's threat was an empty one, since she knew he'd get the charts done by the deadline, but it didn't hurt to make him at least think she was immune to his charm. Unlike every other woman in his universe, apparently.

"As long as it isn't this weekend. My kid sister is home on leave for two weeks, so I'll be spending most of the weekend at my parents'. Big family get-together."

Mari's heart hurt for an instant. Weekends had always meant family time for her too, until first her illness and then her estrangement from those closest to her put an end to the easy sharing. "She's in the Army?"

"Marines," he said proudly. "The little squirt managed to work her way into a Huey command and flies support for Special Ops in…well, over there."

"We'll get you out of here ASAP, then."

"Thanks." He cleared his throat and looked away briefly. "So. How about you? Doing something fun with the rest of your weekend?"

"Nothing special." Mari envisioned the weekend spreading slowly before her and tried again not to think of Glenn, who she knew was off call as well. She'd checked the schedule more than once, just to see her name in print. Lord, really silly, but she couldn't make herself stop. "Still unpacking, decorating. You know."

"Boy, that sounds lame. You want to come home with me? Always got plenty of food."

Mari's throat closed. The kindness of strangers—but Antonelli wasn't a stranger any longer. Their shared struggles and triumphs had forged a real bond between them. "I'd love to, but maybe not on a special weekend like this one. Rain check?"

"Sure. My mom will try to talk you into marrying me, though."

Mari laughed. "I wouldn't want to give her false hope."

He grinned and shot her another sure-to-melt-most-girls'-hearts look just as Abby appeared in the doorway.

Abby asked, "You two have anything to sign out?"

"I've got a thirty-three-year-old in cubicle two," Mari said. "We're waiting on micro to report on the urinalysis. Probably just a straightforward UTI."

"Got it."

Antonelli straightened, coming to attention unconsciously in his chair. "The guy in six is admitted and waiting for a surgical bed and observation. Probable diverticulitis. They're trying to quiet it down with antibiotics and fluids."

"Did he get his first dose of IV meds yet?" Abby asked.

"Yep—triples, all charted."

"Good. Who's on call for surgery?"

"Beecher."

"Did she say she'd be in to see him?" Abby asked.

"Said she'd be by on rounds later this morning."

"Good enough, then. See you both Monday. Get out of here."

Antonelli scraped back his chair, got to his feet, and shot past Abby out the door.

"How's it going?" Abby asked as Mari rose.

"Fine," Mari said. "How are Blake and Margie doing with their volunteering?"

If Abby noticed her quick change in subject, she let it pass. "They'd stay here around the clock if I let them. They both remind me of Glenn." She frowned. "Come to think of it, where is she? I haven't seen much of her all week, and she hasn't called Flann once in the middle of the night. Did you ban her from lurking here at night?"

Mari forced a smile. "Not guilty! Maybe she's finally decided to trust the rest of us to take care of things all by ourselves."

"If she has, it'll be the first time ever." Abby laughed. "But I do think it says a lot she's giving up a little control when you're on call. She obviously respects your judgment."

"I hope so," Mari said, knowing that couldn't be further from the truth. She'd amply demonstrated just how bad her judgment was in Glenn's bedroom. Still, she trusted Glenn not to let their personal crossed signals impact their professional relationship. Glenn was too clearheaded and much too honest for that. "She sets some pretty high standards for everyone."

"None more than for herself," Abby said, "but you meet them just fine. Oh, by the way, Presley reminded me to let you know you're invited to the wedding. She just assumed you knew that, and then realized you ought to get a formal invitation. Consider this formal."

"Oh, but I hardly know anyone!"

"Hey, you're part of the planning committee now. You have to be there."

"Then yes," Mari said softly, "I'd love to come."

"Great! Carrie will fill you in on the specifics." Abby waved and turned to go. "Have fun this weekend."

Mari didn't answer. She didn't have the energy to pretend any longer.

❖

Mari changed into jeans, a lime-green ribbed tank top, and sneakers in the locker room and tried not to look for Glenn as she walked through the ER on her way out. She couldn't really help herself, even though Glenn wasn't on call and, of course, was not around. Hope was hardest to kill when you didn't actually want to feel any.

Traffic was heavier than usual on a weekend morning, and as she approached the unofficial commons, a grassy three-square-block area in the center of town where people frequently sunbathed or sat about on blankets picnicking or simply relaxing, a huge red hot-air balloon with brilliant blue and yellow stripes lofted into the sky. A roar went up from somewhere just ahead and drew her in that direction. The quiet commons had been transformed. A carnival-like atmosphere encompassed the place—adults congregated with cups of coffee while dogs and children ran about. Food tents offering hot breakfasts, fresh baked goods, and luscious-looking fruit ringed half the square, and half a dozen balloons in various stages of inflation were tethered in the center. A big sign announced the two-day balloon festival. She didn't know how she'd missed news of the event, but working nights had given her a good excuse to avoid everyone all week.

Now the tantalizing smell of bacon frying drew her to a tent, and she purchased an egg and bacon sandwich on a fresh-baked biscuit. She actually felt hungry for the first time in a week.

"Thanks," she said, balancing the sandwich in one hand and a cardboard cup of coffee in the other. She turned and almost stumbled into Glenn. "Oh!"

Glenn jumped back, avoiding the coffee slosh. "Hi. You okay? Sorry, I didn't mean to sneak up on you."

"No, I'm fine. Hi." Mari stared just to make sure Glenn wasn't an apparition, considering how hard she'd been wishing she'd run into her. She was dressed in running shorts and a sleeveless V-neck T-shirt. Her hair was damp, her skin lightly misted, and the T-shirt plastered to her chest. She'd been running hard. "Hi."

God, she was repeating herself.

"I saw you across the field," Glenn said. "Just get off shift?"

"Uh-huh." Mari stepped out of the way of a man and woman who wanted to order breakfast.

"Well, I guess I should let you go," Glenn said awkwardly, backing up a step. "You must be tired."

"No," Mari said quickly, "I'm not. I was just getting something to eat. You want something?"

Glenn hesitated and Mari thought she was about to say no. But she nodded after a second. "Yeah, sure if you could lend me some money. I'm light today."

"My treat. Bacon and eggs okay?"

"Actually," Glenn said, breaking into a grin, "it sounds fabulous."

Mari handed over hers. "Here. Take this one. I'll get another. Coffee?"

"Yeah, please. I'll grab us a table over by the trees."

"Great. Just be a sec." Mari turned away quickly so she didn't give herself away. Excitement raced through her and she knew her delight in running into Glenn was written all over her face. She really didn't want to repeat her meltdown of the week before. Really, really didn't.

❖

Mari carried the sandwich and two fresh cups of coffee back to the wooden picnic table Glenn had staked out beneath two tall pine trees. The little shade was welcome. The day promised to be hot and was getting there fast. The square was even more crowded than twenty minutes before. The bright sunny day seemed so fresh and simple. Or maybe she was just happy. Whatever the cause, she intended to enjoy it.

She also intended to enjoy the fact Glenn watched her as she walked toward her. The press of Glenn's gaze slid over her face and down her body and made her tingle. She loved the way Glenn looked at her, as if she was the only person on Glenn's horizon. Foolish, she knew, but the feeling of being so central, so valued, struck a chord in her that made her whole body hum.

"Here—let me help." Glenn rose and took one of the coffees. "I owe you big-time for this."

"I'll have to think of some suitable method of repayment," Mari teased.

Glenn paused, her half-eaten sandwich in her hand. "You do that."

Mari blushed and pretended to be busy with the sandwich she no longer cared if she ate. Her hunger had suddenly shifted to something far more visceral, and far more dangerous. Glenn looked so damn sexy she ached to touch her.

They sat across from one another, the coffee and sandwiches between them, and ate in silence for a few minutes. The silence felt anything but empty. Mari imagined she could feel the very air crackling between them as if at any moment sparks might burst and jump from her skin to Glenn's.

"How did you find the night shift?" Glenn asked.

Thankfully, a safe topic. "About what I expected. Eleven o'clock seems to be the witching hour until about one. And then of course, at six it starts all over again. I kind of liked it. I felt really in charge."

Glenn nodded. "There's something different about nights. It's not just the stillness that comes over the hospital, because it's just as busy, really, but there's always this sense of anticipation underneath the calm. That anything could come through the door at any minute, and you're it. It's all on you."

"You like that, don't you? The anticipation. The not knowing what will test you next."

"You'd think I would've learned not to look for that kind of thing, wouldn't you, but I never lost it. Even when what was coming might kill me, I had that buzz of excitement."

Mari caught her breath. "I'm sorry. I didn't mean to suggest you enjoyed that kind of danger."

"It's okay. I don't have nightmares about it, at least not when I'm sleeping."

"But when you're awake?"

Glenn sighed. "Not even that so much. You don't have to dream about what you carry around with you. It's always just there. This itch between your shoulder blades that something's coming, something you can't stop, something you might not be able to fix."

"Are you afraid?"

Glenn's brows drew down. "No. Maybe angry." She scoffed. "I'd just like to be able to see what I'm fighting, and that never really happens."

"Maybe that's why you like to spend so much time in the emergency room. Because then you know. It's right there and you can see it."

"You might be right. But I'm not really sure it matters."

"No, neither am I. You've taken something that you shouldn't have to live with and turned it into something positive. I'm sorry that you've had to do that, but I think you should be proud."

"Thanks." Glenn stared down at her hands clasping the cup. "It matters what you think."

"I think you're amazing," Mari said softly.

"Do you have plans this morning?"

The question threw her and she didn't have an answer, so she didn't try to think, she just went with what felt right. "No. I'm not working again until Monday. Then I'm switching back to days. I suppose my biggest plans for the day were laundry and vacuuming my rug. It's a pretty small rug."

Glenn grinned. "Can't say that was on my list of things to do." She stood up. "You mind waiting here for a few minutes?"

"Sure. It's a beautiful day and I've been inside all night."

"You're not tired?"

"No!" The last thing she was was tired. Just being around Glenn was exhilarating. She felt better, more alive and more eager for what the day might bring, than she had been all week. "I'm great. Take whatever time you need."

Glenn paused beside her and touched her shoulder, as if reassuring herself Mari really would stay. "Fifteen minutes. I'll be back."

"I'll wait." Mari watched her as she ran across the field to the corner and disappeared. They weren't very far from Glenn's apartment, and she suspected Glenn was going home to change. She didn't know why and it didn't matter. All that mattered was that Glenn said she was coming back. And if she said she was coming back, she would.

Twelve minutes later she appeared—Mari checked her watch when she saw Glenn striding across the green in black jeans and a snowy white T-shirt, her hair slicked back and damp. She looked even better than she had a few minutes before. She grinned and Mari knew she'd been caught looking. Not just looking—wanting. Too late to pretend otherwise.

When Glenn drew near, she held out her hand. "Come on."

Mari didn't even ask where they were going. She didn't really care. She took Glenn's hand and fell in beside her, the clasp of her fingers warm and reassuring and as natural as anything she'd ever experienced. When questions tried to surface in her mind, she resolutely put them aside. For the first time in a week, she was happy.

CHAPTER TWENTY-THREE

I suppose I should've asked you," Glenn said. "Do you mind heights?"
Mari frowned as they walked across the green, slowing every few feet so Glenn could return a greeting. For someone so reserved, so private, Glenn had touched many lives. She was woven into the fabric of this place and Mari knew why. Glenn cared for the community as much as she cared for the individuals. This was a place where roots ran deep and Glenn had found her place, somewhere she might do the same, if she was lucky. She just wished she believed more in luck. Glenn was waiting for an answer, and looking at her, it was easy to forget the past and its hold on her life. Mari smiled. "Heights? You mean like tall bridges and rooftops? No, they don't bother me. We've got plenty of overpasses in LA, and I've ridden over all of them. Major metropolis, remember?"

"Well, this won't be exactly like that, but hopefully better." Glenn grabbed her hand and pulled her down a narrow passage between a jumble of air compressors, tanks, and other equipment into a clearing relatively free of people.

A heavyset, florid-faced man in a bright yellow T-shirt tucked into oil-smeared canvas pants strode toward them. "You're all set?"

"Yeah," Glenn said.

He held out a clipboard. "I need you both to sign these waivers right here. You know, the usual. You won't sue me if we all end up in a tree somewhere."

Glenn signed without bothering to read anything and handed the clipboard to Mari. "Frank is going to take us up for a ride."

Mari looked at the huge tangle of ropes and yellow-and-red-striped canvas lying on the ground. It looked exactly like an enormous deflated balloon. Which it was. "In that?"

Her voice squeaked and Glenn laughed. "Once he pumps a little air into it and fires up the boiler, yes."

"You're serious?"

"You're not scared, are you?"

Oh yes, she was, but not of going up in a hot-air balloon. She'd never done it before, never even imagined wanting to do it, but if Glenn was going to be there, she wanted to go too. And that's what scared her. She wanted to go anywhere Glenn wanted to take her.

Mari looked at the other balloons lifting off around them, most with one or two people aboard who looked like they were actually piloting the craft. Really, how crazy was that—relying on a sheet of cloth tied to an open furnace to fly around in. Frank and another younger man in jeans and a red T-shirt turned on an enormous fan, and the long sheet of colorful canvas began to fill and float above them. Mari was intrigued despite her misgivings. When Frank arranged something that looked a lot like a giant Sterno can under the balloon and lit an open flame, Mari gasped. Flames shot up toward the canvas balloon, which suddenly puffed up and went airborne. Long lines attached to large stakes in the ground kept it prisoner.

"You're kidding. Flames?"

"The hot air makes the balloon rise."

Mari gave her a look.

Glenn held out her hand in invitation. "So, want to go for a ride?"

Yes, anything, anywhere, for a few minutes more with Glenn. The past week's shadows evaporated in the brilliant glow of Glenn's smile. Crazy or not, Mari gripped Glenn's hand. "Tell me we're not insane."

"I promise you'll be fine." Glenn was still grinning, but Mari sensed the seriousness behind her light tone. Glenn could be counted on, no matter what. She knew that in her bones. She'd counted on family, counted on her own body, and both had failed her. She should know better than to count on anyone, anything, but the still strength in Glenn's gaze told her otherwise. This woman she could trust.

"Then let's go." Mari headed for the makeshift set of stairs Frank had pushed up against the wicker basket. They teetered as she climbed, and Glenn steadied her from behind with a hand on her back.

The baskets hanging below the other colorful, gas-filled balloons already floating off in the sky looked tiny from the ground, and when she got inside this one, the basket didn't look any larger up close. A sign had said the basket held five, but Mari didn't see how. There was barely a foot of space left over with the three of them inside. She glanced at Glenn, who was watching her with a faint look of amusement.

"This really isn't funny, you know."

"You did say you didn't mind heights."

"You neglected to mention we'd be up in the air in something the size of a cereal box. And is there even any way to steer this thing?"

"These lines right here help with piloting," Frank said, climbing in with them. "Of course, they're only good for a suggestion. Mostly the balloon goes where she wants."

Mari grimaced but held her protest. She was committed now—no quitting.

Frank began untying the tethers and tossing them down to the ground. The basket bounced like a puppy eager to be let off its leash. "You don't have to worry, miss. I've been piloting this rig since I could hardly see over the top of the basket."

"I hope not this very one," Mari muttered. "They can't have a life span of more than six months." When she watched the canvas lift from the ground as the coiled tube pumped air into it, she didn't actually think it could have a life span of more than a day or two. She prayed for at least another twenty-four hours. "I'm surprised they all don't catch on fire."

Glenn chuckled. "It's a delicate balance."

Mari didn't doubt Frank's lifetime of experience, but she would much rather have been watching the spectacle from the safety of one of the picnic tables. On the other hand, Glenn offered her a taste of adventure, and this one at least was relatively safe. The only thing that might get broken would be her head, not her heart.

That thought brought her up short. Was her heart really at risk where Glenn was concerned? Her body and her sanity were definitely on the losing end of things—being anywhere in Glenn's vicinity sent her heart rate into the stratosphere, and other parts of her body jolted awake with a mixture of pleasure and nagging need. Her mind blanked and basic instincts took charge. She was no stranger to the concept of sex or sexual desire, and even if she didn't have the experience, she knew what she was feeling. Just thinking about Glenn aroused her. The sight of her, the sound of her voice, the merest brush of her hand ignited a flood of desire. She certainly wasn't going to lie to herself about that. The reaction was natural, Glenn was gorgeous, and she rejoiced that her body had finally recovered from the assaults of the last year. But her heart? No, she hadn't let things get that far out of hand. For now she'd let herself enjoy the attraction, within reason.

"It's not too late to change your mind," Glenn said gently. "I want you to enjoy it."

Usually Glenn could read her mind, but thankfully not this time. She didn't need to know Mari had just been debating whether it was wise to lust after her. As if she could stop it. *I want you to enjoy it.* Mari smiled. "I know you do, and I will. I want to go up."

Glenn glanced at Frank. "Good enough. We're good to go."

Mari moved closer to Glenn as Frank released the last ropes holding them down. The bucket immediately shot up, swaying rapidly back and forth.

"Oh!" Mari grabbed the rim of the basket that came about to her waist. She had no trouble at all imagining tipping forward and falling out. For an instant, her head spun.

"Got you." Glenn's arms came around her from behind, her firm body pressed up against Mari's back.

"Thanks. Just caught me by surprise." Mari laughed a little shakily. Maybe heights weren't her thing after all.

"There's no way you're going to fall," Glenn murmured close to her ear.

Mari had never been held so protectively by a stranger in her life. Glenn wasn't really a stranger, far from it, but she wasn't family and Mari wasn't a little girl anymore. She hadn't been cradled in anyone's arms since one of the first nights in the hospital when her mother thought she was going to die. This was something completely beyond her experience, and she would've been happy if Frank the balloon man flew them across the entire country and beyond, as long as Glenn stayed behind her with her arms around her, holding her as if she always had and always would.

"Better?"

When Glenn moved as if to release her, Mari folded her arms over Glenn's to keep her in place. She leaned back just a little until she was in complete contact with Glenn, her back fit into the curves of Glenn's lean form. "Yes, but don't move."

Glenn's cheek brushed hers. "Fabulous view, isn't it?"

They weren't so very high, but Mari felt as if she was floating in the clouds. To the east, the Vermont mountains rose purple and densely forested, the green unbroken by any sign of civilization, their peaks buried in snowy white, clouds or snow, she couldn't be sure. Could there be snow in the mountains in July here like there was at home?

"Not enough to ski on, but it gets pretty cold up there," Glenn murmured, reading her mind again.

"They're beautiful."

"Yes." Glenn's voice sounded low and husky and Mari wondered, hoped, she wasn't talking about the mountains.

To the west, the village quickly gave way to rolling hills and pastures. The nearest city wasn't even visible on the horizon, creating an otherworldly sense of passing back in time. Birds swooped below them, soaring from tree to ground and up again. People on the ground, small colorful patches of them, waved as they passed overhead.

"Oh my God." Mari laughed, pointing when they passed above a large, elaborate out-of-place mansion in the midst of acres of green, clearly meant to mimic some kind of Italian palazzo. Several people sunning by the pool made a quick grab for towels to cover their nakedness.

Behind her Glenn chuckled, the sound reverberating between their bodies, low and exciting. "Happens at least once every year."

Mari tilted her head back to look at Glenn behind her. "You always go up?"

"If I'm free." Glenn rubbed her cheek lightly against Mari's, her lips just grazing Mari's ear. It might have been an accident, the bucket swayed so much, but Mari chose to believe it wasn't. "Always by myself, though."

"I'm glad you brought me up."

"So am I."

"How will we get back?"

"If Frank can't catch a backdraft and turn us around, there'll be a chase car that will spot our landing and drive us home." Glenn rubbed her palm lightly over Mari's abdomen. "You okay with that?"

"Yes." As long as Glenn didn't move, Mari didn't care how long they'd be up in the air or how they'd get back. If the balloon man dropped them off in some little village a hundred miles away and they had to walk back, she didn't care. She had no one to report to, no one who would worry about her. And no one she would rather be with. To her disappointment, though, after forty minutes or so, she began to realize Frank was slowly turning them, adjusting for the wind currents, and they began a circling return.

Eventually the square came back into view and Frank adjusted the flame, turning it low, and did something to make the balloon begin to deflate. As the envelope, as she'd learned it was called, grew ever so slowly smaller and looser, they lost elevation. She gripped Glenn's hand tightly.

"There will be a little bump at the bottom, but nothing much. Frank really is very good."

"I'm fine," Mari said, and she was.

The basket hit the ground and skidded. Glenn held her steady and Mari laughed. "God, that was fun."

"Best ride I ever took," Glenn murmured.

Glenn's arms stayed around her, and Mari wanted to turn within the circle of Glenn's protective grasp and kiss her. She'd never wanted anything so much.

"All set, folks," Frank called from the ground.

Glenn finally jumped out to wait for her on the short steps that Frank's helper had pushed across the grass to the basket. When Mari climbed over the edge, Glenn caught her by the waist and swung her down. The movement was smooth and possessive, and a wave of desire poured over her. Feeling as free as she had soaring in the air, Mari let her hands fall onto Glenn's shoulders and brush down over her chest. When her feet finally touched the ground, she kept her hands where they were. Glenn's breasts strained against the white T-shirt, her nipples small and hard. Mari's palms brushed over them, and Glenn gasped.

Mari wouldn't even pretend she didn't know what she was doing. She wanted her. Had wanted her since the first time they'd touched, since the last time they'd parted. Since Glenn's kisses and caresses had awakened a need that hadn't quieted. Glenn had pulled back, ever respectful, ever honorable, because Mari had said she didn't want a relationship. She still didn't, but she wanted this.

"I want you to make love to me," Mari whispered. "Can we have today?"

Glenn couldn't imagine refusing her. Not when the merest touch of Mari's fingertips, the brush of her breath over her skin, set her ablaze. She'd barely slept three hours in a row all week. She ached for her, and nothing she could do would put out the flames. A day? An hour? Hell, she would've begged for five minutes.

"Yes," Glenn said hoarsely, knowing she was playing with fire a hell of a lot more dangerous than anything she'd faced in her life. Mari wanted to carve out a chunk of time and set it aside, as if it wasn't really part of her life, as if that would keep her safe. Keep Glenn safe, somehow. But Mari didn't know there was no way to ever be safe. Glenn didn't care—she'd learned to stop caring about safety a long time ago. "Now?"

"Oh yes. Now."

CHAPTER TWENTY-FOUR

Glenn clasped Mari's hand as they threaded their way through the crowd and left the commons behind. She kept her grasp loose, giving Mari a chance to pull away if she wanted, giving her a chance to leave if she needed to, if she changed her mind. Her heart hammered and she tried not to think about Mari walking away. Switching off her brain was something she'd had a lot of practice with, in the midst of battle, out on the field or in the emergency room. She could run on autopilot, all her senses alert and finely tuned, locking her emotions away while she fought death. Sometimes keeping the pain and anger and despair locked away meant locking everything else away too, a fair price to pay so she could do her job. She couldn't seem to manage autopilot with Mari, though.

The Kevlar casing surrounding her heart was cracked wide open, letting feelings in and, maybe even worse, feelings out. Longing for Mari burned inside her chest, created an ache in the pit of her stomach, kept her restless and awake all night. But just like that, the touch of Mari's hand, her smile, her laughter banished the ache and replaced it with something sweeter. Something she'd never experienced and never thought she needed. A taste of honey in the desert.

"I'm not going to change my mind," Mari said softly.

Glenn smiled wryly. "How come you can read my mind?"

"How come you can read mine?" Mari shot back gently.

Glenn glanced at her. "I don't know. It just happened."

Mari nodded. "I know what you mean. Maybe some things there are no answers to."

"What do we do, then?" Glenn mused, trying to see over the horizon and finding only shadows. "When there are no answers?"

"Maybe we just believe."

"Can you do that?"

"I wish I could," Mari said softly, striving for honesty because Glenn deserved that. "Until a year ago, I believed without question in so many things. In the unconditional love of my family, in my place in the world, in my future. Now all those things have changed. I'm not sure when or if I'll be able to believe again."

Glenn hadn't really expected anything different. Mari had said in a million ways that she'd lost faith, lost trust, lost believing. Two years she'd said, as if setting some kind of milestone that she needed to reach, as if when she got there all those feelings would suddenly be switched on again. Glenn didn't think that would happen. She'd thought her faith and trust and hope had been switched off forever, but Mari had changed that. She didn't mind as much as she thought she might. She might not be happy about that tomorrow, but today was all that mattered. For now.

"I'm going to need to take a shower," Mari said as she walked down the alley to Glenn's apartment. "I came straight from the hospital and thought I was going right home. Do you mind?"

"No," Glenn said. "I'm not going anywhere either."

"Good," Mari said softly. She paused at the landing outside Glenn's door. "What changed your mind?"

"A lot of things." Glenn leaned against the building next to the door, put her hands in her pockets, watched the heat waves rise off the blacktop in the parking lot. "I didn't get a whole lot of sleep this week—I couldn't stop thinking about how much I wanted to see you. How much I wanted to touch you again."

Mari wanted to smile. She liked hearing Glenn had been almost as miserable as she'd been. "Is that why you stayed away from the ER?"

"Partly." Glenn shrugged. "I figured you didn't want to see me."

"You were wrong." Mari leaned close enough to tap a fingertip to Glenn's chest. "I was hurt at first—"

"Cripes, I'm sorry," Glenn said.

"At first. I'm fine now—I understand why you backed off. I probably would have too, right then. I did tell you I didn't want to get involved, and under the circumstances, you respected that."

"And today?"

"Today is today." Mari tapped her again. "Can we agree on that right now?"

Glenn nodded. "I don't plan on changing my mind either."

"Good." She shivered despite the blazing weather. "Can we go inside?"

Glenn grabbed her hand. "Hell, yes."

Once inside, Glenn showed her where the bathroom was and handed her clean towels. "Take your time, there's plenty of hot water."

Mari gave her a long look. "If you don't mind, I'd like to make this part quick."

Glenn's heart did that rapid-fire machine-gun thing in her chest again and she actually had to work to catch her breath. "Do you need anything else? Something to drink? Something to eat?"

Mari held the folded towels against her chest and moved closer, wrapping her free hand around the back of Glenn's neck. She tugged her head down and kissed her, a slow, smoldering, smoky kiss that scorched Glenn's nerve endings all the way to the tips of her fingers and the soles of her feet. She was surprised she didn't burst into flame like a rocket flare. She groaned against Mari's mouth.

"I don't need anything except more of that," Mari whispered against Glenn's lips.

"Then it would be good if you'd hurry," Glenn murmured.

Mari paused at the door. Should she invite Glenn into the shower with her? Wasn't that what people did when they were trying to seduce a new lover? She didn't know, but for some reason, she wanted their first touch to be in bed, when they were stretched out beside each other, when they wouldn't have to stop and move again until she'd been able to explore every curve and plane of Glenn's body. Until she'd had Glenn on top of her, touching her everywhere. Summoning her courage, she said as firmly as she could, "I'd like it if you waited for me in bed."

"I can do that."

"Naked."

The top of Glenn's head was about to explode. Her hands trembled as she slid them around Mari's waist and kissed her throat. "I'm going to be going crazy until you come back."

Mari tilted her head back and laughed. She loved the control Glenn gave her, and she'd never had the slightest idea that was a possibility, that she wanted to have a woman go crazy for her. Nothing she'd ever read, nothing she'd ever heard, nothing she'd ever imagined had been so wildly freeing and so incredibly empowering as Glenn's desire for her. Her nipples tightened and she throbbed deep inside. She needed to hurry as well, while she could still think. "Two minutes. You can time me."

Glenn chuckled. "Starting now?"

Mari gave her a little push toward the bed. "Start counting."

Glenn stripped by the side of the bed, pulled down the covers, and was thankful she hadn't slept much in the last few days. The sheets were fresh and though the air was hot, with the windows open, enough of a breeze stole through to keep them comfortable until sometime in the afternoon. If Mari was still there by then.

Glenn pushed away thoughts of later and lay down, naked, exposed. With other women, the sex had been perfunctory if heated, sometimes impersonal, sometimes friendly. What she wanted now was something far different. She wanted to touch as deeply as she could, and she needed to let herself be touched. Mari deserved that.

The bathroom door opened and Mari appeared, her hair damp and a towel wrapped around her body. "How did I do?"

Glenn pushed up on her elbows. "I think you broke a record."

"Stay right there. Don't move."

Glenn sent her a quizzical look but followed orders. Mari took in Glenn's naked form. Felt her breath rush out and gasped to pull it back. Glenn was all long lines of muscle and, surprisingly, curves where they ought to be, all of her subtly beautiful.

Mari stopped worrying about whether she would know what to do when the time came. Stopped worrying if she'd made the right decision. Let fear and uncertainty evaporate in the day's heat like the drops of water from her flushed skin. She loosed the towel and smiled inwardly when Glenn jerked and her eyes took on that dark, intense focus. Mari took her time crossing to the bed, feeling her breasts tighten and lift, her nipples pebble despite the temperature. Excitement raged through her. By the time she reached her, Glenn had shifted until she was sitting on the side of the bed as she had been the very first time they'd kissed here. She opened her thighs and pulled Mari between them, pressing her cheek to Mari's bare midriff. Skin on skin, fire to flame.

Mari bit her lip and ran her fingers over Glenn's shoulders and down her back. She'd never get tired of exploring the strength and power beneath the satiny skin. Glenn's mouth pressed against her belly and the soft heat moved through her, coalescing between her thighs. When Glenn cupped her buttocks and kissed lower, Mari trembled.

"Your mouth's incredible, but I need to slow down or I'm afraid this will be over all too soon."

Glenn looked up at her, grinning. "I'm in no hurry, but I have a hard time keeping my hands off you."

Mari gripped her shoulders and pushed back gently. "That's a really good idea. Let's see how long you can *not* touch."

Glenn groaned but obediently stretched out on the bed.

"First, I want to touch you everywhere." Mari knelt beside her. So much to discover. Going slow was going to be a lot harder than she'd imagined, especially with the pressure between her thighs making her head swim.

"You can have whatever you want." Glenn curled her fingers into the sheets as Mari made a little humming noise and leaned over her.

Mari's breasts swayed gently, her hair a dark silky cloud around Glenn's face. Mari kissed her, soft and slow and like she owned her. Glenn liked the feeling. Her thighs tightened and a pulse beat hard between her legs.

Mari eased back and stroked a fiery line down the center of Glenn's body, tracing the curve of her breasts with her fingertips, teasing the muscles in her abdomen until they tightened with need. When Mari stroked the hollow at the base of Glenn's belly, she fought not to whimper.

"You have an amazing body," Mari murmured, brushing her lips over Glenn's nipple.

Glenn hissed. Mari's mouth was hot, her breasts just brushing the surface of Glenn's skin. She wanted to hold them, caress them, taste them. "How much longer?"

"Oh," Mari mused, fascinated by the way Glenn's body jerked and trembled when she caressed her, "a while yet. I know you can be patient."

Once upon a time she could've waited motionless, lying for hours in the scorching heat with the threat of death ready to rain down on her, but now her control was rapidly shredding. Her head was light, her belly heavy, the need for release volcanic. She twisted the cotton harder between her fists, her fingers cramping. Whatever Mari wanted, she would give.

"Turn over," Mari whispered, "I haven't seen all of you yet."

Silently, Glenn obeyed, turning her face against the pillow.

Mari wanted to memorize every inch of her, so starkly beautiful, her face etched in passion, but the more she touched her, the closer she came to losing control. Mari caressed Glenn's back to the hollow at the base of her spine and over the rise of her muscular ass. Glenn's legs parted as her buttocks lifted, and Mari teased the buttery soft skin high up between her legs.

"Be careful," Glenn warned hoarsely. "If you go any higher, if you touch me, I'm likely to explode."

The blood pounded in Mari's head. *She* had done this. *She* had excited this magnificent woman. Need vibrated in the air between them, a living hungering beast. God, she never wanted to stop touching her, but she couldn't think any longer.

"I need you now," Mari gasped, caught by the swift surge of desire rushing to her center.

Glenn flipped over and surged upward, pulling Mari down beside her. Her leg was suddenly between Mari's thighs, pressing tightly into her sex. Her hand cradled Mari's breast, her mouth on the opposite nipple. Teeth scraped against her, and Mari cried out, driving her hands into Glenn's hair.

"Oh my God," Mari cried. "Stop, stop, you're going to make me come."

Glenn pushed her hand between them, cupping Mari in her palm and taking her mouth in a dark, possessive kiss. Mari pushed against Glenn's hand, and when Glenn stroked her once, twice, her world incinerated.

Mari heard a strangled cry, hers or Glenn's, she couldn't tell. Her mind blanked, her body quaked. And then her face was buried against Glenn's chest and she was crying. "I'm sorry, I'm sorry, I don't know why—"

"It's all right, you're perfect. Perfect." Glenn stroked her, rocked her, let her come back to herself. "Okay now?"

Mari laughed unsteadily. "Okay? Oh yeah, okay is an understatement."

"Good," Glenn whispered, guiding Mari down on the bed and covering her again, needing all of her again. Gently, slowly, she entered her and watched Mari's eyes go blank with need. This time the build was slower, deeper, and when Mari crested, her eyes flew open and she searched for Glenn's face, locking onto her as she came apart.

Glenn couldn't breathe, didn't need to breathe, didn't need anything except the look of wonder on Mari's face. Suddenly weak, she rested her forehead gently between Mari's breasts, went still inside her, and waited for Mari's passion to ebb.

"How did you do that?" Mari whispered. "I thought I was going to be in control."

Glenn laughed and settled down beside her. "Oh, you were. Believe me."

Mari gazed at her, her eyes still dazed and sated. She traced a fingertip around Glenn's nipple, then down her belly. "I got sidetracked."

"Uh, I noticed."

Mari laughed. "I haven't finished touching you everywhere yet."

"Why don't you rest for a little while."

"Because I'm not tired. And I'm not done." Mari pushed Glenn onto her back and knelt between Glenn's thighs. "I want to see all of you, I want to watch you come." As she spoke, she traced the outer edges of Glenn's sex with her fingertips.

Glenn arched off the bed, her jaws clenched. When she managed to suck in a breath, she said, "It won't take much."

"That's all right. We can always do it again, right?"

At that moment, Glenn could only agree. At that moment, there was only now. "Just keep doing what you're doing. I'm about to come."

"Good," Mari whispered softly, stroking, teasing, finding the spots that she liked, discovering the places that made Glenn's body bow. And when she found the one that made Glenn groan and tighten all over, she didn't stop until Glenn cried out.

CHAPTER TWENTY-FIVE

The room had grown warmer throughout the morning, and sweat lightly misted Mari's skin. She should've felt self-conscious—she'd never been so close to another human being in her life, never been so exposed, never been so vulnerable. She should've been thinking about how to leave, what to say, how to grasp the tattered tethers of control and wind the clock back to a saner time. She wasn't doing any of those things. For as long as the dream lasted, she wanted to stay in this Spartan room where the merest tease of a breeze danced through the half-open window and the air shimmered with heat as heavy as winter wool. Somehow this room had become the safest place she'd ever been.

"Hungry?" Glenn asked drowsily.

"Mmm. Not sure." Lazily stroking Glenn's hair, Mari lay naked with the sheets tangled around her legs, and Glenn's head pillowed between her breasts. Glenn was the quiet in the center of her being, the peace she'd lost somewhere in the last year, the shelter she'd taken for granted before everything had changed. If she could capture this moment and hold it forever, she thought she would know the meaning of happiness.

"I think your stomach just said otherwise." Glenn rubbed a hand over Mari's midsection.

"I'll take your word for it. I'm having trouble actually feeling my body—I think that last orgasm might have totally short-circuited my nervous system." Mari brushed damp hair away from Glenn's temple and kissed her. "Was I asleep the last few minutes or just comatose?"

"I'm not sure people snore while in a coma."

"I didn't!" Mari groaned. She didn't snore. Did she?

Glenn chuckled, a deep rumble that resonated in Mari's deepest reaches, somewhere beyond the physical, to a place where her soul resided. In an instant, panic roared through her. Safety came with a price, and the price was heartbreak. She knew that, how could she let herself forget? Selfish, foolish, all for a dream she no longer dreamed.

Glenn lifted up on her elbow, gave Mari a long look. "Whatever you just thought, stop thinking it."

"How did you know?" Mari asked softly.

"You shivered, and your pulse jumped." Glenn kissed her, a tender kiss that grew firmer, claiming her even as it soothed. "And we agreed not to do that today."

Mari didn't have to ask what Glenn meant. Glenn always seemed to know what she needed, or at least what she said she needed. The now. That's what she'd asked for. She couldn't offer more, even though she couldn't live in the now. She never had. She'd always counted on the future, planned for it, and once faced with the reality that a future might never exist, she'd reluctantly accepted that life held no promises. And that she could make none. "Can you do that? The now?"

Glenn traced soft circles on Mari's skin, trails of fire and tears. "When you wake up every day knowing the sunrise might be the last you'll ever see, you learn to stop thinking beyond the moment. After a while you forget things were ever any different."

"I know something about that." Mari covered Glenn's hand, ran her fingertip the length of her oh-so-sensitive fingers. She didn't have to explain. Glenn understood what she'd faced during those long months of treatment, the uncertainty and, finally, the resignation. Only a fool would trust to fate. "So you know what I mean, about not plan—"

"Right now," Glenn said gently, brushing another kiss over her lips, stealing her apology, sealing the guilt away, "I'm going to find you something to eat. Can't have you losing strength just yet."

Mari laughed, surprising herself. Maybe Glenn really *could* hold her in the now. She certainly had made her incredibly happy for the last few hours. "Are you really hungry?"

"You have no idea." Glenn's voice was husky, her gaze the stormy gray of a coming gale.

"I am too." Mari wrapped her legs around Glenn's and pulled her completely on top of her, fitting their bodies together, breast and belly and thighs. She arched under her, inviting, wanting, wanton. "Don't go anywhere."

"Never." Glenn's lids fluttered half closed and she groaned. Bracing herself on her arms, she rocked between Mari's thighs, firmly, rhythmically, steadily building, unbearably taunting, ceaseless demanding. "I can't get close enough to you."

Mari gripped Glenn's shoulders, matched her lift and thrust, giving herself over to the heat and the power. When she needed more, she swept the bunched muscles of Glenn's back down to her ass and pulled her even closer, reaching, climbing, clawing her way to the peak. When she exploded, she cried out, and Glenn gathered her up with unbearable tenderness.

Mari buried her face in the curve of Glenn's neck, gasping for breath. "I can feel you everywhere inside me."

Glenn held back the words she desperately wanted to say. *Let me stay. I need you.* She shuddered, a need far different than any she'd ever known roaring through her.

"It's all right," Mari whispered, for the first time misunderstanding Glenn's body language. "Let me make you come."

Glenn jerked in a breath, focused on the now. She knew the terms of engagement. This moment, no more. "Touch me."

Mari pushed on her shoulders, rolling her over, rising above her.

Glenn stroked her breasts, her abdomen, the curve of her hips. "You're beautiful."

Mari swept her hair back with a hand, smiling down at her. "You have a wonderful way of distracting me, but not just yet." She slid her hand between Glenn's thighs and squeezed, fingers already knowing exactly where to press.

Glenn's spine bowed and white heat lashed her brain. Her teeth clamped tight on a strangled groan. Somewhere light laughter cut through the sweet torture. Mari didn't take her over quickly this time. She stroked and teased until Glenn couldn't breathe.

"Please," Glenn gasped.

Mari bent down, her breasts brushing Glenn's, and kissed her. "Please what?"

"Please now."

"Oh yes," Mari whispered, stroking as she filled her, sliding in, gliding out, never stopping. "Now. Now you're mine."

Another lifetime later, Glenn groaned and tried to sit up. Boneless, she gave up and contented herself with stroking Mari's back where she lay curled against her. "I'm done."

Mari laughed and rubbed her cheek against Glenn's breast. "I thought you soldier types had more stamina."

"Clearly out of practice."

Mari grew still. "I never asked, I just assumed…"

"There's no one."

No one. Mari knew what that was like, to be alone. Had known. Knew in her heart that was no longer true. She sat up, smiled brightly. "Someone promised me food."

Glenn felt the change, the click of distance settle between them. Two in the afternoon. They'd had three hundred and sixty minutes, twenty thousand seconds. Enough of a gift to compress into a lifetime.

"Cold pizza? Scrambled eggs?" Glenn sat up, giving Mari the space she'd silently asked for.

"Sounds perfect."

Glenn committed the light in Mari's eyes to memory. She'd remember the happiness of this moment, knowing the truth of it. "Both?"

Mari kissed her. "Yes, both. Everything. I need another shower."

"So do I," Glenn said, letting Mari decide.

"Come with me."

Glenn called Flann a little after one a.m. When Flann picked up the phone, she sounded as if she was wide-awake, just like always. All told, married life hadn't seemed to change her all that much, only the restlessness was gone.

"Why do you never call me with good news?" Flann asked.

"What fun would that be?"

Flann chuckled. "What have you got?"

"Believe it or not, a gunshot wound to the hand."

"Member of the service?" Flann said quickly, referring to those in uniform—law enforcement agents, firemen, first responders.

"No, a ten-year-old boy who for some reason was up long after his parents had gone to bed. Apparently there was a party and they weren't paying too much attention. He found—get this—his mother's twenty-five caliber in her purse and decided to take it apart to see how it worked."

"Jesus. How bad is it?"

"Not bad enough to need ortho. Metacarpal is fractured, but looks like a washout and a splint will take care of it for now. You want me to call them?"

"Nah," Flann said. "If you do, it'll take until dawn for them to get there and then the OR will be backed up tomorrow. You and I can have it done in an hour. Call the OR."

"Already done. Consent's signed and he's in the holding area with his grandmother. His parents—well, I didn't think they were quite in any state to sign consent."

"Pretty sure I was coming in, huh?"

"Never known you to pass up a case."

Flann laughed. "I haven't heard from you at night for a while."

"Yeah, well, I wasn't doing much tonight."

"Saturday night."

"Like I said, the OR's ready."

Flann must've taken the hint. She didn't even bother trying to get a rise out of her. "See you there in fifteen."

Glenn hung up and looked around the empty surgeon's lounge with its outdated, cracked vinyl sofas and mismatched end tables littered with cups and takeout containers, and felt more at home than in her apartment. She'd sat there a thousand times before, just like this, and the only thing that had changed was her. Mari had left soon after their shower and cold pizza meal, and she hadn't been able to do anything since except think about the way Mari had felt stretched out above her, the way Mari had taken her and allowed herself to be taken. By the time she'd decided she was going to make herself crazy if she didn't stop, it was already dark, and the best place to be on a lonely Saturday night was the ER. A couple of the nurses gave her a knowing look when she walked in and scanned the board for a case to evaluate, but everyone welcomed her back. Old home week.

She closed her eyes and let her mind go blank, an old habit that allowed her to be ready for anything at an instant's notice, but kept her from thinking when there was nothing to be done about anything. Not the next mission, the next emergency, the next death on her watch.

A foot nudged her leg. "Yo, sleeping beauty. You done with your beauty rest?"

Glenn cracked an eye and grinned up at Flann. "I only need a couple minutes, but I let you sleep most of the night."

"You doing all right?" Flann asked with unaccustomed seriousness.

Glenn flushed, wondering how much showed in her face. "To tell you the truth, I don't know anymore."

"Mari?"

"Yeah." Glenn couldn't deny her.

Flann's grin widened, part sympathy, part amusement. "Believe me, I've been there, and I'm still there. But take it from me, it gets a lot worse before it gets better."

Glenn shoved herself to her feet. "Thanks, I knew I could always count on you."

"You know what, my mama ought to be taking the biscuits out of the oven right about now," Flann said when they wheeled the boy into the recovery room and left him to the nurses. "Let's head that way."

Glenn nodded. She should be tired, with almost no sleep for two nights running, but the last thing she wanted was to face the empty bed she'd last shared with Mari. "What about Abby—should we go get her and Blake?"

Flann shook her head. "Abby's been working nights all week, and the two of them aren't early risers anyhow. I'll bring them home something from the farm."

"How is it, adjusting, you know, to a family?"

Flann shrugged as they walked out into the dawn. "Weird, but it feels like it's always been this way, or at least it always should've been this way and I was just too dumb to know it. Abby and Blake are as much a part of me as the rest of my family. I can't imagine life without them."

A twinge stabbed at the soft spot behind Glenn's breastbone. An attachment like that, a need like that, was more dangerous than anything she'd ever experienced or wanted to think about. She wasn't cut out for family attachments, hadn't been raised to it the way Flann and the rest of the Rivers sisters were. She was born a loner and had learned to be alone, and maybe she should stop fighting the natural order of things.

"Suits you."

Flann grinned, and they rode in easy silence the short distance to the homestead. Flann parked under the portico and they walked around the back to the porch and through the kitchen door. Ida turned from where she had been removing a tray of biscuits from the oven and looked them over.

"You two look like you've been up all night. Coffee is hot."

"Morning, Mama," Flann said, kissing Ida's cheek and reaching around her for one of the strips of bacon draining on a paper-towel-covered platter.

Ida gave Flann a light slap on the shoulder. "You can take one because I know you've been working hard, but just one." She smiled over at Glenn. "You too."

Glenn shook her head. "I'm good till breakfast."

"Won't be long. Edward and Margie should be down shortly." She looked a little wistful for a second. "Breakfasts are a lot quieter these days than they used to be."

"Don't you worry," Flann said gently. "Before too long, you'll have grandkids spending the night, and you'll wish for a little peace and quiet."

Ida patted Flann's cheek. "Well, I've already got two, now don't I, and one big enough to be coming around on his own. You make sure Blake knows he can stop by whenever he wants."

"Thanks, I'll do that," Flann said, her voice unusually husky.

Ida raised an eyebrow in Glenn's direction. "You've been scarce lately. Working too hard, I imagine."

"No more than usual." Glenn settled with a cup of coffee at her usual place at the table. That might not be strictly truthful, but trying to give Mari the distance she apparently wanted had cut down on some of the time she spent in the ER. The hours they'd spent wrapped up in each other probably weren't going to change that. When Mari had left the day before, neither of them had suggested plans to get together again. Glenn sighed. When she looked up from her coffee, Ida and Flann were regarding her curiously. She straightened, hoping to look nonchalant. "Just getting used to the new routine down in the ER."

"I imagine you miss keeping this one in line." Ida pointed a spatula affectionately in Flann's direction.

Flann laughed. "Oh yeah, like I need supervision." She paused, shot Glenn a look. "Although Glenn might need a wingman these days, seeing how she's starting to make a little more time with the ladies."

"I imagine that's Glenn's business and none of yours," Ida said soundly and pointed Flann toward a chair. "Sit. Your father's on his way down."

Glenn didn't hear anything for a few seconds and then picked out the steady fall of footsteps approaching down the hall. She couldn't imagine being that tuned in to another person, not until she thought about waking next to Mari, feeling the weight of Mari's head on her shoulder, the featherlight touch of Mari's fingertips resting gently on her abdomen, their heartbeats slowly beating in time. Oh yes, she could imagine it with equal parts wonder and fear. What would happen if that fragile, essential connection broke?

"Eggs?" Ida's voice shattered her reverie.

"Oh, sure. Anything," Glenn said.

Edward and Margie sat at the table and the room filled with conversation. Like the rest of the Rivers family Margie was a morning person, and despite it being only six thirty on a Sunday morning, she eagerly questioned Flann and Glenn about the case they'd done the night before.

When Edward got up to leave for hospital rounds, Flann said, "Can I take a care package home for Abby and Blake?"

"Already put one together," Ida said. "Bacon and egg sandwiches. Two each."

"That might be enough for Blake," Flann said, grinning. "He seems to be in the midst of a growth spurt."

"You ought to take it before it gets cold," Ida said.

"Let me help you clean up."

Glenn stood and began to gather the plates. "I'll take care of that, you go ahead."

"Sure?" Flann asked.

"Yeah, I'm good."

Flann clapped her on the shoulder and grabbed the bag Ida had prepared. "Thanks. I'll run by the hospital later this morning and check on our postop."

"I'll do that." Glenn shrugged. "I've got nothing else going on today."

Flann hesitated. "How will you get home?"

"I'll take her," Margie chimed in.

Flann laughed. "Any excuse to drive, huh?"

Margie grinned and Glenn caught a glimpse of the beauty she was going to be in another year or two. Her face was already leaner than a few months ago, her cheekbones strong and arched, her wide blue eyes deep set and the color of the sky on a hot summer day.

"Thanks." Flann kissed her mother, ruffled Margie's hair, and headed out the back door.

In a few minutes, the table was cleared and Ida was sitting on the back porch drinking her coffee and perusing the Sunday paper. Glenn kissed her cheek, said good-bye, and followed Margie down the drive to where the old pickup was pulled up beside the barn. She climbed in as Margie got behind the wheel.

Margie didn't turn on the engine right away, but swiveled on the seat and glanced at Glenn. "Can I ask you something?"

"Sure." Glenn rolled down her window and the breeze off the pasture blew through. A creek ran behind the barn on its way down to the river, dividing two of the larger fields, and the scent of corn and fresh-cut hay lofted in.

"Blake told me about the surgery," Margie said, "and that he and Abby and Flann talked it all over and it's no big deal."

Glenn waited.

"I've seen the videos too," Margie said.

"Uh-huh."

Margie tapped her fingers against the wheel, looked out through the windshield before glancing directly into Glenn's eyes. "Sometimes when you're afraid, you don't want the people who lo…care about you to be scared too, so you pretend you're not." She snorted. "Like pretending to be strong is what matters the most."

Glenn swallowed. She knew a lot about pretending not to be afraid so the ones who depended upon her wouldn't be paralyzed by their own fear. Was that how Mari felt, refusing to let anyone close to protect them from the fear she felt inside?

She refocused on Margie. "You know, Blake's surgery, that's private stuff."

Margie nodded quickly. "I know that. It's okay, I got the gist. He tells me pretty much everything." She grinned. "Well, maybe not everything. You have to have your secrets, right?"

"Right." Glenn wasn't really so sure about that. She didn't seem to have any secrets left where Mari was concerned, whether she told her or not. Mari just sensed how she felt, what she needed. "So what are you worried about?"

"You and Flann, you'll make sure nothing happens to him, right? You know, some weird-ass thing that nobody expects?" Margie sighed. "Because I think he's maybe just a little scared."

"The chance of anything serious going wrong is really, really, really small." Glenn held Margie's gaze. "But anything can happen, anytime, to anyone. You know that, right?"

"I know," Margie said softly. "Like Kate. My dad and Harper and Flann couldn't save her. If all of them together couldn't save her..." She shook her head, took a deep breath. "They don't talk about it, but I know they're really sad that they couldn't."

Glenn clasped Margie's hand tightly. "That's not going to happen to Blake. Flann and I, and Abby too, will take care of him." Sometimes, after the hard truth, hope was the most important gift. Without hope, the struggle was too hard.

Margie's eyes cleared. "Okay, yeah. I knew that. I just wanted to hear you say it, I guess."

"Anytime."

"You'll tell him that, right?"

"I promise."

"Swag." Margie started the engine and dropped the hammer on the old truck. It jolted forward, and they shot down the driveway.

Glenn laughed. "Harper sees you drive like that, she'll kick your ass."

Margie shot her a look. "Yeah, maybe. But then again," she laughed wildly, her hair blowing like strands of red fire around her face, "maybe not. I might be able to take her."

"Yeah, right." Grinning, Glenn leaned back and closed her eyes, indulging herself in memories of Mari. Dangerous, yeah, but sometimes the pleasure was worth the risk.

CHAPTER TWENTY-SIX

I thought you were off at five," Abby said when she noticed Mari in the ER lounge.

"I was. Am." Mari set aside the month-old copy of the *Annals of Internal Medicine* she'd been scanning in the never-ending, never-victorious battle to keep up with her professional reading. "I'm just waiting on a couple of X-rays on the biker in seven. I figured I might as well finish that out since there's four new patients waiting on the board to be seen." She probably would have stayed anyhow, even if she hadn't been right in the middle of an interesting case. She liked finishing her own cases, even if it meant staying an hour or two after her shift was over. But she had another reason for lingering tonight. Glenn was off shift but hadn't left either, and Mari was hoping to accidently bump into her before they both left for the weekend. She hadn't exchanged more than a word or two with Glenn all week, and she was hoping to catch her. She really didn't want to spend another weekend like the last one.

"I don't mind picking it up," Abby said, "if you have plans."

Oh, she did. She hoped. "That's okay, I've got it."

Abby smiled. "In that case, I'm going to grab some dinner while you and Glenn are both still here."

At the mention of Glenn's name, Mari felt her face heat and hoped Abby didn't notice. They'd all been busy the entire week with interviews for the new residency program that was set to gear up in just a few weeks. In between supervising students, meeting with applicants, and taking care of patients, she and Glenn had barely had time to do anything other than review cases. Glenn had seemed her normal self—calm, steady, and focused. Mari doubted she seemed as cool and collected. Every time she saw Glenn her pulse shot through the stratosphere and she seemed to have trouble finding the right words. After they'd parted on Saturday, she'd spent the rest of the weekend trying to keep busy and finding her concentration was completely shot.

No matter what she was doing, she ended up thinking about Glenn. And that almost always led to thoughts of sex. How was she to have imagined something so natural, and so easy, could cause just about every cell in her body to ignite and her brain to malfunction? She understood the biology, even the psychology, of desire, but nothing she'd ever learned came close to the reality. And the worst part was, as amazing as those few hours had been and as exciting the aftermath, she didn't have a clue what she was going to do about it. She knew what she should do, and apparently Glenn agreed. Glenn hadn't given any sign she wanted to repeat their encounter, just as Mari had stipulated. Yep. She had what she'd asked for, and she wasn't the least bit happy about it.

"Got the X-rays back," Antonelli said. "Nasty spiral fracture of the femur—midshaft."

Grateful for the interruption, Mari jumped up and followed him out into the hall. She didn't see Glenn with a quick look around. "Put them up on the board, let's take a look."

The fracture was simple enough to diagnose—the thigh bone in the mid portion was splintered with a long crack running diagonally and the two opposing, spear-shaped fragments overriding each other. The surrounding soft tissues were misshapen and swollen with blood just as she'd expected from the exam, along with the noticeable shortening of the upper leg. "What does that look like to you?"

"Looks like a trip to the OR to me." Antonelli spoke with his usual confidence but after a quick glance at Mari's expressionless face, hastily added, "Spiral fractures tend to be unstable, and in a weight-bearing bone, the potential for limb shortening and gait problems is significant. Open reduction is indicated."

Mari smiled to herself. He was learning to make the transition from battlefield snap decisions to the kind of assessment appropriate in civilian care. She nodded. "Timing?"

"Considering it's almost seven on a Friday night, if we don't get it done now, chances are the ortho boys will want to wait until Monday or

Tuesday, when the swelling is down and they can get it on the schedule electively."

"Pros and cons to that?"

Antonelli frowned. He might be shifting his evaluations to the demands of community medicine, but he was probably always going to be a battlefield medic at the core. And he'd learned at the front that the more rapid and aggressive the treatment, the greater the number of soldiers they saved, with the smallest number of complications. Battlefield statistics supported that approach. He would never recommend postponing care. All the same, Mari wanted a medically sound reason for early intervention under the present circumstances.

"Right now, the soft tissue swelling is minimal. The longer they wait to operate, the more swelling there will be and the more difficult the dissection down to the bone. Plus, the patient's going to be damn uncomfortable if she has to wait for four days until surgery. She's an otherwise healthy, active fifty-year-old and she's gonna want to get on the road to rehab as quickly as possible. If they operate tonight, she'll be in PT by Monday morning. If it was my wife or sister, I'd want surgery tonight. So I say we call and push them to come in and rod it."

Mari nodded. "I agree."

From behind them, Glenn said quietly, "So do I." When Mari swung around with a questioning look, Glenn shrugged. "I happened to notice the films down in X-ray when they were shooting them. Nice work-up, Antonelli."

"Uh, thanks." Antonelli shot Mari a look, as if asking if he really deserved all the credit.

Smiling, Mari shook her head, pleased by Glenn's assessment. Glenn had praised Antonelli, and rightly so, but Glenn knew what Mari'd been trying to teach him, just like Glenn always seemed to know what she was thinking and feeling. Glenn's professional opinion of her was nearly as important as her personal feelings, but those she could read far less easily. Did Glenn think about their intimate time together as often as she did? Did she lie awake, restless at night, her body humming with the memory of desire? Was she finding it as difficult as Mari to pretend she didn't want it again?

Mari wished she knew how to ask, or that Glenn really could read her mind.

Antonelli spoke into the silence. "Zapata is on call. I'll give him a ring. He's a pretty decent guy and will probably come in with a little prodding."

"Tell him you've already called the OR, per me," Glenn said, "and that if he's not available, we'll get Flann Rivers to do it. That will light a fire under his butt."

Antonelli chuckled and strode away.

"I thought Flann was off tonight," Mari said.

"She is. Harper too. A few of us—OR crew mostly—are taking Harper out for a little prenuptial celebration."

Mari laughed. "You're kidding. Like a bachelor party?"

"Well, sort of." Glenn looked sheepish, highly unlike her. "Just tradition, you know."

Mari didn't, but enjoyed teasing Glenn. Enjoyed a conversation that had nothing to do with death, dying, or pain. "Will there be dancing girls?"

Glenn hesitated, brows drawn down as if thinking. "Dammit. I knew there was something I forgot to do. I don't suppose you and Carrie are free?"

"Oh," Mari said, rolling her eyes, "I never took you for such a big dreamer."

Glenn's eyes darkened. "No, neither did I. But you know, nothing ever stays the same."

Mari swallowed. "I know. Change is scary, though."

Glenn ran her hand down Mari's arm and cradled her fingers in her palm. Her thumb swept over the top of Mari's hand, as swift and light as a kiss.

Mari's lips instantly tingled as if she *had* been kissed.

"Not knowing can be scary, I understand that," Glenn murmured.

"I know you do." Mari wet her lips, searching and failing to find the words she wanted, but needing to keep the fragile connection alive, if just for another minute. "I was actually going to ask you out to dinner, but I see that you've already got much more exciting plans."

"Hardly more exciting, but I'm designated driver and I can't back out on them this time."

"Rain check?" Mari's heart actually thudded in her ears. She hadn't thought that possible.

Glenn glanced down the hall, checking they were still alone. Dinner, maybe more. Was that what she wanted? All she wanted? She'd recalled the hours with Mari every night when she tried to sleep, the second she opened her eyes every morning, and every time she saw her in the ER. She'd thought a lot about what Margie Rivers had said to her in the truck too, about strength being the other side of fear. Mari was strong, she had to be to survive what she'd survived, to endure the separation from her family, to face an uncertain future. Glenn respected her for that. She understood the fear that kept Mari from hope too. She understood that war of duty and sacrifice, and she loved her for all of it. In the quiet of the long hours alone, she came to understand herself too. She loved Mari and, for the first time in her life, wasn't afraid of what that meant. "I learned something this week."

"What?" Mari whispered.

"Remember I told you I learned to live in the now in the war?" Mari nodded.

"I didn't just learn it there. I learned it growing up, when I figured out I had nobody on my side but myself. That making it through one day was a victory, and not looking ahead, not counting on anyone or anything, was the only way to avoid disappointment."

"I'm so sorry," Mari murmured.

"That's okay, it got me through and made me tough. Made me who I am. And I did count on a few people. I counted on my unit, I counted on Flann and Harp and the rest of the Riverses." Glenn blew out a breath. More than she'd realized. "But you taught me something more."

Mari's heart beat in her throat so fast, so full, she wasn't sure she could speak. "Me? What did I teach you?"

"You taught me that every day, lived to the fullest, is just one link in the chain of forever. That it's safe to go to sleep and believe in the sunrise. You made me believe that when I open my eyes, everything that matters to me will still be there. I want that to be you, Mari. And I want you to believe that I'll be there for you."

"I...I don't know if I can. Believe." Mari grabbed Glenn's hand. "But you make me wish I could."

Glenn nodded. "I know that too. But you know what? I'm patient, and I'll wait."

"That's not fair. To you, I mean."

Glenn smiled, a rakish smile that carried no hint of sadness. "No one ever said life was fair, but it is what we make it. What we choose. I choose you, Mari."

Before Mari could answer, Glenn leaned forward and kissed her, just as she did everything—filled with certainty and strength. Mari gripped her scrub shirt, leaned into her.

Antonelli cleared his throat. "Zapata tried to give me the runaround until I suggested Flann could handle things just as easily as him. He'll be here in half an hour."

Glenn took her time stepping back, glanced over her shoulder at Antonelli. "You're learning."

Antonelli looked between Mari and Glenn and flashed his lady-killer smile. "Yes, ma'am. I am."

"Well," Glenn said, her gaze on Mari. "I'd best head out. Don't want them to have too much fun without me."

"You'll want to see to the dancing girls as well," Mari said teasingly.

"Oh yes. I won't forget that." Glenn took a step, looked back. "Call me, anytime."

Mari watched her walk away, her heart full and her soul in turmoil. Could she let her go? Did she dare try to keep her?

Glenn pulled out of the parking lot just as the sun dropped below the crest of the mountains, painting the road in intersecting patterns of light and shadow. Walking away from Mari was about the hardest thing she'd ever done. She'd wanted to press her for an answer, for some sign that Mari felt what she felt, and knew she couldn't. Mari needed to come to her of her own free will, in her own time, and all she could do was hope that time would one day come. If it didn't, well, she wasn't going to think about that. The need that clawed at her belly was like a hunger, an aching void she couldn't fill. Living with that need would be torture, had been torture, every day. The only thing that helped was catching a glimpse of Mari, spying that fleeting smile, the lingering look that said Mari was searching for her too in the midst of a busy day. Every time she did, she knew she was right to wait, to hope, saw the road ahead as clearly as she'd ever seen anything in her life. She wanted this woman, this one woman, and whatever it took, as long as it took, she'd do—

The IED exploded right under the belly of her vehicle. The blast deafening, the detonation blinding. She braced automatically, her transport airborne, spinning, tumbling, end over end. She landed with a bone-jarring thud in a scream of metal and shattering glass, her head striking steel, pain lancing down her spine. Through a wash of blood obscuring her vision, she fumbled for her safety harness, finally found the clasp, and once released, tumbled to the ground. The scent of fuel penetrated the copper scent of blood.

No, not ground, still inside, had to get out.

Couldn't burn. Wouldn't die in flames.

She crawled, wiping blood from her eyes, peering around for the rest of her unit. Couldn't find her med kit. Up ahead a Humvee on its side, trailing a glistening line of fuel on the road. Pushed to her feet, staggering, dizzy. Found the door, braced her leg against crumpled metal, felt the edge slice through her BDUs, into her thigh. Ignoring the searing pain, she pulled, strained, finally popped the door. Single occupant, unconscious, strapped in. Couldn't find her KA-BAR to cut the straps. Worked him free and dragged him up clear, had to stop to vomit, kneeling in the road, the trooper slung over one shoulder. RPGs lit the sky. She staggered for cover, fell again, threw her body over the trooper.

"Medic, medic," she whispered before the dark took her.

❖

While Mari waited for Dr. Zapata, the young orthopedist on call, to come in from the suburbs a half an hour or so away, she checked over the pre-op numbers, made sure Antonelli got a consent signed, and explained to the patient and her spouse what they could expect for the rest of the evening.

"Dr. Zapata will go over the surgery in detail," she said in response to their anxious questions, "but from the experience I've had with fractures like this—"

The curtain enclosing the cubicle rattled back with a loud clang, and she glanced over her shoulder, annoyed at being interrupted.

Antonelli filled the space between the tiny cubicle and the hall. His face was white.

"We need you out here."

Mari smiled at the woman with the fractured femur and her worried spouse. "The surgeon will answer the rest of your questions. I'll be back as soon as I can to check on you." She stepped aside and closed the curtain. "What's going on?"

"We just got a STAT call from the sheriff. MVA, two victims en route, both unresponsive."

"Did you page Abby?"

"Yes." Antonelli blocked her path as she started toward the trauma bay.

Annoyed, Mari stopped short, already mentally cataloging what needed to be done. "Who's on for surgery tonight?"

"That asshole Williams. Mari—"

Mari sighed. "I wonder if we could get Flann and Glenn back here from their—"

"Mari, it's Glenn."

"What? You already got her?" Mari looked down the hall, expecting to see Glenn stride around the corner with her battle-ready expression, directing everyone to their stations.

"No, no. *Listen.* The sheriff's local. He recognized her. One of the victims *is* Glenn."

CHAPTER TWENTY-SEVEN

Icy fingers squeezed Mari's throat. Time froze. The sound of her thundering heart drowned out all thought, leaving only primal fear.

"Where is she?"

Mari skirted around Antonelli, shouldered him aside when he tried again to stop her, and raced toward the admitting area. Antonelli, with his longer legs, caught her easily and grasped her arm.

"Don't." Mari jerked free, her voice a whip crack in the unnatural silence. Where was everyone? In receiving, waiting for the injured. Waiting for Glenn. No, that couldn't be. She couldn't even bring that picture into focus. The vision made no sense, and yet, beneath the denial, a terrible truth tried to bubble free. Nothing lasts—not life, not love, not dreams. "No. No, that it isn't true. I will not accept that."

"Mari," Antonelli said, dropping his hand and keeping pace. "You don't want to do this. Abby's on her way down right now. We'll take care of Glenn."

Mari stared straight ahead. A crowd of hospital personnel and security guards formed a corridor from the double doors of the emergency room toward the treatment area, ready to escort the victims.

No. Glenn was not a victim, she was everything that a victim *wasn't*—a warrior, a leader, a healer. Mari ran outside past the blur of faces, barely slowing enough to clear the half-opened glass doors as they slid back, into the bright glare of the floodlights illuminating the emergency zone in the lot outside receiving. The area was empty save for an emergency van and two parked police cars. The sky was ridiculously clear, moonlit and star-studded. Mockingly beautiful. She scanned the hillside below and the winding road down to the village she'd walked that first night with Glenn.

Antonelli followed her out, stood silent vigil with her.

"Where are they?" Mari asked.

"Two minutes out," Abby said, coming up behind them. As she spoke, a faint siren wail grew louder, as if summoned. "Mari, take triage, Antonelli, take the trauma bay—"

"Mari can't triage," Antonelli said. "I'll do it."

"What? Why not?"

"Because they're..." Antonelli stared helplessly from Mari to Abby.

Abby peered at Mari. "Oh God. All right—yes, Mari, back inside. Let us take care of this."

"I'm all right."

"Of course you're not. As soon as I know what the situation is, I'll brief you. Until then, you're backup, non-patient care. I mean it." Abby blew out a breath, squinted into the dark in the direction of the sirens. "If there was time, I'd get Carrie in here to wait with you..."

"Don't send me away." Mari drew in a long breath. "I want to see her. I won't get in the way. I'll wait, just please—"

Abby squeezed her shoulder. "The minute she's stable, I promise."

Mari turned to go inside, spun back to meet Abby's gaze. Abby knew, they all knew, what might lie ahead. "I don't want her to be alone if..."

"We are not going to let that happen. And Glenn will never quit. You know that, if you love her."

"Yes." Mari grasped onto Abby's fierce strength, needing to believe.

"Good. Now I need you inside. Make sure the staff is ready and we've got the support teams standing by. Can you do that?"

Mari nodded, stony calm sweeping over her, blunting panic and doubt. The battle had begun. "Yes. Trauma admitting and room two?"

"That sounds good. We don't know the status of either one."

A nurse came out to join them. "EMT radioed—they're coding one of them en route."

"That one goes to trauma admitting." Abby pointed at Mari as the night filled with the wail of warring sirens and explosions of red flickering lights cutting through the trees just below them. "Go."

Mari hesitated, every instinct driving her to stay. Glenn was hurt, alone, and she didn't know…*if you love her*. Only her training convinced her she'd be in the way for the first few critical moments. She trusted Abby and the others she'd come to think of as family, and turned on wooden legs to hurry back inside.

Bruce met her halfway down the hall. "Is it true? Is it Glenn?"

"I think so."

"Flann just called, she and Harper are on their way. Five minutes max."

"Thank God," Mari murmured. "Are you ready? You have respiratory here, X-ray?"

"Setting up now."

"What about the blood bank and the OR?"

"Just about to call."

"I'll take the OR, you notify the blood bank."

Bruce jogged away and Mari saw in her mind's eye what she knew was happening outside. The emergency vans careening to a stop, doors already swinging open, paramedics jumping out and dragging the gurneys free—the injured strapped down, helpless, panicked, and in pain. All she wanted was to be by Glenn's side, fighting whatever battle needed to be fought, denying death this one critical time. She shivered, forced the image away, willed herself to think. *Do*. Do what needed to be done. She punched in the extension to the OR, told them to get anesthesia and OR techs on standby.

She hung up the phone, and the cacophony of voices filled the hallway, shouting over one another in a chaotic chorus she'd heard hundreds of times. As her training kicked in, each note in the madness rang out crystal clear. A male medic shouting out vital signs, Abby calling for blood, Antonelli yelling for a trach tray.

Steeling herself, Mari whirled, focused on the first stretcher rocketing toward her, the patient with a cervical collar obscuring their lower face and blood covering the upper portion. Short sandy hair, and a medic astride the stretcher, rhythmically compressing the chest. Full arrest.

Mari's stomach twisted. *Please, please, not her.*

As the team hurtled by, she saw the glint of a gold ring on the left hand. Not Glenn. Not Glenn.

"Trauma one," Abby shouted and was gone.

Right behind them, Antonelli guided another stretcher pushed by a female EMT reading out blood pressure, pulse rate, pulse ox from the mountain of monitors piled beside the patient.

The patient.

Pale, so pale, a large gash running from the hairline at her right temple across her forehead, and blood, so much blood. Cervical collar, IV lines, EKG leads on exposed flesh. Mari pushed to the side of the stretcher, ran to keep up, gasped, "Glenn."

Glenn's eyes were open, staring and unfocused, her pupils wide and dilated. Mari registered somewhere in the midst of the kaleidoscope of images the flicker of movement in the storm-gray pupils, reactive and equal, normal.

"I've got her," Antonelli said.

And Mari had to step aside to make room and they were past her and Glenn was gone. Galvanized, she sped down the hall after them. The EMT pushed the stretcher into treatment room two and everyone converged around Glenn, blocking Mari's view. Suddenly helpless, she stood in the opening of the cubicle and wondered at the value of all her training when the only thing that mattered at that moment was saving Glenn, and she could not help. Nothing mattered, nothing at all, except Glenn.

Reality receded to the tableau beneath the blinding spotlight and she just stood there, waiting for the unknown. Just as she had been doing since the moment the doctors had informed her she had a potentially terminal illness, and life as she had known it had ended.

Hands grasped her shoulders and Mari shuddered. Flann bent down, peered into her eyes. "You okay?"

"Yes." Her voice sounded hollow, empty. Dead.

"Stay here. Let me get a look at her and I'll be right back. Okay?"

Mari nodded.

"Stay right there," Flann said firmly. "She'll want to see you. All right?"

Mari dragged in a breath. She was done being dead inside. "Yes, yes. I'm here."

Flann strode into the treatment room and the crowd around Glenn's bed gave way as if the sea were parting before an inexorable force. Mari followed close in her wake. No one was keeping her away from Glenn any longer. Flann leaned over the side of the stretcher, and Mari hovered by her right side.

No breathing tube. Saline soaked gauze on her forehead, still actively bleeding. Mari scanned the monitors. Pulse ox 95. BP 80 systolic. IVs running wide open. Stable.

"Glenn," Flann said in a strong clear voice. "You with me? You know me?"

Glenn blinked slowly, winced.

"Glenn?"

"Yeah."

"Good. You know where you are?"

Glenn blinked again and her eyes rolled. She wet her lips. "What about my unit?"

Flann glanced at Antonelli, raised an eyebrow.

"She kept muttering there was an IED," Antonelli said. "She thinks she's in Iraq."

Flann gripped Glenn's shoulder. "It's Flann, Glenn. You're at the Rivers. Car accident. We're all okay."

Glenn swallowed and groaned softly. "No fire?"

"No. You're okay. Where does it hurt?"

"Everywhere." Glenn's lids flickered closed. "Damn."

"Chest, belly? Glenn, hey, tell me where."

Mari focused on the X-rays that came up on the screen on the wall over the bed. "Fluid in the right costophrenic angle. Rib fracture."

Flann followed her gaze. "Not too bad, though. Damn, I like putting in chest tubes too."

"Belly films look all right," Antonelli chimed in.

"Looks like you're taking a trip down to CT to make sure everything's where it should be inside your head," Flann said. "I'm headed to the OR but Harp will be here."

Glenn grimaced. "Mari. Tell Mari—"

"I'm here." Mari nudged Flann aside, gripped Glenn's arm above the tangle of IV lines. "Right here."

"Don't...worry."

Mari laughed weakly. "Never. Just let everyone look after you for a change. Rest now."

Flann pulled off her gloves. "Antonelli, you and Bruce take her—"

"I'll go down with Antonelli," Mari said.

Flann gave her a look, slowly nodded. "All right. If there's any change while you're downstairs, let me or Harp know right away. When you get back up here, one of us will take care of that laceration."

Glenn said softly, "Just don't let Antonelli do it."

Antonelli laughed.

"Don't sweat it," Flann said. "We'll make sure you're still handsome."

Mari backed just far enough away so the staff could get Glenn ready for transport.

"What about the other one," she asked Flann.

"I'm about to explore his belly. Damn lucky Glenn pulled him out of his Hummer. The thing blew up right after the first responders got them clear. Looks like he ran through the intersection at about a hundred miles an hour, T-boned Glenn, and totaled her Jeep. If Glenn hadn't been in something that big…" She shook her head. "Damn lucky for both of them."

Luck, fate, chance—was that really what life was all about? Maybe. But what did it matter? Glenn was alive and here, now. And so was she.

CHAPTER TWENTY-EIGHT

"No focal swelling," Harper muttered as cut after cut of the head CT scan appeared on the computer screen.

Mari stared unblinking, searching each view for some hidden enemy, reluctant to be convinced. The calculating, cool part of her mind scanned and correlated, while the emotional part she usually kept contained and shut away while she worked kept screaming, *This is Glenn—Glenn!—and she's in danger.* Mari took a shaky breath. "With the size of that laceration, she must have taken a serious hit. She's going to have a hell of a headache."

"For sure." Harper grinned. "She'll never admit to it. She'll just want to rub dirt on the sore spots and get back in the game."

"I know. God, she could have—"

Harper draped an arm around her shoulders and squeezed. "She could have, but she didn't. She's going to be all right. Could-haves don't matter in this game. Only what is."

"Only what is," Mari whispered. Only now. *This* now, and as she was beginning to understand, the next one. Relief so potent she was briefly light-headed washed over her. "I'm so glad you're here. You and Flann and Abby—everyone."

"Where else would we be, huh? Glenn's family."

Tears pricked her eyes. "Yes, I know."

Harper made a few notes on Glenn's chart and dropped it on the small desk facing the glass-enclosed room where the big scanner revolved around Glenn's head. "We'll run her chest and abdomen too, but there's no sign of anything worse than a cracked rib or two. She'll need to stay in at least overnight."

"Can't you keep her longer? You know she'll want to go right back to work."

"Abby can probably hold her off awhile, but you know what Glenn's going to say. If she'd been at the front, she'd be back with her unit in the morning."

"This isn't the damn front," Mari said, her fear giving way to rage. Some careless, irresponsible driver had nearly killed the best person she knew, the woman who had already given so much for so many. The woman she loved.

"It is to her," Harper said gently.

Mari closed her eyes, let the targetless fury drain away. "I know. You're right."

"I'm going to call and get a room for her upstairs. As soon as we get that laceration closed, we'll get her settled."

Mari waited until the scans were done and helped the ICU nurse transport Glenn back to the ER. Abby came in a few minutes later.

"Flann called down. She's going to be a few hours. Ruptured spleen, fractured liver, avulsed duodenum. The guy's a mess. I'll do this."

"Can I help?" Mari asked.

Abby cocked her head, surveyed her. "Sure. That will free up one of the nurses, and we're slammed out there."

Mari cut sutures and dabbed blood from the field as Abby anesthetized and closed the eight-inch laceration on Glenn's forehead. Somehow, Glenn slept through most of the procedure, or maybe her body just kept her submerged so the healing could begin.

"It looks great," Mari said softly as Abby finished the last suture.

Abby's eyes above her paper mask smiled at her. "Thanks. Nice assist. She'll have a little bit of a scar, but the orientation's good so it won't be too noticeable in six months or so."

"It won't bother her." Mari doubted Glenn even realized how unbelievably attractive she was. And a scar? Nothing could mar her incredible beauty.

"Her room is ready," Abby said, "so we can get her upstairs. Coming up?"

"Yes." Mari appreciated that everyone just assumed she was staying with Glenn for as long as it took to be sure she was out of danger. Did everyone know what she had barely begun to recognize?

That Glenn was the most important thing, everything that mattered to her?

"Carrie's outside in the family waiting area if you want to give her an update while the staff get Glenn ready to transport. I'll call you when they're ready."

"Thanks. I'll go find her right now." Still Mari hesitated, unable to leave. Glenn's vital signs were stable, everything checked out fine, but what if she wasn't there and something happened? What if while she was gone Glenn—

"She's going to be all right. Sore as hell for a few weeks, and she'll need some tending that she won't want, but I'm sure you'll figure out how to get around her." Abby's tone was gentle, knowing.

Knowing Abby knew what Mari feared, and why, gave her comfort and strength. "I might need a little help in that department. She's one of the quietest people I know, *inside*, but staying quiet? Not so much."

Abby laughed. "Don't worry, we'll gang up on her."

Glenn softly muttered, "I can hear you, you know."

Mari stroked her cheek. Glenn's eyes opened, momentarily clear and oh so reassuringly strong. "Good. Then you know you're outnumbered."

Glenn's smile flickered, and she sighed deeply. Asleep again, safe.

"I'll be right down the hall." Mari finally backed away, watching Glenn's chest rise and fall, slowly and evenly, checked the EKG and blood pressure tracings moving steadily across the monitors one more time. Glenn was going to be all right. They were both going to be all right.

The instant Mari reached the waiting area, Carrie jumped up.

"Sometimes I hate not being one of you clinical types," Carrie exclaimed. "I had to stay out here and all of you were running in and out and oh God is she okay?"

"She's going to be. Banged up, but nothing time won't fix." Mari opened her arms as Carrie flew at her.

"Are you okay?"

"No. Yes. Just give me a year or two…" Mari buried her face in the curve of Carrie's shoulder, and the tears she'd been holding back for hours flooded free.

Carrie rocked her, crooned wordlessly, and held on.

"Sorry, sorry," Mari gasped when the worst of the burning in her chest had passed. "She's fine, really."

"Harper told me." Carrie led Mari to a sofa against one wall, drew her down, and enclosed her in the circle of her arms. "Doesn't mean it's not terrifying all the same."

"God, you're so right." Mari wiped her face with her palms and took a deep breath. "You heard what happened?"

Carrie nodded. "You know Glenn pulled the other driver out of the car right before it caught on fire, right? She saved the idiot that ran into her and could have killed her."

"Of course she did. That's Glenn."

"She's a hero," Carrie said.

"She always has been."

Carrie leaned back, read her eyes. "And I'm guessing she's yours now."

Mine now. Mari smiled. "Oh yes, she is."

"I thoroughly approve."

Mari laughed, a bubbling sensation she barely recognized at first as joy coursing through her. "I feel so lucky to have found her."

"Oh hell, she's the lucky one." Grinning, Carrie gave her another hug. "After all, she's got you."

"Yes. She does." Mari gave in to the comfort of Carrie's embrace another minute longer. "I should get back. They're going to take her upstairs soon."

"All right. I'll let everyone else know how she's doing. You just concentrate on taking care of yourself."

"Me?"

"Glenn will be rightly pissed if you don't take care of yourself while she's recuperating. That means eating right, sleeping right, and not worrying."

"I don't know how I'm not going to worry." She trembled, seeing the stretcher zooming past her, glimpsing Glenn's still form, remembering the blood and the terror.

"By reminding yourself she's all right and thinking about all the amazing things the two of you will share."

"Yes," Mari whispered. "I can do that. Now."

❖

Every single person in the hospital, in the entire community, maybe in the entire county came by Glenn's room into the late hours of the night. Mari, curled up in the chair by the side of Glenn's bed, was aware of them, sometimes just shadows, pausing in the doorway for a few seconds, then moving on. Just checking to be sure Glenn was taken care of, leaving a little positive energy behind. Around midnight Antonelli came in, reviewed Glenn's vital signs on the computer printout by her bed, listened to her heart and lungs. When he was done he bent down by Mari's side and whispered, "You should go home. Get some sleep. She's had a little sedation and is going to be out all night."

"She might wake up."

"Not for four or five hours."

"You're still here."

He shrugged. "I'll watch her for both of us."

"Yeah, well…I'm so glad you were here tonight."

"Me too. Mostly I'm really glad I have such a good teacher."

The tears came again and Mari was too tired to even be embarrassed. Antonelli silently handed her a tissue and she wiped her eyes. "We were all lucky."

"Damn scary night, just the same."

Mari nodded.

"If you don't want to go home, at least crash in the on-call room for a few hours."

"He's right," a woman said from the doorway.

Mari looked over and something brought her instantly to her feet as Antonelli slipped out. "I know. It's just really hard to leave her."

"Mm-hmm." Ida Rivers walked to the foot of Glenn's bed and studied her for long, silent moments. With a brisk nod, she put her arm around Mari and drew her to the door. "She's not in pain and she's strong as an ox. She'll mend quickly. I'm Ida Rivers, by the way."

"I know. All your children look like you."

Ida smiled. "When you see them next to their father, you'll say the same thing."

"I'm Mari Mateo. Carrie's cousin."

"Glenn's girl too, if I understand right."

Mari caught her breath. "Yes. You do. I am."

"The first thing she's going to worry about when she opens her eyes is you."

Mari surrendered. "I'll run home, shower, change my clothes. I don't know how I can sleep."

"Good enough." Ida squeezed Mari's hand. "She's not going to want to stay in here, either. She'll come to the homestead for a day or two so we can make sure she doesn't overdo."

Mari hadn't thought beyond the morning. Of course Glenn would need time to recover, and she'd need to be with family. The family who had chosen her, whom she had chosen. "That's perfect. I have a feeling she'll listen to you."

"For as long as the lot of them do, which in this case will be about a day." Ida laughed. "You're welcome to come by and stay as long as you want. We've got more than enough rooms."

"Thank you. I'm going to need to work, especially with Glenn out. But if you wouldn't mind me dropping by..." Mari sighed. "I know she's going to be all right, in my head at least, but—"

"The heart needs something different." Ida gave her a squeeze. "Breakfast starts at six, dinner at five. We always have leftovers. So you just come around when you're free. Glenn will want you there."

"Thank you," Mari whispered.

Ida glanced into the room at Glenn. "No need to thank me for taking care of my children."

Mari returned to Glenn's side and kissed her softly on the cheek. "I love you."

CHAPTER TWENTY-NINE

Mari knew she wouldn't sleep, but Ida's voice in her head kept telling her she needed to try, and she woke up twelve hours later. A spurt of adrenaline jolted her out of bed and she speed-dialed the page operator and asked for Glenn's floor.

"Oh, hi, Mari, this is Kimberly. I was just going off shift."

"How's Glenn?"

Kimberly laughed. "Harper was by around six this morning, signed Glenn's discharge, and personally wheeled her out just as I was coming on."

Mari sighed. Of course Glenn had left the instant she could. "Thanks."

Mari rang off, hesitated a moment, and called the page operator back.

"This is Mari Mateo, a PA in the ER. Can you connect me to Dr. Edward Rivers's home number?"

"Sure can. Hold on."

Ida answered on the third ring. "Hello. Rivers."

"Mrs. Rivers, it's Mari. I'm so sorry to disturb you, but—"

"She's here," Ida said. "Sleeping still, I'd wager. Harper was by a little while ago and said everything looks just fine."

Mari's breath whooshed out. "Thank you."

"What about you? Have you eaten?"

Mari laughed. "I just this minute opened my eyes. I slept almost all day. I'm fine."

"You have time to come by for something to eat?"

"I wish I did, but I need to get to work. You'll let me know if there's any change, though, won't you?"

"You can stop worrying about that. She's sleeping and when she's not, she's eating, and under orders to do nothing else. Come to breakfast in the morning."

"If you're sure…"

"Course I am. You take care of yourself now."

"I will. Tell her I called, please."

"Done. Now I'll see you in the morning."

A shower, a cup of coffee that she drank on her way up the hill to the hospital, and a fresh sliced deli sandwich seemed to put her back on track. That and knowing Glenn was being cared for and healing.

Abby pursed her lips when Mari walked in and gave her a thorough study. "How are you feeling?"

"I'm good."

"I've been working on the schedule, switching things around to cover for Glenn. I can get someone in here for you tonight too."

"No. I want to work."

"Good, because I need you."

"I need to be here too." Mari shrugged. "I want to be here. Mrs. Rivers—Ida—is looking after Glenn."

Abby nodded. "I know. Flann told me. Everyone is getting updates and passing them along, otherwise the place out there would be overrun." Abby smiled. "Glenn is very popular."

"I don't think she has any idea just how much."

"Of course she doesn't. That's the sweetest thing about Glenn."

Mari's face heated. There were many sweet things about Glenn. "I'm going out there in the morning."

Abby chuckled. "If it's quiet, you can finish up a little early. And if you need to, you can take my car. I'll catch a ride with Flann."

"Thank you. Thanks for everything. Coming here is the best thing I've ever done in my life." Mari didn't say what Abby must already know—the staff in the ER, the friends she'd made, Carrie and the Riverses—they were her family now. This was her home. And she had Glenn, a woman she loved.

"I'm very glad you're here."

Her shift passed quickly. A steady line of patients, noncritical thankfully, kept her busy until six in the morning. The board was finally empty except for several patients who'd already been seen and were awaiting rooms upstairs.

"I'll keep an eye on the rest of them," Baker, Mari's PA trainee, said.

"Thanks. Let me just clear it with Abby. Good job tonight."

Baker smiled, her eyes sparkling at the praise. She was growing in confidence from a serious student to an intuitive clinician. Not everyone made that leap, but she had. "No problem. Tell Glenn we all said hi and to get well soon."

Mari's throat tightened. "Yes, I will."

❖

The sunrise was a brilliant wash of orange and red flames dancing over the mountaintops. Mari drove with the windows open, exulting in the cool morning air that would be gone in just a few hours, fleeing before the sultry summer heat. God, it was beautiful. She laughed aloud. She'd forgotten what happiness felt like, and the excitement that a new day brought when anything was possible.

She slowly made her way down a long gravel drive flanked by broad green fields to a magnificent brick and white-columned house with sweeping wings that looked in many ways like a miniature of the hospital, and of course it would, probably being as old or older. The multi-paned windows sparkled, urns of red and white flowers bedecked the formal front porch, and stately chimneys crowned each end gable. She parked and got out, hesitating as to whether to try the tall front door or wander around to a side entrance, when she smelled what could only be the aroma of fresh-baked bread. Ida, she guessed, was baking.

Following the delicious aroma, she walked around to the back of the house and up a few stairs to a wide, homey porch and an open doorway enclosed with just the screen. "Hello?"

Ida's voice called back, "Thought I heard a car, but the rest of them usually pull all the way under the porte cochere. Come get some coffee."

Mari entered a kitchen twice the size of her apartment, anchored by a huge table in the center with at least a dozen chairs, framed on two sides by wood-topped counters, glass-fronted cabinets, and a giant cast-iron stove where Ida dished food onto a platter. "Oh, I'm not sure I can eat—"

Ida turned and gestured to the table. "You're hungry. Your stomach just hasn't caught up yet."

Mari sat dutifully and, when coffee appeared beside the food, realized she was ravenous. "Oh my God, these eggs are amazing."

"Just laid this morning, that's why." Ida sat with a cup of coffee. "Edward's gone on rounds, Margie is off to get Blake for their shift over in the ER, and Flann was just here checking on Glenn."

"She's doing all right?"

"She's doing as she's told. Sleeping and eating and taking the pills that Harper prescribed."

"Thank you so much. All of you."

Ida sipped her coffee. "How are you?"

"I'm wonderful," Mari said and meant it with every fiber of her being.

Ida nodded. "Then everything is as it should be."

"Not quite," Glenn said from the doorway. "I don't have any coffee."

Mari dropped her fork, her heart leaping into her throat. "Glenn."

Ida turned in her chair. "I thought we'd be seeing you this morning. Sit down. You'll need food with the coffee."

Mari devoured her with her eyes. She looked thinner by ten pounds and way too pale. The row of tiny perfect stitches along her forehead was starkly black against her skin. She wore a T-shirt with a faded logo of a sports team and sweatpants. She was the most beautiful woman Mari had ever seen.

"I need to water those begonias out back before the sun gets too high," Ida said and disappeared out the back door.

Glenn's gaze, riveted on Mari, was a beacon brightening a day Mari had thought perfect until now. Now she understood what it meant to be completely whole and unafraid. Glenn's smile, whimsical and inviting, called to her and Mari rose. She went to her, caressed her uninjured cheek, and kissed her. "Come sit down."

"Just give me a minute." Glenn draped an arm around Mari's shoulders, held her close. "I thought I heard your voice. Thought it was a dream at first. But it wasn't, was it?"

"No," Mari whispered against Glenn's throat. "Not a dream. Real." She tilted her head back, met Glenn's calm, patient gaze. "Just like now. We're real. I love you."

"I thought I dreamed that too."

"You didn't."

"That's a dream I wouldn't mind having every night." Glenn sighed, leaned against her a little. "You're all I've been thinking about. I'm so glad you're here."

"Always," Mari whispered.

"I love you. I never imagined how amazing that would feel."

Mari closed her eyes, pressed her cheek to Glenn's shoulder. "Neither did I. I don't know what I'd do if anything happened to you." She looked up, found Glenn's eyes. "I wish I could be sure about how long I can offer you."

Glenn brushed her thumb over Mari's lips. "You love me, don't you?"

"Oh yes."

"And that's not going to change."

"Never."

"I feel the same. That's all we need. The rest is just living."

Mari kissed her. "Then I want to live with you by my side."

"You will." Glenn smiled. "And for starters, I think I need breakfast."

A joyful peace settled deep in her heart as Mari looped an arm around her waist. "Sit and get started on this enormous plate of food. I'll tell Ida it's safe to come back in."

When Ida returned, she said, "Flann and Harper said no work for you for a week. They didn't say you can't go home, which I imagine you want to do. You know the routine. Don't overdo."

"Yes, ma'am," Glenn said and polished off her breakfast with heartening energy.

Ida nodded, apparently satisfied. "I'll pack up a basket for you to take so you have something to eat for a couple of days. Don't imagine either one of you will be doing much cooking."

❖

Mari pulled in behind Glenn's building and turned to face Glenn. "Are you sure you can handle the stairs?"

"As long as I go slow, I'm doing okay. My head's good, but the ribs are pretty sore."

"Let's get you upstairs and into bed, then."

Glenn grinned. "I've always liked that you could read my mind."

Mari flushed. "I don't think that's a prescribed activity."

"There are a lot of ways to interpret recovery, and one thing I need more than anything else is you."

"Let's start with the stairs, and we'll go from there."

"Will you stay today?"

Mari reached for Glenn's hand and leaned over to kiss her. "Honey, I'm staying for as long as you want me."

Glenn cupped her cheek and kissed her. "I love you. So that's easy. Forever would about cover it."

CHAPTER THIRTY

Mari woke with a warm hand pressed to her middle and Glenn's body curved against her back, Glenn's face pillowed in her neck. After four mornings waking the same way, she knew she would never tire of it. Glenn possessed her just as she did everything else—with a quiet certainty that left her feeling safe and desired and stronger on her own than she'd ever imagined.

"Mmm."

"Does that mean you're awake?" Glenn murmured, her fingers circling slowly, teasing Mari's skin into wakeful need.

"I believe I might be, but I'm not sure yet." Smiling, eyes still closed, Mari pressed her hips into Glenn, rewarded by a swift intake of breath. Knowing she could excite her was another of those wonderful revelations she'd quickly become addicted to and hoped to repeat at every opportunity. As soon as Glenn was fully recovered. The waiting was torture, since every time Glenn looked at her she throbbed. Coming back from the ER to Glenn's welcoming kiss, sleeping beside her with their heated skin sliding in a seductive dance, kept her constantly on the edge of desire. "Maybe you should just keep doing that a little bit longer."

Glenn chuckled and her hand drifted lower, inviting Mari's thighs to open.

Mari half turned toward her, kissed Glenn over her shoulder. She caught her breath when Glenn's fingers slipped between her parted thighs. They were playing a dangerous game, one she loved and was quickly losing. "All right, I'm awake."

Glenn kissed her again, the tip of her tongue playing over Mari's lips in time with the glide of her fingers ever lower. She coaxed Mari's mouth to open, to let her in.

Mari gripped Glenn's shoulders, turned completely toward her, and pressed her breasts to Glenn's. "How are your ribs?"

"Perfect."

Mari laughed, the sound breaking on a sob as Glenn slid effortlessly inside her. She arched, struggling for a little sanity. "Is that a lie?"

"No," Glenn rasped. "Truth. I've been patient, and I'm done waiting. I want you."

"I'm here. And oh God, I'm yours."

Glenn buried her face in Mari's throat and gave herself to the sensation of heat and belonging that pulled her in, body and soul, with each slow, deep stroke. This was home. "I love you."

"Glenn," Mari whispered, "you're going to make me come."

Mari's grip on her shoulders tightened, and Glenn focused on the beat of Mari's heart pounding faster and faster against her own, the soft sounds of wonderment and need breaking from her throat, the lift and pull of her hips. Every hour she'd spent waiting for her body to heal, holding Mari close to her while they slept, part of her had been longing for this, needing this and only this to be completely whole again.

"You're everything I want," Glenn said as Mari tightened around her, her body wire taut for an instant, a cry torn from her throat. When Mari relaxed with a long, satisfied sigh, Glenn grinned. "You're so sexy when you come."

"Am I?" Mari said drowsily. "That's handy. Because I very much like it when you make me come."

"Anytime, say the word." Glenn kissed her. "How about now?"

Mari laughed, shook the pleasure fog from her mind and framed Glenn's face, kissing her until Glenn groaned. "If your ribs don't hurt anymore and your headache's gone…"

"Gone, perfect, no pain anywhere." Glenn sounded a little desperate. "Except this one place. Terrible, terrible pain."

Still laughing, Mari gently eased Glenn onto her back and propped herself on an elbow beside her, trailing her fingertips up and down the center of Glenn's torso. "Here?"

"That's nice, but…"

Leaning down, Mari kissed the purple bruise over Glenn's chest. "You're sure about this?"

"Yes, yes, positive." Glenn's eyes pleaded.

Careful but sure, Mari stroked lower, watching Glenn's abdomen tighten, her thighs tense. When she slowly circled Glenn's clit, Glen muffled an oath.

"Sorry. Should I stop?" Mari couldn't help teasing just a little. She loved knowing Glenn needed her, craved her touch. Loved her.

Glenn growled, gripped her wrist and pressed her hand down harder. "Don't be cruel."

"Oh," Mari whispered, kissing her as she picked up her tempo, "only in the best of ways."

Glenn's head rolled back, her neck strained, and a long groan shuddered from her chest.

Content, Mari rested her cheek against Glenn's shoulder. "I love you."

"Oh, baby, I love you too."

"You know we have to get dressed right away."

"Uh-huh." Eyes still closed, Glenn stroked Mari's face. "I'm coming."

"Not right now," Mari kissed her. "But later for certain."

❖

Mari gripped Glenn's hand, her eyes shimmering with tears. Margie sat beside her in an airy floral dress patterned with bluebells the exact color of Blake's tie. They looked fresh and eager and full of possibility, the kind of possibility Mari welcomed now. Ida and Edward, Carson's husband Bill and their toddler, and members of the bridal party filled the front row just ahead of them. Mari had heard the words before, thought she'd known their power, but nothing moved her as much as listening to two women she admired and cared for hold each other's hands in front of family and friends and the entire community and speak the vows of love and devotion and desire.

Harper slid the ring onto Presley's finger and looked into her eyes. "With this ring, I thee wed."

Mari didn't try to stop the tears as Presley lifted Harper's hand and slipped on the matching circle of gold. "To have and to hold…"

Glenn's fingers closed around hers.

"I love you," Mari murmured.

Till death do us part.

About the Author

Radclyffe has written over fifty romance and romantic intrigue novels, dozens of short stories, and, writing as L.L. Raand, has authored a paranormal romance series, The Midnight Hunters.

She is an eight-time Lambda Literary Award finalist in romance, mystery, and erotica—winning in both romance (*Distant Shores, Silent Thunder*) and erotica (*Erotic Interludes 2: Stolen Moments* edited with Stacia Seaman and *In Deep Waters 2: Cruising the Strip* written with Karin Kallmaker). A member of the Saints and Sinners Literary Hall of Fame, she is also an RWA/FF&P Prism Award winner for *Secrets in the Stone*, an RWA FTHRW Lories and RWA HODRW winner for *Firestorm*, an RWA Bean Pot winner for *Crossroads*, and an RWA Laurel Wreath winner for *Blood Hunt*. In 2014 she was awarded the Dr. James Duggins Outstanding Mid-Career Novelist Award by the Lambda Literary Foundation. She is a featured author in the 2015 documentary film *Love Between the Covers* from Blueberry Hill Productions.

She is also the president of Bold Strokes Books, one of the world's largest independent LGBTQ publishing companies.

Find her at facebook.com/Radclyffe.BSB, follow her on Twitter @RadclyffeBSB, and visit her website at Radfic.com.

Books Available From Bold Strokes Books

21 Questions by Mason Dixon. To find love, start by asking the right questions. (978-1-62639-724-8)

A Palette for Love by Charlotte Greene. When newly minted Ph.D. Chloé Devereaux returns to New Orleans, she doesn't expect her new job and her powerful employer—Amelia Winters—to be so appealing. (978-1-62639-758-3)

By the Dark of Her Eyes by Cameron MacElvee. When Brenna Taylor inherits a decrepit property haunted by tormented ghosts, Alejandra Santana must not only restore Brenna's house and property but also save her soul. (978-1-62639-834-4)

Cash Braddock by Ashley Bartlett. Cash Braddock just wants to hang with her cat, fall in love, and deal drugs. What's the problem with that? (978-1-62639-706-4)

Death by Cocktail Straw by Missouri Vaun. She just wanted to meet girls, but an outing at the local lesbian bar goes comically off the rails, landing Nash Wiley and her best pal in the ER. (978-1-62639-702-6)

Lone Ranger by VK Powell. Reporter Emma Ferguson stirs up a thirty-year-old mystery that threatens Park Ranger Carter West's family and jeopardizes any hope for a relationship between the two women. (978-1-62639-767-5)

Love on Call by Radclyffe. Ex-Army medic Glenn Archer and recent LA transplant Mariana Mateo fight their mutual desire in the face of past losses as they work together in the Rivers Community Hospital ER. (978-1-62639-843-6)

Never Enough by Robyn Nyx. Can two women put aside their pasts to find love before it's too late? (978-1-62639-629-6)

Two Souls by Kathleen Knowles. Can love blossom in the wake of tragedy? (978-1-62639-641-8)

Camp Rewind by Meghan O'Brien. A summer camp for grown-ups becomes the site of an unlikely romance between a shy, introverted divorcee and one of the Internet's most infamous cultural critics—who attends undercover. (978-1-62639-793-4)

Cross Purposes by Gina L. Dartt. In pursuit of a lost Acadian treasure, three women must work out not only the clues, but also the complicated tangle of emotion and attraction developing between them. (978-1-62639-713-2)

Imperfect Truth by C.A. Popovich. Can an imperfect truth stand in the way of love? (978-1-62639-787-3)

Life in Death by M. Ullrich. Sometimes the devastating end is your only chance for a new beginning. (978-1-62639-773-6)

Love on Liberty by MJ Williamz. Hearts collide when politics clash. (978-1-62639-639-5)

Serious Potential by Maggie Cummings. Pro golfer Tracy Allen plans to forget her ex during a visit to Bay West, a lesbian condo community in NYC, but when she meets Dr. Jennifer Betsy, she gets more than she bargained for. (978-1-62639-633-3)

Taste by Kris Bryant. Accomplished chef Taryn has walked away from her promising career in the city's top restaurant to devote her life to her six-year-old daughter and is content until Ki Blake comes along. (978-1-62639-718-7)

The Second Wave by Jean Copeland. Can star-crossed lovers have a second chance after decades apart, or does the love of a lifetime only happen once? (978-1-62639-830-6)

Valley of Fire by Missouri Vaun. Taken captive in a desert outpost after their small aircraft is hijacked, Ava and her captivating passenger discover things about each other and themselves that will change them both forever. (978-1-62639-496-4)

Coils by Barbara Ann Wright. A modern young woman follows her aunt into the Greek Underworld and makes a pact with Medusa to win her freedom by killing a hero of legend. (978-1-62639-598-5)

Courting the Countess by Jenny Frame. When relationship-phobic Lady Henrietta Knight starts to care about housekeeper Annie Brannigan and her daughter, can she overcome her fears and promise Annie the forever that she demands? (978-1-62639-785-9)

Dapper by Jenny Frame. Amelia Honey meets the mysterious Byron De Brek and is faced with her darkest fantasies, but will her strict moral upbringing stop her from exploring what she truly wants? (978-1-62639-898-6)

Delayed Gratification: The Honeymoon by Meghan O'Brien. A dream European honeymoon turns into a winter storm nightmare involving a delayed flight, a ditched rental car, and eventually, a surprisingly happy ending. (978-1-62639-766-8)

For Money or Love by Heather Blackmore. Jessica Spaulding must choose between ignoring the truth to keep everything she has, and doing the right thing only to lose it all—including the woman she loves. (978-1-62639-756-9)

Hooked by Jaime Maddox. With the help of sexy Detective Mac Calabrese, Dr. Jessica Benson is working hard to overcome her past, but they may not be enough to stop a murderer. (978-1-62639-689-0)

Lands End by Jackie D. Public relations superstar Amy Kline is dealing with a media nightmare, and the last thing she expects is for restaurateur Lena Michaels to change everything, but she will. (978-1-62639-739-2)

Bitter Root by Laydin Michaels. Small town chef Adi Bergeron is hiding something, and Griffith McNaulty is going to find out what it is even if it gets her killed. (978-1-62639-656-2)

Capturing Forever by Erin Dutton. When family pulls Jacqueline and Casey back together, will the lessons learned in eight years apart be enough to mend the mistakes of the past? (978-1-62639-631-9)

Deception by VK Powell. DEA Agent Colby Vincent and Attorney Adena Weber are embroiled in a drug investigation involving homeless veterans and an attraction that could destroy them both. (978-1-62639-596-1)